RUSTLER MOUNTAIN

More from Maisey Yates

Santa's on His Way

RUSTLER MOUNTAIN

MAISEY YATES

KENSINGTON
PUBLISHING CORP.

kensingtonbooks.com

ISBN: 978-1-4967-5347-2 (ebook)

ISBN: 978-1-4967-5346-5

First Kensington Trade Paperback Printing: March 2025

10 9 8 7 6 5 4 3 2 1

Printed in the United States of America

To Helen Breitwieser, for everything.

To Flo Nicoll, for being such a great friend.

And to Megan Crane, Jackie Ashenden, and Nicole Helm, for always being the ones to pick me up when I fall down.

This book wouldn't exist without all of you.

Welcome to Rustler Mountain!

Founded in 1849, this California gold rush town sits only eight miles from the Oregon-California border and served as a home base for thousands of people who crossed the country to make a new fortune for themselves in the American West.

In spite of its gold rush history, Rustler Mountain is perhaps best known for being the town where one of the most dangerous outlaw gangs of the West was apprehended.

On this site in 1867, the notorious Austin Wilder—leader of the gang that was responsible for a string of stagecoach, bank, and train robberies from 1845 to his death—was shot dead by Sheriff Lee Talbot on Main Street in front of the Rustler Mountain Saloon. His brothers and co-conspirators, Jesse and William, were arrested and tried for robbery and murder, then hanged on the courthouse lawn.

Butch Hancock, another member of the gang, escaped and was never caught.

The spirit of the Wild West, with its outlaws and heroes, lives on in Rustler Mountain to this day, where its well-preserved historic Main Street pays homage to the past.

—plaque at the head of Main Street, Rustler Mountain, Oregon

Chapter 1

Millie Talbot had never been called brave.

Mousy, timid, plain, homely, missish. Yes. *Jilted*, perhaps. Brave, no.

But as Millie stood there staring at the ranch house that sat smack dab in the middle of the Wilder homestead, she thought she might be a little brave for coming there.

Austin Wilder was an outlaw, after all. Maybe not so much in the present moment, and maybe never in the way his five times great-grandfather had been, but he had certainly raised a significant amount of hell in his youth.

An apple that had fallen very close to the tree.

Rustler Mountain traded on its history, and as a result the lore and legends of the Wild West often felt nearer to the present day than they might otherwise.

The town still felt divided the way it had been back then. Into the lawful and the lawless.

As a result, the Talbots didn't mix with the Wilders.

Ironic that now she needed him.

She'd been rehearsing the speech that would get him on her side since yesterday, when she'd finally come to the conclusion that he and his family were her only options if she hoped to solve two of her current pressing problems.

She'd written the speech.

She'd discarded it.

Help me, Austin Wilder, you're my only hope.

All the girls in middle and high school had whispered about him. A bad-boy fantasy or something like that. He'd ridden his horse down Main Street, right into the high school once. Defiant and cocky as always.

She'd heard about it. She'd been in eighth grade, so she hadn't actually seen it.

It had been more common for him to ride his motorcycle into town with his brothers, Carson and Flynn, flanking him, their friend Dalton Wade bringing up the rear, the bikes so loud you couldn't hear anyone talking over the roar of the engines.

They'd had legendary brawls with the Hancocks, who were also descended from outlaws—but did not mix with the Wilders, for historic reasons—and had near showdowns in the streets with the good citizens of town.

Austin had been arrested for any number of petty crimes in his youth. Moonshining, vandalism, and grand theft auto. Though he'd never been convicted, due to a lack of evidence.

They were the Undesirable Element about town.

They had their own saloon, their own haunts and hangouts, just as the other faction in town did.

Of course that had made him and his brothers ripe for speculation with any teenage girl in town who was inclined toward men.

Almost.

Millie had never had bad-boy fantasies.

She was the ultimate good girl.

And if she didn't have the library in common with him, she never would have come here.

But that was the thing.

For all his crass-talking, hard-drinking, brawling ways, he had always been a patron of the Rustler Mountain Library.

In Rustler Mountain, there was the good and the bad, and never the twain shall meet.

Except at the library.

She clung to that now. Their common ground. The reason he might help her. The reason he would even know who she was.

She reminded herself of all that now as she tried to force herself to walk up the porch steps so she could knock on the door.

This meeting had seemed easier when it was theoretical. Well, that was life.

Everything had seemed easy just two months ago. Now it was all different and terrible, and she was about to fling herself on the mercy of Austin Wilder.

Mercy she wasn't sure he possessed.

But he was a *reader*. That made her feel they had something in common. It made her feel she had a hope of reaching him.

When she was a girl, and her mother was the head librarian, she used to watch him from behind the reference desk. He always came in alone. He was about five years older than her, so he had always seemed tall and remote.

He still did, honestly.

He wore outlaw the way her father had worn his sheriff's badge.

Not surprising, because the town's history was emblazoned everywhere. Their best-selling souvenirs were bricks from the original redbrick streets in town, which had been etched with the words: *Rustler Mountain, Last Stop for the Wilder Brothers.*

However, for all that the townspeople loved their history, the actual historical society was underfunded. The museum had closed a decade ago. It had once occupied the original courthouse, which was now being used as a town hall, with all the wonderful artifacts in boxes in the basement.

Gold Rush Days, once a staple of town tourism, running all through the month of June, used to bring in schoolchildren and visitors from out of town to see living history, gold panning, and a reenactment of the last stand of Austin Wilder. The historical figure, not the man she was here to see.

She wanted them back. Those events had been the pride and joy of her father, and he'd wanted to see them restored.

Something Millie was working on.

But Millie needed votes. Votes she would have had if her now ex-fiancé hadn't cheated on her with Danielle LeFevre, the daughter of the former mayor, now town mayor herself.

Danielle was also Austin's half brother Flynn's half sister. Which was the kind of small-town complication that was all too common. Millie had never had the feeling that Flynn was close with that part of his family, not that she knew the LeFevres or the Wilders well enough to be sure.

It was a gamble, and she was—historically—not one for games of chance.

But she was desperate.

The way voting on town matters worked in Rustler Mountain was . . . quirky was maybe a nice way of saying it.

Town council members had votes, but so did members of Rustler Mountain's founding families.

When she and Michael were engaged, she'd had enough votes. Michael was a Hall. The five times great-grandson of Rustler Mountain's first banker. Michael was friends with the Langleys and the Hugheses, and they would generally vote with him. She could no longer count on those votes.

But the vote it hurt worst to lose was her father's.

He'd died two and a half months earlier. The loss was fresh enough that there were still days she found herself standing there washing dishes or pruning the roses in her front yard, or putting a book back on the shelf at the library, and she'd be jolted by the sudden realization that John Talbot was dead.

She'd lost her mother ten years earlier, so she was no stranger to loss.

But with her dad gone. . . .

She was the last remaining Talbot in town.

And it seemed that without him, she didn't matter at all.

It certainly didn't help that right after his death, she'd found out Michael was cheating with Danielle, and her wedding had been called off and. . . .

Well, here she was.

Danielle was also a member of a founding family and had run on a platform of building Rustler Mountain up, but her idea of the way to go about it was very, very different from what Millie thought needed to happen. She proposed that the part of the budget Millie wanted for the historical society should be "earmarked for town council travel."

Millie had four members of the town council on her side, as well as the Millses, the Bowlings, and the Lins.

She and her opposition were dead even.

And that was where Austin came in.

She needed the Wilder vote.

She could only hope that she was right in thinking she might be able to get it.

She doubted that anyone in town would believe her if she told them that he was a regular at the library.

But he had been since he was a boy, and he remained one now.

They didn't speak when he came in. But he did come, once every two weeks, and he spent an hour or so perusing the shelves, coming back to the desk with a stack of books of just about every imaginable variety.

Around town, Austin had a reputation for being remote, cold, and hard. For being, essentially, the reincarnation of his ancestor.

He'd changed, though, after his father's death, after his half sister had come to live with him and his brothers. The brawls had stopped.

But the town's memory was more than a century long, so his reputation remained.

Austin had already lived longer than his father, his grandfather, and his great-grandfather. Who had basically all lived just long enough to procreate, and then gotten themselves killed doing something dangerous or illegal.

She had to hope there was more to Austin than that. She wanted his vote.

She also wanted some artifacts from his family for the museum.

If she could go into that meeting with his vote and with offerings of new attractions and insights for the grand reopening of the museum, she would feel. . . .

Well, she would feel like maybe she was a Talbot in more than just name.

Austin's family had a legacy of living fast and dying young. Hers was a legacy of staying strong and steady. Millie often didn't feel strong or steady.

She needed to be now.

"Have courage," she whispered to herself as she walked up the steps. She could have used his phone number. She had it in the library system.

But she felt that would be a violation of her sacred librarianship vows.

Not that she had actually taken *vows*, but she did take her job very seriously. The truth was, she knew which books everyone in town checked out. With knowledge came power and great responsibility. She had to be vigilant. She couldn't just go telling everybody that Ronald Miller had checked out a book on herbal remedies for erectile dysfunction.

She simply had to check the book out, keep her expression neutral, and perhaps murmur a couple of things about the weather.

She never said anything about the weather to Austin Wilder, however.

She took a breath, and gathered herself up, stomping up the porch steps, trying to use the vigorous nature of her steps to boost herself up.

Then she knocked. Firmly.

She was coming here to talk about the town. The past and the future.

She cared about both with all that she was.

A little ember began to burn in her chest.

She might be mousy a lot of the time, it was true. She couldn't deny it. But when she got started talking about subjects she felt passionate about, she found her fire.

She was passionate about *this*.

And maybe passionate about beating Michael.

Maybe.

She waited for a moment, listening for the sounds of footsteps after she knocked.

She heard nothing.

She knocked again.

"Can I help you?"

She whirled around, putting her hand on her chest as if it might catch her heart as it tried to slam its way past her breastbone. "Oh," she said.

There he was, standing in the dust behind her, cowboy hat planted firmly on his head, cowboy boots planted firmly on the ground.

He was wearing battered blue jeans, and a belt with an ornate buckle. His expression was unreadable, his square jaw set firm, his mouth a grim line. His dark brows were locked together, eyes glittering with emotion she couldn't name.

He was backlit by the sun filtering through the towering pines behind him, and he looked as dangerous as he was rumored to be, as the many generations of his family were always purported to be.

"Austin?"

He looked her up and down, his gaze bracing.

"You're the librarian," he said.

At least he recognized her. She sometimes had the sense that she was nothing more than floral wallpaper to the men of this town. Even to her own fiancé.

Who hadn't even noticed her when she'd walked in on him with. . . .

She didn't need to reflect on that right now.

"Yes. I am. I. . . ." She cleared her throat and tilted her chin upward. "That's not what I'm here about."

He was so tall. So broad. And somehow it felt very different to be staring him down here, without the reference desk between them.

That, she realized, was her territory, and he, the outlaw, was a trespasser in it.

Here?

She was the one who didn't belong.

She swallowed hard.

"I was going to say, I know I don't have anything overdue."

"We don't make door-to-door attempts at repossessing books, Mr. Wilder."

He snorted. "No one in my family has ever rated the respect of being called *mister*. Just call me Austin."

It wasn't an overture of friendliness, but a flat statement of fact. She didn't know quite what to make of it. "Okay."

"What brings you up to Wilder Mountain if you aren't here to repossess a copy of *The Life-Changing Magic of Tidying Up?*"

"You . . . you turned that in two weeks ago." She clasped her hands up at the center of her chest. Someone in high school had once said she made "mouse hands" when she was nervous, and every time she caught herself doing it, it infuriated her.

She lowered them quickly.

"So I did." He stood there, staring, making her feel tiny even though he was standing down on the ground gazing up at her on the porch.

"You have *The Elements of Style* and a Jack Reacher book right now," she said.

"I actually do know which books I have out right now."

"Right. Well. I came up here because I wanted to talk to you. About . . . I'd like to ask you about a couple of things. The first is that I'd like to talk to you about any artifacts—journals, letters, or family heirlooms—you might be willing to donate to a new endeavor I'm working on."

He crossed his arms across his broad chest, and she couldn't help but notice how muscular his forearms were. And his chest under the tight white T-shirt he wore. Which was a silly observation, really. He was a cowboy. A working man. Of course he had muscles.

The heaviest thing she lifted was a weighty reference book.

He frowned. "Why?"

"I want . . . I want to reopen the museum. I have so many documents in the library. Historical journals and newspapers. All the artifacts that used to be on display at the courthouse are just gathering dust and . . . maybe I could put them on display at the library or in a different building in town—I'm still working on that part—but I want to have this information available again."

"Then what do you need me for?"

"I'm a Talbot. The stories I have about my family, whether lore, legend, or fact . . . they are innumerable. But when it comes to the Wilders, there's nothing but speculation."

"And you want what?" He huffed. "Our side of the story?"

"Well . . . yes."

"Make no mistake, Miss Talbot, what you really want is a boogeyman. You like your heroes and your villains, and you don't like it complicated."

"That isn't true," she said. "I want to portray the real history of the town."

"And so you're done with reenactments of my ancestors being shot in the streets?"

Her mouth dropped open, and then she shut it again. "I have no control over a private company's Wild West shows."

"I'm not asking about the Hancock's Wild West Show. Their historically inaccurate nonsense is their own concern. Their family never had scruples and I don't expect them to have any now. What I'm talking about is the historical society–sanctioned reenactment of the showdown that occurs under the guise of education."

"I . . ." She stumbled over her words. "That's part of the other piece of the conversation."

"We've never spoken more than four words to each other, and you have two favors you want to ask? Damn, darlin', that is bold."

She knew that wasn't supposed to be a compliment, but she took it as one all the same. "I need to be a little bold with this one, so I thought I'd take a shot."

"Oh, careful. I find that triggering. Considering a Talbot did in fact shoot my ancestor."

"Sorry," she said quickly.

For the first time she wondered what it was like to have your family history centered on being the one who was shot dead.

She was related to the one who'd done the shooting.

"I'm kidding," he said. Then he sighed heavily. "Come on inside."

He walked up the porch steps, and then past her. She could smell hay, sweat, and something indefinable on the wind as he moved by her. It didn't smell bad.

On the contrary, he smelled like the land. Like hard work and sunshine. Like dirt and trees.

It made her heart trip over itself, but she quickly gathered her wits. Austin Wilder was the kind of man who turned female heads wherever he went. It was impossible to ignore him. But one thing Millie had going for her—she was focused.

And she would remain focused now.

He held the door open and led her inside the house. She wasn't sure what she had been expecting, but she found herself fascinated by this place. It was clean. A large open space, a living room, kitchen, and dining area all combined into one. There was a large bookshelf next to an overstuffed chair. Everything was old, well-worn, but scrupulously kept.

She didn't think there was a speck of dust to be found in the whole place, and it was just . . . not at all what she had expected from a rancher who was descended from one of the Wild West's most notorious outlaws.

For a man with a tarnished reputation, he kept a very clean house.

"Have a seat," he said, gesturing to a spot at the square oak dining table.

There was no decor in the place, nothing that spoke of whimsy. A wooden floor, the walls covered in wood paneling, the ceiling also wood, with large log beams.

There were blinds, not curtains, over the window. And there wasn't so much as a throw pillow on the couch. No vases with flowers, or anything like that.

It was nearly military, all that cleanliness combined with the simplicity.

"So what makes you think this is something the town wants? Something you can be successful with."

"I think you misunderstand me. This isn't a moneymaking venture. We have a building. The Talbot family. And I want to use it for this. The library is already in possession of a great many documents that I can use. But what I really want is to make the exhibit as interactive as possible. And I want people to get a deeper look at the reality of this place."

"All right. And to do that you want . . . to go through all my family's old shit?"

"Yes. And you know, if you . . . have any heirlooms you might possibly be interested in donating."

"We have a collection of things in the attic."

"They're labeled and sorted, aren't they?" she asked.

Because she could see it. He took good care of what he had.

He was an enigma, Austin Wilder. A man who read books, had a meticulously clean home, everything in its place, and yet possessed an outlaw reputation.

"They are," he confirmed. "How did you guess?"

"You seem like the type."

He chuckled. "Most people would say that I don't."

"Most people haven't watched you check books out for the last twenty years."

He laughed dryly. "Fair enough. So when you put forward your plan for the new museum, you're confident that the town council is going to approve it? We both know they have a chokehold on what happens on Main Street."

"Yes," she said, "they do and . . . that's where I need . . . my second favor."

"Your second favor relates to the town council," he said, the words deadpan.

"Yes."

"Just how do you think I can help you with a whole panel of

people who think I'm as bad as every other Wilder who came before me?"

She cleared her throat. "It doesn't matter what they think. You have the vote. The founding family vote."

He rubbed his chin, and the sound of his whiskers scraping against his palm sent an electric response all down her spine. "I see. So you don't just want to take my family heirlooms and journals to make a museum. You want me to physically come and exercise a vote I've chosen never to exercise even once."

Well, when he put it like that.

"I was hoping you might," she said.

"All for what? For your family's continued glory?"

"I told you," she said, sputtering now. "I . . . I don't want that. I want to present history in a real way and—"

"And continue with your sensationalized versions of history."

"They aren't *mine*," she said.

"You're a Talbot."

As if that was the end of the discussion.

"And you're a Wilder but—"

"I think you can see yourself out," he said.

She was so shocked that she almost couldn't comprehend what he'd just said. "What?"

"You heard me. You can see yourself out."

"I . . . I . . . ."

"Is no not enough? Then how about *hell* no."

And with that, he stood up and gestured toward the door. And Millie Talbot found herself right back out on the front porch with no artifacts, no ally, and no hope.

Chapter 2

*Pa is dead now, and that means I've got to keep the boys safe,
to keep them fed. We've been at Fort Stevens since he died. The
plan is to head south, for gold.*

—Austin Wilder's journal, May 10, 1848

"Can you believe the audacity of that little mouse?" Austin hadn't
stopped ranting since Millie Talbot had left his house and taken herself back on down the mountain.

"Unbelievable," his brother Carson said.

"Absolutely unconscionable," his other brother, Flynn, said.

"I don't know." Cassidy, the youngest child and only girl, looked
up at him with a sly expression in her eyes. "I think maybe you're
the asshole."

"Is that so? Well, that's the thanks I get for feeding and clothing
you for the past fifteen years, you bratty little mite."

Cassidy did not fear him in the way she should, because he'd had
to reform when she'd come into his life. A good thing, he felt, but
damn, it would be nice if she understood that he used to be intimidating. He used to scare women and children in the streets.

Not on purpose, but his very presence had been a dark cloud. A
long shadow, etc.

It still was, he supposed. But to Cassidy he was just . . . her big
brother.

She shrugged. "I'm just saying. This is actually what you want,
Austin. You want people to understand our family better."

"I don't care if people understand our family. What I care about is the truth. And the jumped-up version of history this town consideres its claim to fame is just bullshit."

"What does it matter?" Flynn asked. "I mean, seriously. Who cares if we're the outlaws. Hell, it does me good when I go down to the bar and try to find a woman."

"Operative word being *try*," Carson said, his voice dry.

"I do just fine, big brother."

"Ew," Cassidy said.

"Flynn," Austin said, looking at his half brother, "I thought you'd enjoy the chance to poke at Danielle."

Flynn snorted. "She's basically a stranger. She and Michael have barely said a handful of words to me. Even when I did have to spend the holidays with them."

"Your half brother Michael or her new boyfriend, Michael Hall?"

Flynn's face contorted. "Oh. God. She's really with. . . ." He shook his head. "Just when I think I can't want more distance between myself and my mother's side of the family. This is why I'd rather be an outlaw than ever be associated with one of them."

Cassidy was also wrinkling her nose at the whole Michael/Michael thing. "I don't care about the outlaw reputation stuff."

"It's not the reputation," said Austin. "I'm not doing this for reputation. I'm doing it because. . . ."

Because he was thirty-five. Because all the other men in their family had the bad luck to die before they reached this advanced age. And here he was.

Here he was staring down a future that he hadn't really figured he'd have. Not that he had been living the kind of life that had killed those who'd come before him. But he had been sort of convinced that it was a family curse.

His namesake, Austin Wilder, had in fact been killed in a shootout on the main street of town. He knew, also, that Austin Wilder had been an outlaw. By any definition of the word. He had robbed stagecoaches, trains, banks—basically, if it wasn't nailed down, he was happy to try to take it.

He hadn't been a murderer, though. Austin was convinced of

that. Because his great-great-great-great-great-grandfather had kept a detailed journal for most of his life, and if he had killed someone, it would have been written in those pages, in black and white. The journal had never existed to absolve the man. There were some damning things written in it.

But Austin knew there was more to the story than he had in those pages.

Millie Talbot had access to other letters. Journals. Artifacts. She had said so herself. That was the one thing that tempted him to play ball with her. Except . . . there was his pride. And pride was a pretty big factor in his life. Really, in everything he did.

He wasn't that far removed from his bloodline.

He might not be a criminal—currently—he might not be a cheater, a gambler, or a drunkard, but he *was* bloody minded, with a stubborn streak wider than Outlaw Lake.

And the idea of agreeing to help out a Talbot with anything, the idea of going down into town and participating in that travesty they called a town council meeting, was enough to make his blood boil.

"I thought you were thinking you might find yourself a wife," Carson said.

Austin regretted sharing that. He had gotten drunk a couple weeks ago and told his brother that he was starting to think about the future, which he had never done before. But once his birthday had passed and he'd turned thirty-five without incident, making him ancient in the Wilder timeline, he had begun to think about what life looked like on the other side.

So yeah, he had thought about a wife. Kids. He was trying to set the record straight when it came to the family. If there were no descendants. . . . Well, it made the whole thing seem kind of pointless.

Flynn was never going to have children. Flynn was never going to do anything but run around town, and indeed the entirety of Jackson County, being an abject manwhore. Carson had tried his hand at love and marriage, and it had ended so suddenly, and in such a devastating way, he knew full well his brother was never going to try again.

After Alyssa's death, Carson had looked at him and said that he figured he was going to live well past thirty-five, because he was going to have to live with the grief, and the weight, of having lost his wife.

Austin wished he could have said something comforting in response. He wished he could've said he didn't think fate worked like that.

But he did. So all he'd been able to do was raise a glass and get blinding drunk in a show of support.

"That's not really a present action item," Austin said.

"You're on borrowed time at this point," Cassidy said, cheerfully.

"You're just smug because the women in the family don't have a long history of dying at thirty-four," Flynn said.

"Yes," Cassidy said dryly. "The half sister who got left on your doorstep on Christmas Eve fifteen years ago is smug. Super smug."

"So what exactly do you think I should do?" Austin asked, looking at Carson.

"I think you should consider giving her what she wants. Or the very least, go down there to that town hall meeting and cause a ruckus with your mere presence. Can you imagine?"

"To what end?"

"Why are we here?" Carson asked. "I think that's the better question."

"Because this is our homestead," Austin said. "And it doesn't matter how the town treats us, and it doesn't matter that we will always be the bad guys, this land is ours. This is Rustler Mountain. On the banks of Outlaw Lake. This is our country."

"So what exactly is the problem with putting yourself in a position where you can actually impact what's happening in town?"

"Because I . . . don't like people," Austin said. "Present company excluded. Most of the time."

"Yeah," Flynn said. "Most of the time."

It was the truth. Austin felt deeply entitled to his land. To the house that they still owned on Main Street, even though it was boarded up. The house that the original Austin Wilder had bought for his wife, so that she could have a beautiful home. So that their children could have a future. One that he had never gotten to see.

And he loved his family. His and Carson's mom had left when they were little, because their dad was a cheating asshole and couldn't keep a woman to save his life. Their mom had left them because they'd been wild hellions who had done whatever they felt like, whenever they felt like it.

They'd earned that abandonment, he supposed.

Flynn's mom hadn't lasted much longer, though she'd been in and out of his life over the years instead of being totally absent. And Cassidy was the product of an affair that had happened outside of town, which was how she had found herself abandoned on the doorstep as a little girl. But by then, their dad had already been dead, and it was up to the brothers to raise her.

They had done it. They'd stopped making moonshine—other than for their own private consumption—they'd stopped fighting, they'd stopped being menaces. Mostly. Because Austin had wanted to do something for Cassidy that no one in their collection of parents had seemed to be willing to do for them.

Change.

The truth was, Austin had loved his dad.

He had been a charming bastard. It wasn't a mystery how he had managed to get all those women to have children with him. He had been likable. Rough, sure—he'd been the one who'd taught them how to throw a punch. But he'd taken a giddy pleasure in being a rebel, and he'd passed that on to his boys.

It was just that he didn't have any staying power. He wasn't reliable. He hadn't done a very good job of running the ranch that Austin himself now ran. The ranch was the reason Austin had gotten so involved in reading.

Because he had been able to learn all the things he needed to know to be the man of the house. God knew he'd needed that information. It had been essential for him to figure out how to take care of everything and everyone. Because his dad might grill a mean steak and spin a great yarn, but he wasn't going to make sure that there was enough money in the bank to pay the power bill and keep the lights on.

He wasn't going to be there at night to tuck his kids into bed, he wasn't going to make sure that anything other than steak was well-stocked in the larder.

He wasn't going to get a designated driver to make sure he got home safely.

And hell, at the time Austin hadn't thought anything of it. They'd all done stupid shit all the time. Austin had been a teenager, tall for his age and too strong for his own good. He'd gotten up to all kinds of trouble whenever possible, living down to his reputation, because why the hell not? He'd dragged his brothers along too, right with him into purgatory.

But then, like a one-two punch, their dad drove his bike into a tree, and Cassidy had been dropped on their doorstep, and he'd known it had to change.

He supposed there was a particular sort of masochism inherent in staying in a town where everyone had known from the day you were born that you were the bad guy.

But it was their land. It was their birthright. Along with their history. That was why he was going through all the journals of the original Austin Wilder. It was why he was writing his book. Incidentally, it was why he had checked out *The Elements of Style*.

The Jack Reacher book was just for fun.

He really hated to consider it, but he had to wonder if his brother had a point. If participating in the town meeting might actually make his life easier. If what Millie had actually been offering him was a path into . . . the future.

Maybe it was time for him to take his position in the group of founding families.

It would be better for all of them.

Because whether or not his brothers thought they were going to have families or futures including love and marriage and all that, he wanted to plan for the possibility that they might. He was the family patriarch, as dubious an honor as that was in this family, and it meant that the future mattered to him.

They were living the legacy of all the people who had lived on this land before them. And anyone who came after would be living theirs.

The sins of the father and the grandfather and the great-great-grandfather. On and on.

He was also curious as hell what information Millie Talbot had access to. Because he had some suspicions about what had actually gone down the day that his ancestor had been shot in the street. He would dearly love to get his hands on the letters and journals written from the Talbot side of things. She had said that the Talbots were the only ones with representation in the museum, but he had to wonder how curated that representation was.

"I'll consider it," he said.

He pushed up from the table and walked over to the oven, where he pulled out the chicken pot pie he had been baking. Not made by him, obviously. He had picked it up in Jacksonville, which was a town about thirty-five miles away. Sometimes he just didn't feel like dealing with the dynamics in Rustler Mountain, in which case he took the long drive. And if he wanted to go to the Walmart, he had to take an even longer drive into Medford.

He didn't mind rural living. In fact, he thought it was perfect. There was nothing but views for miles around, and he had his family to talk to if he was ever lonely. Plus, there were enough towns not too far away where he could find a woman for a little bit of company if the urge took him.

What would it be like to have a slightly easier relationship with the people about town? Was it even possible? Well, if he dug up the information he thought he might be able to find, he might even change history.

That, though, would probably not make him any more popular around here. The town's heroes were enshrined in glory. Their villains firmly kept in the shadows.

He brought the pie tin over to the table and slammed it down in the center on top of a stone trivet. "Eat up, you filthy animals."

Everybody grabbed paper plates and disposable utensils and ate the pie with relish. After which he brought out a second pie—this one blackberry—for dessert.

He dug into the pie and began to chew thoughtfully. "If I go down and give her our vote, they're just going to continue with that Gold Rush Days nonsense."

"It doesn't really affect you," Carson pointed out. "I mean, because you don't participate in anything, and you don't go to anything. So even if the end result is that it goes on, and they continue to take our family name in vain, what does it really matter?"

"Here's the thing," said Flynn. "They aren't really taking our family name in vain. The Wilders were outlaws. I get that it bothers you, Austin, but it's the truth."

"No," Austin said. "It's not what bothers me. What bothers me is that the Wilder brothers were painted as being terrible people. In reality, they did what they had to do to survive. They were complicated. Austin Wilder loved his wife, he loved his children. He wasn't only a bad man. He was . . . a good man who did bad things."

And Austin needed to believe that was a real thing. A possible thing.

"I don't know about that," Carson said. "I think if you get all your earthly goods by nefarious means, you might not actually be a good person."

"The mountain that we're sitting on was bought with stolen gold, Carson. If you're going to be all high and mighty about it, then maybe you shouldn't have a seat at the table."

He was mostly kidding. Mostly.

"Hey, I am Team Wilder," said Carson. "I swear on the name of Butch Hancock the Traitor."

At the mention of Butch Hancock, Flynn raised his middle

finger to the sky and Cassidy pantomimed spitting on the ground. Butch Hancock the Traitor was notorious in their family lore. The town might not think much about him, but as far as they were all concerned, he had abandoned his friends when they needed him most.

And Austin suspected, he had betrayed them.

Based on some of the things in the diaries . . . he was just suspicious.

"All right," he said. "I'll do it. But I'm not happy about it."

"I am," said Cassidy. "This is interesting. Nothing interesting ever happens around here."

He didn't say that, in fact, too many interesting things happened to them. The problem was that they tended to be bad. Tended to involve loss.

But maybe this was his opportunity to make something good happen for their family. Hell, that would be a boon.

And if he actually got his book written and published, a real, in-depth look at the complexity of a Wild West outlaw who had been a good husband, a good father, a caregiver to his siblings. . . .

It might change the way people thought of the Wilder family.

Maybe it did matter to him. More than he had realized.

Maybe their reputation was more of a factor than he had previously believed.

But either way, Millie's proposal might be the first step to changing it.

He just wished it didn't mean joining forces with a Talbot.

Chapter 3

Four days without food and I couldn't stand it anymore. Not for me, but for the boys. I could hear their stomachs growling when they were trying to sleep. I sneaked into another camp and took a rasher of bacon. But when we started cooking it up, the smell filled the air and I was afraid they'd know it was us who took it. But no one came to our camp or said anything.

—Austin Wilder's journal, May 30, 1848

Millie felt as if she was heading to the gallows. Which was sort of amusing, all things considered. Because not a Talbot in history had ever been sent to the gallows. But Jesse and William Wilder had been hanged publicly on the courthouse lawn on charges of robbery and murder.

She supposed it was really no wonder that Austin wasn't a huge fan of town history. But it wasn't her fault that his ancestors had been outlaws.

It felt relevant, though, as she put on a dress that only a few months ago she knew Michael would have pretended to like. She was getting ready to endure public humiliation at the town council meeting where she was going to get outvoted, and there was nothing she could do about it.

If this was her lesson in strength, she was going to be irritated. She had really hoped that the lesson was going to be that she could gain victory as long as she was willing to put herself in uncomfortable situations.

Maybe it was a sign of growth to be okay with the fact that she had to go even though she was going to lose.

Okay was perhaps a strong word.

She wasn't going to be a no-show. She had too much pride for that. She wished she had had a little bit more pride before now.

Wished she had had just a little bit more pride when she had been dating Michael. Because then maybe she would have seen all the relentless red flags in their relationship. But the problem was she had just been so. . . . She really didn't like the truth. Because the truth was that she had been so surprised any man was paying attention to her that she had been willing to overlook the way he managed to give compliments that hurt. The way he had twisted any given situation and made her question herself.

It was always going to be a broken dynamic when one partner thought they were the catch, and the other one thought they were lucky.

She knew that now. But she had been surprised he'd wanted to date her for as long as he had. Let alone ask her to marry him. She felt the odds of that happening again were low.

Wow. Be sadder, Millie.

She looked at her reflection in the mirror and wished that the woman staring back at her didn't look quite so tired.

Someone was going to mention that when she walked into the town council meeting. She just knew it.

She wrinkled her nose, and that made her laugh, because it was silly. And it reminded her of her mom. She could remember her doing that, sitting at the library desk, dealing with a difficult patron with endless grace and wisdom, and then turning to where Millie was sitting behind her, scrunching her whole face to let Millie know just how much her mom actually disapproved of the person's behavior.

That was an interesting side effect of losing her dad. It had brought the loss of her mother closer to the surface too.

But she would hold on to the good memory for now. And she would let it boost her out the door and into her car, down the main street, then left to the old courthouse building.

It was a two-story redbrick structure, with a white roof that had a steeple, with an American flag perched up on the top.

There was a wide green lawn where arts and crafts markets were held every Sunday in the summer, and where there was a community picnic on July Fourth. Invariably, there were at least ten differ-

ent varieties of doodle dog wandering around wearing bandannas,
leading their owners on leashes. She supposed she had to admit that
even if her museum was voted down, there was still a robust sense of
community in Rustler Mountain.

During Christmas there were people who made old-fashioned
candy on different street corners and carolers in Victorian clothes
walking the sidewalks. There was Butch Hancock's Wild West
Show, which might be controversial—to Austin at least—but
brought heavy traffic into town every weekend in the summer, with
rodeo events and blacksmithing demonstrations by Jessie Jane Hancock on an old-fashioned forge.

Gold Rush Days was just the most . . . it was the most educa-
tional event, and the museum would be a place where that history
could be experienced all year long.

What she wanted mattered.

She scowled as she found a parking space and squeezed her little
Camry into it. She didn't need to be placating herself already. Telling herself that it was going to be okay if she lost before the actual
loss was ridiculous.

She would *win*. She *would* win.

Except she knew everybody who would be at the meeting and
she knew exactly how they were going to vote.

This was the problem with living in the same small town for
all of her life. She loved it here. She really did. But everyone had
a prescribed role to play. Austin could act as if it was irritating that
everyone thought of him as a villain. But he had played that part by
leaving her metaphorically tied to the train tracks. As for everybody
on the town council, and the other founding families . . . half of
them were acting like they were still in high school. And what could
be done about that?

She hated it. But there wasn't much that she could do about it.
Except leave. And she wasn't going to leave. This was her home.
This was. . . .

She felt as if she might float away all of a sudden, sitting there
in her car with her fingers still wrapped around the steering wheel.

Because home meant her mother in the library, and her father at the sheriff's office, and the family name, and now she felt untethered.

She was still a Talbot.

But it didn't seem to matter when she was the family representative, not the way it had when it was her dad. Not even the way it had when it was her mother, who had been the very opposite of a stern librarian. Who had offered a safe place for everyone in the community to come in to learn.

She had known that she could never be her dad, so she had set out to try to give the community what her mother had.

She had completed an online degree to get her master's in library science through an online program and had maintained a support position at the library throughout. Because her mother had been sick. Then partway through Millie's degree, her mother had died. She had always been glad that she hadn't gone away to school.

But it had meant that she hadn't really met other people. She was with the same people she had always known, and who had always known her. Then when Michael had shown an interest in her, she had thought everything was changing.

In hindsight, she suspected he had probably just wanted to be with a Talbot. He had believed there would be a certain sort of cachet in being with her.

But she wasn't her father. She didn't walk around with the heroism of the past stitched into her very bones. He'd done that. He had worn his badge with ease and authority. He'd been affable, but firm when he needed to be.

He'd been the legend of the Wild West sheriff come to the modern age.

Like his father before him, and his father before him.

And then Millie had come along. She was the only girl in generations of Talbots, and her parents had never been able to have another child. She hadn't felt compelled, or even able, to carry on the lawman legacy of the Talbots.

She didn't think it was a coincidence that Michael stopped being so careful about his affair after her dad died.

He'd clearly decided not to preserve the future he'd been planning with her, because it wasn't going to give him what he wanted.

A chance to climb the social ladder in a town where said ladder was barely a step stool.

She made a short, frustrated growling noise, hit the steering wheel, and got out of the car. She shut the door, not bothering to lock it, because she never did in Rustler Mountain, and crossed the grass before taking the steps two at a time up to the front door of the courthouse. She pushed the black door open and walked inside, her shoes echoing on the dark wood floor.

She could still remember when this place had been the museum. She missed it. Profoundly.

It still smelled the same inside. Hundreds of years of moisture, age, and different wood varnishes mingling together, creating this specific scent only found in historic buildings. There was something about it that felt welcoming to her.

She wanted to get down to the basement to look at all the artifacts.

She wanted. . . . She felt grounded again. The history of this place, of the people who'd walked these halls, was important.

She wanted to preserve this piece of the past for the future of the town, and for the future of everyone, really. Because she truly believed that history had to be preserved so that people could truly understand the times they lived in now.

Yes, the Wild West was interesting. It was sensational. There were stories of daring cowboys, of wild outlaws. There were also grave stories of injustice. Examples of humans choosing to be the worst versions of themselves over and over again. The way they continued to do. The way they split themselves into groups and marginalized people who didn't look like them. Who didn't think like them.

She thought if humanity was ever going to move forward, people had to really understand where they had come from.

She believed it wholeheartedly. Just as she believed that books were the key to changing a person's heart. That stories were really what taught people that we're all more alike than different.

So she cared about her little corner of the world. Her little piece of history.

Because she thought all of those things mattered. That children would go through the library and come out different from when they'd come in. That they would come out of living history demonstrations with a deeper understanding of how much progress had been made in the world. And how little at the same time.

She used her passion to steel her nerves as she walked down the hallway and into the meeting room.

It was already full, with most everyone milling around a table in the corner that held cookies no one ever ate, and open bottles of wine that had been donated by Alana from White Owl Vineyards. There was no shortage of vineyards in the area. The climate was great for growing grapes, and there were many fine local wines, which also helped draw tourists to the area. There were wine trail tours that started in Jacksonville, and moved from Ruch to Applegate, and then on to Rustler Mountain. Big vans full of people growing increasingly tipsy as the tour went on. A party atmosphere in every sense of the word.

And of course that was the kind of thing Danielle wanted to foster, which put Alana on Danielle's side. Unfortunate, because it wasn't that Millie was opposed to the wine tours. She wanted to support local business in all its forms.

It was just. . . . She didn't want to lose what made Rustler Mountain unique.

Marietta Hensley caught her gaze right when she walked in, and it was not a friendly gaze. Marietta was one of Danielle's dear friends.

Millie wondered what the discussion was around Michael, Danielle, and the fact that their relationship had started with infidelity. Somehow *Millie* had come out of it as the villain to the people who swore fealty to Danielle.

Actually, she didn't wonder. Because she didn't really want to know what array of nonsense had been presented as justification for that.

She was almost certain the biggest get-out-of-jail-free card for Michael and Danielle was that he and Millie hadn't been married yet. Like that made it better.

"Hi, Millie. You look tired." Her expression of faux concern was almost comical.

Almost.

"Thanks. I am," Millie said. Marietta clearly didn't know what to say to that, so she slowly sidled into a group of people who were already in conversation.

Good to know she still had the ability to kill a social interaction with a well-placed truth.

She searched the room desperately until some of the milling bodies moved and she caught Heather Lin-Stewart's eye.

Heather scooped up a clear plastic cup of wine and crossed the room, handing it to Millie. "Do you think you're going to win?" Heather asked.

Heather was probably Millie's best friend in the world. She had always been nice to Millie. Even in high school.

Heather had gone away to college and had made more friends. She'd gotten married and had kids. She was busy in different ways than Millie, and even though they lived close together it was hard for them to find time to just hang out.

But she had been slated to be a bridesmaid in Millie's wedding and had offered to personally castrate Michael when Millie had caught him cheating. She was there when it counted.

Like now.

"I don't think so," Millie said.

"Meh," she said, pulling a face. "I have so many great letters for you. Correspondence that Gin Lin got from China, old gold-mining equipment. Copies of some of the claims. My dad cleaned out the storage unit at the back of the property, and it was packed to the gills with that kind of thing."

"We'll figure out a way," Millie said, sounding much more hopeful than she felt. "Even if I have to open the exhibit up in the back room of the library and do rotating displays." It was a possibility. It didn't make her happy, but the truth was, it was a possibility. And maybe she needed to start thinking in terms of compromise.

Even if she didn't want to.

"Well, Danielle is hideous," Heather said.

"Inside," she said. "Outside, she's the opposite of hideous."

"I know. It would be really convenient if horrible people signaled it. Like poison dart frogs."

"Yes. It would. As it is, half the time you're poisoned before you even know you need to look out."

Not that she and Danielle had ever been friends. But she definitely hadn't imagined that the woman was sleeping with Millie's fiancé.

Everyone was beginning to file into their seats, and Millie and Heather were moving in that direction also when a hush fell over the room.

Heads began to turn toward the door, and Millie turned to look as well.

Her heart stopped.

There he was, standing in the doorway, dressed in all black, looking every inch the outlaw.

Black cowboy hat, black shirt, black jeans. Black boots.

Good thing she'd never had a crush on him.

"*No*," said Heather.

"*Oh*," said Millie.

"Did you know he was coming?"

"No. He totally. . . . He said no."

He scanned the room, and the minute his eyes connected with Millie's, she found herself completely frozen in place. Like a little sheep that had been spotted by a wolf.

And then he began to move toward her, every step fluid, languid, not doing anything to dispel the feeling that he was predator to her prey.

"Can we have a word?" he asked.

She could feel every eye in the room on her. She really hadn't expected that. Not at this point. Yes, she had known they would all look at her when she made her presentation and when it was time to vote. They would all look at her and vote no, and feel triumph or pity depending on who they were and which camp they were in. But she hadn't expected everybody to be staring now, while Austin Wilder stood there in front of her, looking into her.

"Sure," she said, glancing at Heather and then turning to face him. He tilted his head toward the door, then turned away from her, clearly indicating that she was supposed to follow him. So she did.

Her footsteps seemed loud in the room, and it felt as if everyone had gone completely quiet. As if everyone was watching them.

They went out to the hallway, and he turned toward her, arms crossed over his broad chest. "I might be convinced to vote for you," he said.

"Really?"

She felt a rush of relief, and suddenly her knees were weak. But she was pretty sure that was from relief, and not the fact that he towered over her. She had been so overwhelmed by him yesterday, she hadn't fully processed just how tall he was.

She only came up to the center of his chest. He made her feel like a mouse. Fitting, since many of the people in that room had called her Millie Mouse when they were in high school. But she was not a mouse. Or maybe she was, but she was a very determined one, who had gone up the mountain and come down with Austin Wilder. To her own astonishment.

"What changed your mind?"

"Well, I wouldn't go saying I did anything quite so dramatic as change my mind. But I had a think about it. I don't have any affection for the Wild West shows, or any reenactments that include the death of my namesake. Having said that, what I do have affection for is history. And I would be willing to give you some of the information I have about my family if I could get access to letters and journals from the perspective of yours."

"Why?"

He lifted a broad shoulder. "Research."

"For?"

"Something that isn't your business. I'm not looking to pick out a china pattern with you, Millie. I just want to see what you have about the Talbots. And anything that might exist about the arrest of the Wilders, and the shooting of Austin."

"Sure. Of course." She wondered if she should offer to give him a little bit more say in the different events connected with the Gold Rush Days. But she found she didn't want to give him a say. She wanted tradition. Because she felt especially attached to it right now. Because of her dad. Because of how much she missed him, and how much he had loved Gold Rush Days.

How much her family's past had meant to him.

That the Talbot family had cleaned up the streets, not just of Rustler Mountain, but of the West. Because the Wilder brothers had been a scourge.

She looked up into Austin Wilder's face, with those thoughts still whirling in her head.

"And this is all you want? You'll vote yes, and you'll give me access to information on your family?"

"Conditionally. I'll vote yes, but if I don't like the way you proceed, then I won't give you anything of my family's."

"That's fair."

"Good. Now let's go."

When they turned and walked back into the room, she felt a ripple go through the crowd. She hadn't considered what it would look like for her to walk into a room, elbow to elbow. . . . Well, elbow to the top of her shoulder, with Austin Wilder.

She, Millie Talbot.

Maybe this was her moment of infamy.

She hadn't realized she'd wanted one until this instant.

But having the ability to shock people, rather than simply arouse pity, was nice for a change.

He sat in the back, and she moved to the spot where she had been intent on sitting earlier, next to Heather.

She could feel Danielle looking at her, her blue gaze pointed. She could also feel Michael staring at her. They didn't know what she had done. They had no idea what she had planned, they didn't know why Austin was here, or how she knew him.

That made her feel powerful.

For once, she was completely unpredictable. And that was extraordinarily intoxicating.

She wasn't mousy. Okay, maybe she was. But she was more than that.

And when it was her turn to speak, she walked to the front of the room with conviction. "You all know me, and I'm only going to cover the proposal you were sent after the previous month's meeting. I am proposing that a portion of the budget be allocated back to the historical society. To Gold Rush Days, and to the reopening of the Rustler Mountain Museum. This would be good for tourism, not just the traditional kind that we are all accustomed to, but school groups as well. I truly believe that only by looking at the past can we really see the way forward to the future. I am ready to put this plan to a vote."

And then it was Danielle's turn to speak.

She stood up, a sugary smile on her face. "Thank you so much, Millie," she said, her grin so broad and brittle that Millie was sure it was going to break her face. "That was a lovely speech. But the reality is that times are hard economically. We need to lean into projects that will directly increase revenue to the town."

Completely unlike her, and absolutely out of character, Millie blurted, "And how exactly is travel for you and your friends going to do that?"

Danielle was undeterred, which was why she was the mayor and Millie was not. She continued to seem nonconfrontational, smiley, and unruffled. "Because education for myself and other members of the council is helpful in figuring out how to effectively manage the community. And it isn't that I don't believe in the importance of history. I do. Of course. As you know, I am descended from the first doctor ever to live in Rustler Mountain. And of course I would love to honor our history in a permanent way such as a museum. But, the economic times being what they are, I just feel that it isn't the right moment."

Danielle swanned around acting as if she herself was currently a physician, when in fact no one in her family since that first doctor had ever been in the medical profession. Her family actually owned a real estate company. Which was fine. But she could take it down a notch.

Millie felt as if she was boiling in her own rage. Because already this woman. . . . It took so much nerve to look at her in the face like this.

Michael couldn't make eye contact with Millie. She took a small amount of comfort in that.

"All those in favor of maintaining the budget with an increase for rising costs, indicate your support with a show of hands."

Half the hands in the room went up, just as Millie had known they would.

"And all those in favor of Millie's suggestion?"

It was truly heartening to watch the show of support she had. She raised her own hand, and so did Heather. Everyone sitting on her side of the room followed suit.

Then she heard footsteps, heavy, coming down the center aisle. She knew exactly who it was. Somehow it sounded as if those footsteps were being made by black boots.

"I'm in favor of Millie's proposition," he said, his voice deep, commanding. Menacing, a little.

Michael stood up and faced Austin. Suddenly it was as if she was looking at a showdown in the middle of town.

All those years ago.

"You never exercise your voting rights. Nobody in your family does," he said.

"And rumor has it, you didn't exercise your right to be a faithful fiancé."

A small gasp went through the room. Nobody had ever mentioned that outright. Everybody pretended it hadn't happened.

Michael sputtered. And Danielle was frozen with rage.

"That doesn't have anything to do with our budget," Danielle
said.

"Maybe not. But the fact that I haven't chosen to exercise my
right before doesn't have much to do with anything either. It's my
right as a member of one of the town's founding families."

"I think whether or not the Wilders are included as one of the
founding families could and *should* be up for debate," said Danielle.

"But it's not," he said.

"I don't think that felons—"

"Do you mean my ancestors?"

Danielle's eyes narrowed. "Not exclusively."

"Careful," Austin said. "I've personally never been convicted
of a thing. Also, you're treading dangerously close to insulting your
own family."

Silence filled the room and he hooked his thumbs in his belt
loops and looked around, making sure to cast an eye over everyone.
When he looked at her, it was like being touched by electricity.

"You may not like the way that my family helped found this
place," he said. "But they did. In fact, they invested a fair amount of
the money they stole in these streets. So if you have a problem with
our role, it's too damned bad."

"I think there should be a codicil that states there must be warning before somebody shows up and—"

"But there isn't," Austin said, his voice hard, definitive.

She could watch Danielle making projections behind her blue
eyes. Trying to figure out what the next move was. If she dug in
and tried to get her way at the expense of protocol and any sort of
pretense of civility, then she would possibly lose the allies she had.
Because while her close friends might not care if Danielle was being
entirely scrupulous, the majority of people did.

While Danielle's friends had sided with her over Millie's demolished wedding, when it came to the general populace she and Michael were on thin ice after the affair. Millie supposed that should be salve for her broken heart. That most people at least recognized the cruelty of it.

Though she had a feeling most people thought Michael couldn't really be blamed. After all, Danielle was much prettier than Millie.

"Well, that's . . . that's settled?" Danielle looked around the room. "Everyone realizes that this means the budget will be set and we will be planning and executing Gold Rush Days again. I'm not sure it's going to be easy to drum up the number of volunteer hours necessary. In fact," Danielle said, a militant light in her eye, "that is one piece of information your paperwork was missing. We might have the money, but do we have the ability to execute? You can't be the only person running things."

"I'll do it," Austin said, before everyone had even taken a breath.

Millie whipped her head toward him. "Really?"

"Yes. It's about time the Wilder family had a say in how we're represented anyway."

"You had a say in how you were represented," Michael said, his tone arch. "By your own behavior."

"Careful now," Austin said, his mouth curving into a half smile. "If we start talking about behavior, this might go a direction you won't like."

"We won't be engaging in revisionist history," Michael shot back.

"Oh, does that mean that you're going to include information on how your ancestor tried to collect exorbitant interest from mine because he was Chinese?" Heather asked, her gaze filled with fire.

Michael sputtered. "Maybe the plaques on the bank need an update."

"Calling it revisionist history is assuming the whole truth got told in the first place," Heather said. "And I know full well that isn't true."

Heather looked at Millie and smiled slightly.

Millie smiled back. "And as part of the museum reopening, I aim to present deeper insight into the history of the town," she said. "I hope to correct some of the narratives that were told."

"Will there be a children's museum?" The question was asked by one of the men who had voted against the endeavor but also had small children. Clearly, now that his side had lost, all he really cared about was how the museum might benefit him.

"Yes," Millie said. "There will be a general store. One that replicates the original general store in Rustler Mountain."

"And what building exactly are you going to use?" Danielle asked.

"I'm hoping to use the old Waterford building my family—I mean that I own." There was no one but her. Not anymore.

It still didn't feel as if it was just her building.

"You're going to have to get approval."

"I know," Millie said. "Fortunately, that approval goes through the county." *Not you.*

But she didn't say that last part out loud, because they were trading fake niceties. Fake civility.

"All right. You have your earmarked budget," Danielle said. "Let's move on to the next order of business."

But Millie couldn't hear the rest of the meeting, because her ears were buzzing, and her entire body was floaty and tingly. As if she had ascended to a cloud somewhere high above this room.

And when it was over, she found that what she really needed was to get back home. To silence, to isolation. To take a minute to gather her thoughts. She waved at Heather and scurried out of the room as the meeting adjourned. But as she put her hand on the door, she felt an iron grip on her elbow.

"Wait just one minute."

She turned and her gaze met the furious blue of Austin Wilder's eyes.

Chapter 4

*Desperation makes a man do things he never thought he'd do.
Winning makes a man feel invincible. The two put together make
a man dangerous. Or so I've found.*

—Austin Wilder's journal, October 15, 1848

This whole thing had gone to hell in a handbasket. And as a Wilder, he was more than familiar with that state, but he hadn't exactly been thinking it was one he was going to get himself into *here*.

Maybe he should have guessed that the old courthouse would be the site of his demise, just as it had been for earlier Wilders.

Hell and damn.

He had managed to get himself ensnared in running this thing. But he had walked into some kind of . . . high-school fever dream, and he hadn't liked the way people in that room seemed to think they were better than Millie Talbot. Any more than he liked the way they clearly thought they were better than he. The way they thought they could change the rules just because it suited them.

No. If there was one thing he didn't like, it was a lack of fairness.

He was too intimately acquainted with it. He had been tarred by a very specific brush from the time he was born. Black sheep since day one.

And for a while he'd actually lived it. Why not?

He'd walked around like he owned the place. An outlaw who could go wherever he wanted. Who would ride his horse down Main if the mood struck him and damn all the motorists honking behind him.

Being the bad seed was the birthright of every Wilder who had ever come into the world and Rustler Mountain. His inheritance. And he supposed today was the ultimate expression of the stubbornness that kept them all here anyway.

He knew it would seem completely unhinged to somebody who didn't live here. Hell, maybe it seemed unhinged even to people who did live here. But he refused to be run out, on a rail or anything else. Just like all the Wilders who had come before him.

They were stubborn, and he aimed to honor that legacy.

Or maybe they all died so young, they didn't have the chance to get as sick of all the bullshit as they should have.

Well. That was an interesting thought. He might be less amused by all of this when he was ninety.

Or, he had to change the script.

He'd done it once. When they'd cleaned up their act to raise Cassidy, he and his brothers had done it.

So what if they did it on a broader scale? What if the name *Wilder* meant something different in the town going forward?

Of course, the town had no real motivation for letting it mean anything different. Because it was just so damned convenient to have this outlaw legend. Danielle might not have an interest in history the way Millie did, but she clearly gave a shit about tourism. And he had overheard snippets of those wine trail tours.

When they went down Main Street, the guides hammered on how Austin Wilder had bled out right there in the dirt.

He was used to hearing his own name in connection with that horrific image. It didn't really jar him anymore.

Yeah, basically nobody had an investment in changing that narrative.

Nobody but him.

What if he settled down? What if he had children? What if he was able to pass on a different legacy to them? If he could finish his book . . . he could change the story.

He just had to survive Gold Rush Days first.

"Don't you go scampering out of here like a mouse that got caught in the grain sack. You need to stay and talk to me."

"I do?" She looked up at him, her eyes wide. "Please don't call me a mouse."

He blinked. "Don't scurry like one."

She shook her head, her dark hair swishing with the movement. "No. That's what they used to call me in school. Millie Mouse. Because I was. . . ." Her nose twitched, her gaze darted off to the side.

"I cannot see why they would call you that," he said, his tone dry.

"Then why did you do it?"

"It's obvious why they called you that—sorry you didn't get my sarcasm."

"Well. That's. . . ." People started to filter out of the meeting hall, and he could feel her becoming increasingly uncomfortable.

"Come on," he said.

Still holding her elbow, he propelled her out of the building, down the front steps, and around the corner. His boots sank into the soft ground, and he cursed the overly watered grass. They could use that water for the ranches, but instead it was being used here to make this lawn as green as possible. All right, maybe he could understand the axe that Millie had to grind with the way the funds were allocated in this town.

"How do you see this thing working?" he asked.

"Which thing?"

"I have to help you plan Gold Rush Days. What does that even mean? I've never even been to one of these events, much less *planned* one."

"You're the one that jumped in," she pointed out.

He looked past her head, across the near-vacant side street at the little restaurant on the corner, filled with snug, cozy diners enjoying soup and hamburgers in peace.

He wished he were them. Instead he was standing outside in the wet grass trying to figure out what in the hell he'd gotten himself tied up in.

Because it turned out he had a heart.

What an inconvenient time to discover it.

"Yeah, I did jump in," he said. "Because I couldn't stand . . . all *that*."

"Are you telling me that you volunteered because you felt sorry for me?"

He sighed. "A little bit."

Her cheeks went pink. And for the first time, he looked at her and saw something other than a Talbot.

Something other than the town librarian.

She was pretty. Maybe in a mousy way, but still pretty. Her dark brown hair was glossy, and she had freckles on her nose. Her eyes were hazel, with flecks of green and gold fringed by dark lashes. She was petite. He tended to prefer tall women, and she was. . . .

A Talbot.

He gritted his teeth. "And I want access to anything you have about your family."

"I don't understand what you think you're going to find."

"I think that Austin Wilder was betrayed."

"By who?"

"Well, Lee Talbot for a start."

"How can an outlaw be betrayed by a sheriff?"

He chuckled. "Oh, honey. That you even have to ask that question shows me you don't poke your head up out of your hole all that often. Mainly, I don't think that the Wilder brothers ever killed anybody."

"But they were tried for murder."

"William and Jesse were. Austin wasn't. He was shot dead in the street."

"He had a gun."

"It was the Wild fucking West, Millie. The goddamn preacher had a gun strapped to his hip. That's not notable. Austin was never tried. He was never convicted. And he was definitely betrayed by *someone*. I think it was Butch Hancock. I think he's the one that told law enforcement of the Wilder brothers' identities, so he could skip town with the loot they got from their last robbery."

"What makes you think that?"

"Some things in the journals I have. And I want to see if you have anything that corroborates my hunch."

"I have never seen anything to suggest . . . anything like that. The story I have is . . . the story. That there were witnesses to the last robbery Austin and his gang committed, and their reports led authorities to the house on Main Street where Austin, Butch, Jesse, and William were hiding. Out of respect for Austin's wife and children, they took it outside, where things got violent."

"I don't believe it. I never have, and I never will."

"I don't see what difference it makes." She shifted, her arms wrapped around herself like she was clinging to all the preconceived notions that lived within her. "They were cattle rustlers. All the ranching success the Wilders started with has a basis in stolen cattle. And frankly, once the town found out about that they would have taken vigilante justice into their own hands."

They both knew that back then cattle rustlers often found themselves strung up a neighboring tree, without ever engaging the judicial process.

"This is Rustler Mountain," Austin said. "It was a wild time in a wild town. I don't think they were the only rustlers hiding out in the hills around here. The West was wild, and that was one thing. It's another to accuse them of murders I don't think they committed."

"I just don't see how it would change anything to go kicking over rocks."

"Of course you don't. Because you're held up as a good citizen because your bloodline goes back to a great lawman. And I'm supposed to be bad because my ancestry is filled with outlaws and villains. Believe me, it's much more complicated than that."

"I'm . . . sorry if anyone made you feel that way."

"That's a weak-ass statement."

"I am sorry that they've made you feel that way. I know they have. I live here too and know how judgmental everyone can be. It's wrong. Even though you did cause a lot of trouble back then. . . ."

"And you barely made a squeak," he said.

She glared at him. "Fine. I'm mousy. You've made your point.

And I'm actually not arguing that. . . . If there are incorrect things in public record, they should be corrected. I don't think there are."

"Based on?"

"Extensive research. I'll give you access to everything," she said. "But I'm telling you, if anything like that existed, I would know. I volunteered during Gold Rush Days when I was in middle school and high school. I worked in the museum. I handled a lot of the artifacts. I've read most of the letters."

"And you think that's everything?"

"Obviously it isn't everything. For one thing, there's not enough information on the miners that came from China. They were definitely erased from the history of the town at first. And Heather's family just found a lot of new documents when they were cleaning up their property."

"And that's my point. You don't have *everything*. Or at least, you can't know if you do."

"But the account of the shooting would be with my family. And I've been through my father's things."

He realized then that he hadn't actually considered how recent her father's death was. His own had been dead more than fifteen years. It had been a hard loss. But one he had dealt with more or less. He didn't think much about it anymore. The loss wouldn't be distant for her.

And he wasn't a total monster.

"I'm sorry. About your dad."

She blinked. "Oh. Thank you. I'm . . . not really okay."

But she was here. Fighting for this museum.

"It's hard to believe how things just keep moving. Even when you don't want them to."

A mystified expression passed over her face. "Yes. It is. That is exactly how I feel. Like everything keeps moving at a relentless pace, even though I don't really have the energy to deal with it. I showed up today thinking that I was going to lose."

"Why does it matter so much to you to win?"

"I mean, partly because my fiancé cheated on me with Danielle, and I don't want her to win."

Right. He'd pulled that one out in the meeting. It had been town gossip so widespread, it had made its way up Wilder Mountain, and that was saying something. That Sheriff Talbot's daughter had been jilted less than two months after her father had died, and only a couple of weeks before her wedding.

It was funny, because he didn't *know* Millie. But he had seen her. Every week since she was nothing more than a sprout. And he hadn't been much more than one himself. He remembered her mom always being at that desk, sitting behind a big box of a computer that was probably older than he was. She had always been kind to him. One of the few people who had never treated him as if he was inherently bad. Ironic, because she had married into the Talbot family.

He had been sad when she passed. He had felt as if he'd lost a member of his own family, but he didn't have the words to articulate that feeling, or anyone to share it with.

He didn't much feel inclined to share it now. Because she had actually been Millie's mother. And to him she had just been the lady at the library. But the library meant more to him than it did to most people.

When he'd first gone in when he was a fifth grader, a grumpy old man had told him he should get out because the Wilders weren't welcome.

He'd shouted very loudly, in the high soprano of a ten-year-old boy: *Fuck you, asshole, I'll go where I want!*

And Millie's mother hadn't gotten mad at him. Instead, she'd given him a library card, and said everyone was welcome at the library.

No one had ever told him he was welcome before.

Millie had taken her mother's spot at the desk. Her hands were always efficient as they passed quickly over the keyboard, checking out his books. And he could remember the day that a diamond ring had shown up on her left hand. But he hadn't commented on it, because he didn't make comments to her about her personal life, or really much of anything.

He remembered feeling a little bit perturbed by the sight. Irritated that she had a life outside the library. She was a whole human who didn't just stop existing when he wasn't around. He couldn't articulate why.

Much as he couldn't articulate the grief he had felt over her mother's death.

He also remembered the day the ring disappeared. Which was when he had pounded the ground for information, provided to him by his brother Flynn's best friend, Dalton, who always seemed to know what was going on around town.

"I might be from a family of ne'er-do-wells," he said now, "but I don't like cheaters."

That was one of the few sins he hadn't committed in his day. Of course, he'd never been in a relationship that was more than physical.

"You don't?" she asked.

"I'd stay single if I thought I couldn't stay faithful. Hell, the thing is, you end up single if you behave that way. My dad is a prime example." He snorted. "Well. He was."

"Right." He could see that she was withholding a whole lot of commentary. Everybody knew about their dad's philandering. And if they didn't know every detail, they at least knew about how Cassidy had been left on their doorstep only ten months after their dad's death, the product of some out-of-town affair that he'd had.

"They won't last," he said.

She looked up at him, and suddenly he saw that same core of steel in her eyes that he had first seen when she came to his house. Totally at odds with the way she had been scurrying to safety earlier.

"I don't care if they do," she said. "I'm not heartbroken. I'm angry. I'm angry that I almost married somebody who was doing that to me. That if he hadn't stopped caring about what I thought, I would have walked down the aisle and made vows to somebody who was lying to my face for months. That is actually so scary, and so much worse than catching him in bed with somebody else." She shook her head and looked up at the sky. "It's actually kind of convenient. Because she is my political nemesis in many ways."

"Are you aiming for politics?"

"No. If I wanted to be a politician then I would've become one. I want to be a librarian. And I want to restore the historical programs in town. I don't want to run anything, and I don't want to engage in machinations. I just mean . . . Danielle and I have different goals for the town, I think."

"It's a good thing you aren't planning to go off and be the mayor, I suppose. The library needs you."

The assertion was a little more heartfelt than he had intended.

She looked down, her cheeks going slightly pink, and he was sure she looked . . . pleased. Even though she didn't smile, her eyes sparkled with a different sort of light. Just for a moment.

"I do have plans for Gold Rush Days. I'm not actually starting from nothing."

"That's good to know."

"I have all the plans that previous organizers used in a little folder."

"Great," he said. "A folder."

"You can't pretend that you won't actually be really good at this," she said.

"Why do you think that I'll be good at this?"

"How many books have you read on adjacent subjects? Budgeting, running businesses, all that kind of stuff."

He didn't like that at all. He'd never given it one thought, all the years he'd been checking books out, that the librarian might remember, and be putting a case together about his character based on what he read.

"No, that's not fair," he said. "Isn't my library activity proprietary information?"

"Maybe, but I'm the person it's proprietary with."

"Touché," he said.

"Let's get together tomorrow," she said. "We can meet back at the courthouse. I got the keys to the basement from Donna, who kind of unofficially still heads up the historical society."

"Why is it unofficial?"

"There hasn't been any funding. So when the museum closed, and all the programs ended, she didn't really have anything to do."

"I did like the living history stuff."

"You said that you never got involved in anything like that."

"Well, when I was in school, I didn't exactly have a choice. It was mandatory to go to Gold Rush Days. I'm pretty good at gold panning."

"Good. Maybe you can run the gold panning demonstrations for the kids."

The idea of actually trying to influence youths sent a shock of fear through him. Not much scared him. Kids . . . a little bit.

"You don't look keen," she said.

"I'm just fine. I'll see you tomorrow. We'll go look through all those different things in the basement."

"Austin," she said, just as he turned to go.

"What?"

"Thank you for being my hero."

Chapter 5

Along the way we met up with Butch Hancock. He's a real
outlaw. The kind that thinks nothing of robbing trains and banks.
It makes the mail coaches seem like work for little boys. I'm coming
around to his way of thinking. The riches to be had are worth the
risk.

—Austin Wilder's journal, December 5, 1849

She wanted to bite her own tongue out. That was the most ridiculous thing to say, and she felt . . . ridiculous about it. The words kept echoing in her head all the while she was trying to have a nice evening at home, washing the jitters of the whole day off her body, washing away the discomfort of every interaction she'd had in that meeting house.

They played in her head when she tried to sleep. And when she got up the next morning to get ready to go meet him again.

Her *hero*.

It was so overdramatic and so . . . bleah.

Except in the moment, it had felt true. Because Danielle had tried to throw a curveball and he hadn't let her. She honestly wasn't sure if she would have thought on her feet quickly enough to fix the issue. Heather would have volunteered to help, of course, but Heather had kids. And a full-time job. Millie couldn't expect her friend to give up her free time.

Austin had a whole ranch to run. She wasn't sure quite how either of them was going to pull this off. Cows and library patrons kept different hours. That meant their schedules might not be entirely harmonious.

She drove back out to the courthouse, though today she was filled with a different kind of energy. While she was embarrassed, she wasn't feeling as grim as she had been.

She had won. And it was taking some time for that fact to fully sink in. Or maybe it didn't feel like anything as simple as a victory, because now there was just work to do.

Work with Austin.

She should be used to him. She saw him so often—she probably saw him more often than anyone in town did.

As she got out of her car, she imagined being back at the library desk. Imagined him walking in and walking past her, off to peruse books. Or imagined him coming in and leaning over the counter in that way he did, asking for the books he had ordered or placed a hold on.

He was a patron of the library, like anyone else.

Like anyone else.

Like anyone else.

Like anyone el—

The mantra came to a dramatic halt in her head as she rounded the back of the courthouse building—where the basement entrance was—and saw him standing there, thumbs through his belt loops, a cowboy hat on his head, his face darkened by stubble he hadn't bothered to shave away this morning.

She knew he was handsome. She'd watched him grow taller and broader. Watched his jaw turn square and his nose sharpen. She'd watched his hair go from tawny gold to a warm brown. She'd seen the boy become a man over all these years, and his handsomeness was a sort of undeniable reality that existed alongside all the other truths she'd learned while growing up. She knew it in an academic sort of way.

It didn't feel academic out here.

Not since he'd grabbed hold of her elbow. Not since she'd called him her hero.

Not now that she was standing near him without a desk between them.

Not when she was so aware of how tall he was.

How small she was.

Not, regrettably, small enough to scurry into a hole in the side of the building and disappear for a minute. She was a mouse with none of the perks.

"Mornin'," he said.

"Good morning to you too," she said.

"I didn't say it was good. I just said it was morning."

She was actually kind of happy he wasn't being agreeable because that meant she might be able to tamp down the fizzing sensations in her veins that seemed to get worse the closer she got to him.

She wasn't used to feeling fizzy. She didn't like it.

She didn't even know what it was. It would be easy to say it was attraction, but she'd been attracted to Michael, and he hadn't made any of her internal systems go haywire.

"I can take you down here and show you the corner of the basement where they keep everything about the Talbot family. I just have to be finished by nine thirty so I can get over to the library."

"I'll be headed that way myself."

"You don't have any orders coming in today."

"Doesn't matter. I'm going to go ahead and return the books I have and look around for a couple of other things."

He was probably the most dedicated patron the Rustler Mountain Library had. At least, the most dedicated patron under the age of sixty-five.

"Right."

She took the keys out of her pocket and jammed them in the stubborn deadbolt in the door, jiggling them before she was able to get it to turn.

"It feels criminal," he said. "Having all this history shut away in boxes."

"It's common. A lot of things are archived."

"Does this count as archives? Things being shoved in boxes and neglected in a basement?"

She shrugged. "Technically, I think so."

"I don't like it."

"Neither do I. This history belongs to the townspeople. It should be accessible to everybody." She grimaced. "It's very librarian of me."

"To want everybody to have free access to information? I guess so."

They stepped inside the room, and she turned on the light switch. The fluorescent fixtures hummed before lighting the room in a pale glow.

"I seem to recall that what you're looking for is in the back right-hand corner. But I'll show you the way."

She was very aware of the sound of his footsteps behind her. Of the fact that they had exchanged more words in the past few days than they maybe ever had. Well, she supposed if she added up the number of times they had greeted each other and said goodbye, it was technically more words. But this was different.

Not that she really knew much more about him than she had yesterday. Except that he didn't like cheaters. And apparently he couldn't stand bullies, so that was nice. Even if it was a little bit lowering to need rescuing from bullies at the age of thirty.

No. She hadn't needed rescuing. She had been holding her own. She just might not have gotten the victory without him. Those were two different things. A moral victory would've been hers either way.

There were large pieces of furniture covered by sheets, shelves filled with pottery and baskets. Bins of clothing, fragments of dishes that were tagged and dated. And there in the back corner, where she remembered, were three large boxes labeled with the Talbot name.

"How come your family didn't keep all this?" Austin asked.

"My grandmother thought that it ought to go to the museum. We used to have it at my grandparents' house. I remember going over and looking at it when I was a kid. Along with a lot of my grandfather's World War Two memorabilia. He really loved history. And he wanted to hang on to all of it. But my grandmother . . . she wanted to share it. After he died she donated it to the museum. I think my mother probably encouraged that a little bit."

"Librarian," he said.

"Yes. And I think even my dad was relieved, because I don't think he wanted to feel like he had to keep all of it safe. It's a lot of pressure. Of course, we didn't count on everything ending up in boxes in a basement."

"You donated it to the museum. Couldn't you take it back?"

"I don't think so. It belongs to the historical society. If we had given it to them as a loan, maybe."

"So when the museum closed, that must have felt defeating."

"Well, my grandmother wasn't alive to see it. Neither was my mom. She would have been so sad."

"I know she would've been," he said.

There was something that sounded an awful lot like warmth in his voice, and it was unexpected.

She looked at him, his face washed out by the fluorescent lighting, yet still handsome. "She was a good woman, your mother," he said, responding to the question in her eyes. "She always made the library feel like a place where I was welcome. You can imagine I didn't always have that experience."

"Really?"

"Millie," he said. "Your dad arrested me. And you can honestly ask me whether or not I felt welcome in town?"

She shifted uncomfortably. "Well. Did you commit acts of vandalism?"

He snorted. "Yes."

"Oh. Well."

"I was told from the time I was born that I was bad. Innately. My dad made it seem fun. He said we could go where we liked, do what we wanted, because we couldn't earn our way to being good, so we might as well live down to the expectations of those around us. He said that was being free. Not giving a damn." He shook his head. "So yeah, I did that shit. I broke windows, I started fights. I sold illegal alcohol, underage too. But it didn't start there. The first time I went to the library, an old man told me to leave."

Her stomach twisted. "How old were you?"

"Ten."

"I'm sorry," she said.

"It's fine. Ancient history."

But she knew that he was lying, because obviously ancient history mattered to him. The things they were looking for now were far more ancient than his being yelled at in a library when he was ten, and he still cared. That, she supposed, told her a great many things about Austin Wilder.

"Your mom told me I could stay. It's why I kept coming back. The library was the only place I ever really went that wasn't . . . for us."

She frowned. "What do you mean?"

"Oh, come on. You know. There's a saloon for us, and a grocery store for us. There's a diner we like, and we don't go into your fancy Scallywag's Coffee."

She did know. That was the thing. She'd always thought the outlaws-versus-lawmen story was . . . local flavor. He made it sound terrible.

"Right," she said, her throat getting tight. "I . . . I'm glad you felt you could go to the library."

"Me too," he said.

Silence stretched between them as an ache in her chest started to expand. She busily redirected her focus. "You can actually check things out, we just have to document it."

"Well, I am well-versed in the act of checking things out."

"So if you find some letters or a journal that you want. . . ."

He walked over to the shelves and took the lid off one of the boxes. "This is full of documents."

"A lot of it is boring. Bank statements and deeds, a couple of mining claims."

"I didn't think your family ever did mining."

"They didn't really. As far as I know, they just had the claims to help keep a wide buffer around their property so that they didn't have people putting mining rigs in where they didn't want them."

"Right." He looked thoughtful, though.

"Maybe I'm wrong," she said. "But as far as I know, the Talbots weren't miners."

"I might take this whole box," he said. "Then come back for the rest."

"You're really going to go through all of this?"

"Yes."

"What exactly are you doing with this research? Other than going on a personal quest for information."

He let out a long, slow breath, and he seemed to be debating something. "I'm writing a book."

"A book? Like . . . an entire book?"

"Yes. Not just historical record, I'm turning Austin Wilder's journals into a novel."

She didn't know why it surprised her. He loved books. He loved reading. Maybe even more than she did, so the idea that he might be working on a novel shouldn't surprise her, and yet. . . . She felt dumb, in that moment, confronted by the fact that she clearly had more prejudice against him than she had realized, by the fact that even she somehow held on to this idea that he was something he wasn't.

She had watched him come into the library every single week, for all these years, and yet she still didn't apply adjectives like *imaginative, deep thinking,* or even *intelligent* to him. He was a cowboy. And more than that, he was. . . .

He was a Wilder. She was a Talbot.

"I'm sure it's great," she said.

"I don't know about that. Mostly right now it's a collection of scenes. And I don't know if anybody would ever be interested in reading it. But it's a story that I'm interested in. And I figure since I have all this insight into who he was, I'm in a pretty decent position to write it."

"But you need to fill in information from other points of view."

He nodded. "Yes. As far as town history goes, I'm pretty well steeped in it."

"Sure. Still, I bet it's going to be helpful to you, being involved in the Gold Rush Days."

He chuckled. "Maybe. Though I remember the whole routine from back in the day."

"There are some books in the library about getting published."

"Thanks. I . . . do you remember Jennifer Allman?"

She squinted. Jennifer had been older than Millie, younger than Austin. She had left for college, and she hadn't come back. "Yes. Vaguely."

"She's a literary agent. I got in touch with her when I first had the idea for the book. I pitched it to her. But she wanted me to get back to her when it was finished."

"Ah." She wondered if their connection was just professional. Or if there was some other reason he had thought to get in touch with her. How had he known she was a literary agent, when Millie hadn't?

The thought made her fizzy again. It shouldn't.

"Let's just get all this signed out on the sheet."

There was a clipboard hanging up on the wall, a sign-out sheet for all the documents, a place to put your name, the date, and the reference number of the items you were taking. No one had checked anything out for three years.

Austin wrote his name, boldly, in all capital letters as if he was making a declaration.

When they exited the basement, Millie let out a sharp breath, her lungs tortured, likely from the stale air they had just left behind, not anything else.

"I'd better go," she said, looking at her watch.

Her mother's watch.

She had inherited all of her mother's jewelry when she had passed. She had often thought that there was a certain gift in having advanced warning that a loved one was going to pass away. Having experienced it both ways, she could confirm that if she had to choose, knowing beforehand was her preference.

She'd had weeks while her mother was in hospice to sit with her, to hear the story behind each piece of jewelry. To ask her about her childhood, to collect moments and stories, and to say what needed to be said.

With her father . . . one day he had been there, and the next he was gone.

One day he had felt hale and hearty and indestructible, and the next he was forever beyond her reach.

The only good thing, she supposed, was that he never had to grow weak. In many ways, she imagined that if her father had been forced to choose a way to go, it would've been exactly how he'd gone. The heart attack that no one had expected.

Himself until the very end.

But when she looked at her mother's watch, she remembered the story her mom had told her about how her dad had given it to her for their fifth anniversary.

She could remember that moment. The way her mom had pressed it into her palm, and looked at her with those kind blue eyes. Millie did not have her mother's eyes.

She took a breath, trying to shift some of the heaviness that had landed on her. It was all this talk of the past. "I'll . . . I'll get in touch with you about planning. . . ."

"I'm going to see you in a minute."

"Right."

She turned and hurried to the car. She doubted that he was actually going to make conversation with her when he came to the library. He never did.

She got to the library with fifteen minutes to spare before opening and unlocking the door, turning the sign early, and flicking on all the lights, starting up the computer.

The building was large and bright. A far cry from the basement space that had comprised the library until Millie was eight or so. There had been a levy to build all new libraries throughout the county, and large new buildings had gone up in each town. Finding money to keep the lights on had been the real challenge, and Millie felt blessed that Rustler Mountain had considered funding the library a necessity.

The library and the fire department were both well-funded. She supposed that was a function of being distant from major towns. Rebel Heart Books in Jacksonville was the closest bookstore, and it was nearly forty minutes from them.

And if disaster struck, the rural fire department acted as EMTs as well as putting out fires.

With the closest hospital over an hour away, an active fire department was a necessity.

She had just sat down behind the desk at ten o'clock when her first couple of patrons came in. Some of her favorite library ladies who always came for the new romance releases on Tuesdays.

They often competed for books on hold, though Marjorie preferred historical romance while Alice liked vampires.

She was busy helping a patron find a new cozy mystery series to start and had almost forgotten that Austin was supposed to come by, when she heard the door open again and turned to see him striding in.

Every head turned when he entered.

Marjorie whispered something to Alice, who shook with laughter, her shoulders bobbing up and down.

It hit Millie then, that they were lusting after him.

Good God.

It hit her, with even stronger force, that she might've been doing the same earlier.

No. It wasn't. Because that fizzy feeling wasn't anything remotely familiar, and she knew what lust looked like.

And frankly she could do without it. Having been once reduced by the unwieldy force of lust, she could happily go without for the rest of her life.

She was not someone who inspired it, apparently. Not the way Danielle did.

Really, she wasn't hurt. Really, she was not heartbroken.

Really, she was just mad.

And didn't need to be pondering it right now.

"Anyway," she said, turning back to the patron she had been working with, "I think you'll really like this series. It's set locally."

"Thankfully, we don't have actual murderers locally," the woman said.

"Not recently."

She went to the desk and took a seat, and Marjorie and Alice came to check out their books, followed by the cozy mystery patron. And then, Austin came to stand behind her, looming very tall.

She ignored the fact that her hands began to tremble just slightly.

He had two more Jack Reacher books and *Bird by Bird* by Anne Lamott. "This is a good one," she said, pointing to *Bird by Bird*.

"Good," he said.

"I haven't read Jack Reacher," she commented.

"Why not?"

"I don't know. Would I like the books?"

"They're violent. And they're about a very large man who solves his problems by being large. So, I don't know, you have to make your own determination."

She smiled. She couldn't help herself. "That is a pretty good endorsement, actually."

"I don't know what you read," he said.

"A little bit of everything," she said.

"It's just, I realize that you know everything I read."

She blinked. It was true. She did. That made her feel powerful in a way. She could look right into his imagination, and he had no idea about hers.

"I do," she said. "Suddenly I feel drunk with power."

"Well. We can't have that."

Suddenly she heard a very loud throat-clearing noise, and she looked behind Austin to see a short man who only came up to his shoulder and had been previously obscured by Austin's body. He was standing behind Austin looking impatient. "There are other patrons," he said.

Austin looked at the man. Millie fought to keep a disdainful look off her face. She did not know this man's name. Which meant that he didn't often come into the library, and he probably hadn't lived here all that long. He was certainly demanding that things work at a pace they did not work in Rustler Mountain, and she discovered right then that she and Austin had something else in common, beyond their love of the library.

Neither of them took kindly to somebody who wasn't from around here telling them how to do things.

"I'll be with you in a moment," she said. "I'm just finishing my conversation with this other patron."

"I need your phone number," Austin said.

She sputtered. "Oh."

The man let out a hard sigh. "Are you flirting or are you checking his books out?"

"Flirting," said Austin, without looking at the complainer. He reached his hand out. "Give me your phone."

She did. He punched in a number, and then called, then hung up quickly. "There. Now I'm in your call data. You can text me and let me know when you want to meet up." He took a stack of books. "Thank you kindly, Ms. Talbot. I'll see you around."

Then he turned and walked out of the library, and she struggled to take her eyes off the door long after he had gone through it.

"I have an appointment," the man said.

"Well," Millie said, turning her focus to checking out his books. "I'm sure there won't be any traffic on the road. You ought to get there just fine."

She looked down at her phone, looked down at Austin's number. Then she clicked *add to contacts.*

Create new.

Austin Wilder.

She sat there and stared at it, and she wished that she could go back to the Millie of two months ago who had been devastated and quite certain there would never be anything else in her life that meant anything, with her mother gone, her father gone, and her only romantic relationship dead and buried.

She wished she could go back and tell her that she wouldn't even believe what was happening now. Nothing huge. Nothing life-altering. But definitely different from anything she could have imagined.

There was something about that she found oddly cheering.

Chapter 6

I know I'm not a good man, and that's never mattered much to me. I managed to keep us all alive, and living is dirty business. I rode through Jacksonville today and saw an angel. It was the first time I wished I was closer to God.

—Austin Wilder's journal, May 12, 1855

"How about we go out tonight?"

Austin looked over at his brother. "You go out every night."

"Yeah. I do." Flynn didn't look the slightest bit chagrined at the accusation. "But we ought to get Carson to go out."

"Carson doesn't need to drink any more than he already does."

"Granted. But we probably aren't going to get him to stop drinking cold turkey. We might be able to get him to drink with other people around, instead of drinking alone."

Carson's decision to be the one to settle down, to get married, had been surprising. He was a pretty damn locked box on a good day. But since his wife had died, he had shut down completely. Yet he still showed up for family dinners. He made conversation. But when it came to the subject of how he was doing? He wasn't sharing that information. Not ever.

He was a fan of self-medication. And Austin couldn't say that he approved of the behavior. But he also couldn't say that Carson had ever asked his opinion.

"I already told Dalton that we would be down there in about twenty minutes."

"Damn. Give a man a chance to pretty up a bit."

"What does that even look like for you?" Flynn shook his head.

"It's going to take more than a quick shower to get that ugly mug into shape."

It was funny, because Austin was good-looking by any metric. He wasn't conceited about it. It was just a fact.

"Yeah. That's why I have such bad luck with women."

He had always thought it was bad luck that the Wilder family was so damned good-looking. It was certainly how the original Austin Wilder had managed to snare himself a wife who had been too sweet, too pretty, and too good for the likes of him.

That love, that marriage, was also the closest he had ever come to redemption. Not that he had really taken advantage of it. But it was part of the complexity of it all, to Austin's mind. He'd been a good husband, yet in many ways what people would call a bad man.

Over the years, though, other Wilder men had proven that they often used their good looks for bad ends. Their dad was a good example. Four kids with three different women, and he had done all of them wrong.

"I'll be quick."

He stood up as Cassidy rounded the corner. "Are we going out?"

"Didn't invite you," said Flint.

"I didn't know that I needed an invitation to go to a public venue," she said, looking fierce.

Cassidy was a half-pint, probably like her mother, though he had only met the woman the one time, and he had been too shocked by the fact that she was actually leaving her nine-year-old daughter on his doorstep to think much about her height.

Cassidy lived in a little house about a half mile down the road from his. On the same ranch property. Carson had bought a piece of land and built a new house on it when he had gotten married, a gorgeous cabin that sat on the edge of Outlaw Creek, where he ran his own ranching operation.

Flynn had inherited a piece of land from his maternal grandfather. Only a couple of miles away from the Wilder Ranch.

Still, they found themselves together most nights. And tonight was going to be no different. Though apparently they were going out on the town. Austin felt he'd had a little bit too much of town lately.

"You're going to put a damper on things," Flynn said, still sniping at Cassidy.

Austin ignored them, going into the bedroom to quickly change his shirt, boots, and hat.

"Want to be the designated driver?" Cassidy asked.

"Sounds like a job for you, sprout," he said as they headed outside to the truck.

She scowled, but she still hauled herself into the driver's seat. He and Flynn piled in next to her.

"Nice of you boys to ride bitch," she said, starting the engine. Not for the first time he wondered if they had done Cassidy a disservice by . . . being the only influence in her life.

Though he wasn't sure she would've fared any better if her actual parents had been around. Their dad had raised them, after all.

And as far as her mother went . . . she'd abandoned her daughter. So, really, there was nothing she could have taught Cassidy anyway. A person who would do that couldn't possibly have anything to recommend them.

Flynn took his phone out of his pocket and dialed up Carson. "Hey," he said. "We're going out. Want to come down to the saloon?"

"No." He could hear his brother's surly voice down the other end of the line.

"We're coming by your place," Austin shouted.

"You can't escape," Cassidy added.

"Fuck you." Carson's words were loud and clear.

And true to their word, they pulled up to his house and squeezed him into the very small halfback seat in the truck.

"You didn't have to come along," Austin said.

"I did so. You would've come into the house and dragged me out."

"They're not going to serve you if you're already drunk," Flynn said.

"I'm sober, asshole."

"Forgive me. It's after five o'clock, so what the hell do I know?"

It took about five minutes for them to get into town proper, and the main street was already heaving with activity. Cars parked against the curb, and pedestrians crossing in and out of the crosswalk. It was the tourists who wandered outside the crosswalk. It drove him nuts.

Tourists didn't do him a lick of good. He was a cattle rancher. It didn't make any difference to him if people were traipsing around enjoying the wineries and country music concerts in the park.

That turned his thoughts back to Millie. She didn't care about tourism either, not the way most business owners around town did. She served the local community. But she seemed to care a lot about the overall health of the town. And of course the legacy of her family. The spurious legacy, in his opinion.

He couldn't spare any grief over her father, who had pigeon-holed him in exactly the way everybody else in town did. Except he had done it with power. And that had been a pretty shitty thing. He grumbled as Cassidy drove around the corner and found a parking spot a good piece away from the bar.

"We're overrun," she complained.

"Damn straight," said Flynn.

"Wow. I thought I was the sad one who was being forced to go out. You all sound grumpier than I do."

"Hardly," Austin said.

"If you don't get out of this truck so that I can unfold myself from this back seat, you're going to find out just how grumpy I am," Carson said.

They piled out of the truck and headed toward the Watering Hole Saloon. The old brick building was lit up bright tonight with its old neon sign boasting a cowgirl in short shorts leading her horse to water. There was a line of motorcycles parked at an angle against the curb out front, and some rusted-out pickups on either end.

There was a different bar down at the other end of the street where there were no motorcycles. They served martinis, and they did not have a bar top with a bullet hole in it. They didn't have bad checks taped to the wall, shaming the people who'd written them.

The floor wasn't sticky with spilled liquor and the walls weren't bowing out from the boom of overly loud live music.

Which were just a few of the reasons he never went to that other bar.

Flynn led the way inside and Austin followed, with Carson behind him, and Cassidy bringing up the rear.

He could feel the energy in the room change when they passed through the swinging saloon doors into the party. Except, unlike yesterday's meeting in the courthouse, this was his kind of party.

And if there was any place in town where the Wilders were greeted like friends, it was this bar. Because the truth was, heroes weren't much of anything without outlaws.

This was the place that celebrated that truth.

"Howdy, Wilders," said Gus the bartender by way of greeting.

"Howdy, Gus," said Austin. "Beers all around. Whatever you have on tap that you like."

"So generous," said Flynn. "I didn't know you were taking us all out for a night on the town, Austin."

"Does that include me?"

Austin turned and saw that Flynn's friend Dalton Wade had just rolled in. Dalton's ancestors weren't Rustler Mountain founders, but he was from a longtime ranching family up north in a town called Copper Ridge. He wasn't from California, so that made him okay.

Austin was aware that it was petty to have an issue with a state whose border was only eight miles away.

But he had it all the same.

As was his right as an Oregonian, born and bred.

"Sure," he said.

"Well," Dalton said. "The rumors must be true. Austin Wilder has gone soft. You didn't even pretend to tell me no. You didn't even pretend you were going to throw a punch."

"Excuse me? What rumors are there?"

"That you're helping plan Gold Rush Days," Gus said, setting a beer in front of him on the scarred bar top. "With that little librarian."

"A Talbot," Dalton said.

"I am aware of who the librarian is. Since I'm a card-carrying member of the library system."

"Well, aren't you full of surprises," said Gus.

"It only surprises you, Gus, because you've never set foot in the library. And I know that because I've never seen you there. I have *not* gone soft."

"You must have a little bit," said Flynn, tempting his ire, because he was much more likely to punch his brother than he was to punch Dalton or Gus. "Because there was a day when you would never have done a single thing to help a Talbot."

"Her father, sure. The dishonorable sheriff can rot in peace."

A flash of Millie's devastated face passed through his mind, and he felt guilty. Maybe he was getting soft. Because he sure as hell couldn't remember a time before this when he would've felt guilty for wishing the sheriff exactly what he deserved.

He gritted his teeth. "Her father," he said, reaffirming his pronouncement, "sure. But if you could've seen the way all those jackals were treating her, well, you would've jumped in too."

"Probably," Flynn relented, along with Dalton.

"Not me," said Cassidy.

"Because you're a woman. So you wouldn't have felt honor bound to step in."

"Haven't you ever heard of women supporting women?" Cassidy said. "The sisterhood is alive and well, thank you very much. But not for a Talbot. Also, since when do you have honor?"

Damned little termite. She didn't fear him the way she should.

"Harsh," said Dalton.

"I'm harsh, Dalton," she said.

"I'm familiar," he said.

Carson didn't seem to be paying attention. He was texting.

"Are you trying to talk Perry into coming down?"

"Maybe," said Carson.

Carson's friendship with Perry Bramble was one of those great mysteries in life. They had met as pretty small children and formed an instant friendship, even though they were as different as could be. Perry was as sweet as Carson was growly.

She'd been a little blond thing racing around the Wilder Ranch with them. She'd always been large-eyed and upset about the different illegal and dangerous pursuits they'd gotten up to, but she was loyal to Carson all the same.

Things had gotten very dark the last couple of years with Carson, and Perry had been right there, all the way. Just like always.

Even when Carson had gone away to the Army Rangers, Perry had stayed his best friend. She had been the best man in his wedding.

"If she's still in the florist shop, she'll probably head down."

Austin had no doubt she would, because as far as he could tell, Perry would do anything for his brother. He had thought that maybe. . . . It had always seemed odd to him. That of all of them, Carson had been the one who'd gotten married, to a girl he had met while stationed out of town, even though he'd had Perry all along.

But then, he supposed with some people there just wasn't chemistry.

"She's on her way," Carson said.

"Can we get another beer, Gus? We have one more joining us."

This was another reminder of why they were still in Rustler Mountain. Because for all that they had issues with the town, they had a community within the community. A pretty big one too.

It wasn't just the land—they had some damn good friends.

And he was not soft.

He was not going to let that bother him. No. He wasn't. Because he didn't answer to anyone. He was Austin fucking Wilder.

The swinging saloon doors opened, and he expected to see Perry walk in, but no. It was a grinning Heather followed by a nervous-looking Millie, in a floral dress that went down almost to her ankles.

She looked more like a member of the temperance society than someone out on the town.

And she had sure as hell had never been in this joint even once in her life.

He'd remember.

The only nice girl who ever came here was Perry, and it was only because Carson wrapped himself around her like the Dark Knight whenever she did. Heather Lin-Stewart and Millie Talbot were the last people he'd ever expected to see in this place.

"Did you invite guests?" Flynn asked.

He shot his brother a mean look. "I did not, Flynn, and I think you know that."

"I don't know anything about you anymore. Apparently, you go around saving mousy damsels in distress now."

"Don't call her that," he said.

If his order made him a hypocrite, that was just fine.

Heather spotted them and smiled widely, grabbing Millie's arm and bodily dragging her over to where they stood. "I wanted to thank you," Heather said.

"Heather has had some wine," Millie said, looking baleful.

"Really?" Flynn said, looking Heather up and down.

"I'm married, Flynn Wilder," Heather said, lifting her ring. "But thank you. That is very flattering."

She did indeed look pleased.

"We were having dinner," Millie said. "We saw you walk in, and Heather wanted to extend her thanks for what you did at the meeting."

The fact that Millie was leading the conversation and controlling it so forcefully was a little bit interesting.

"Is that so?"

"Yes, I told her that she should come in and thank you and buy you a drink," said Heather. "Since you *are* her hero."

That word again. It jolted him. It hadn't escaped his notice the first time Millie had used it, but he sure as hell hadn't intended to let himself marinate in it. Nor had he intended to remember it had even happened. But he did. It was pretty damned hard not to.

"Thank you," said Millie. "Heather, some thoughts are inside thoughts."

"No," Austin said. "Heather doesn't need to keep any thoughts inside."

"Well, we agreed that it was pretty amazing, you just breaking in there like an outlaw. Like you were actually going to have a showdown with Michael. Who sucks," said Heather.

"He does suck," Austin agreed. Because he wasn't going to argue with a drunk woman when she was right.

Carson laughed, which was a rarity. "Yeah. He's the worst."

"You know him?" Millie asked. She seemed to be engaging in the exchange in spite of herself. As if her desire to avoid being rude was at war with her desire to escape quickly.

"Oh yeah, a little bit," said Carson. "Kind of from school. He was a prick then, and it doesn't surprise me to know he's a prick now."

Her lips twitched. "Well. He isn't . . . yeah."

"Let's get a table," said Heather. "Sorry. I'm an organizer, I can't help it. You know I manage all of the Wellspring medical offices in Medford. So it's kind of my thing. Standing here, we are sort of cluttering up a major throughway."

"Heather," Millie said. "We should probably go."

"No," said Heather. "I told Allen that I would be home at midnight, so I'm going to be home at midnight. This is my night out. And we've never been here before. Oh my gosh, remember when we used to watch people use fake IDs to get in here in high school?"

Millie looked at Austin, helplessly, and he had the urge to step in and be her hero again. Although right now that would mean saying that they could leave. Or even should. He found himself reluctant to say that.

"Fake IDs? How would that even work here?" Cassidy asked.

"Oh, back in the day they didn't check IDs here," Carson said. "It was a free-for-all. How do you think we were out starting bar fights before we were old enough to drink?"

Austin laughed. "True, we had to get in the bar somehow."

"They just didn't check?" Millie asked.

"They didn't care," Austin said. "Not here. Of course, Gus keeps things a little more on the up-and-up. I think there was a crackdown when we threw one of the Hancocks through the plate glass window out front."

"You did not!" Heather said, her eyes widening.

"I mean, I didn't," Carson said. "That was all Austin."

"Well, he was being a prick."

"There's a cluster of tables over there," said Flynn, interrupting Austin's story. "We'll push them together."

Flynn, agent of chaos that he was, was clearly all too willing to engage in this diversion.

Probably, he was also happy to flirt with a married woman. Because it involved no commitment. She clearly wasn't going to do anything with him, but he could flatter her endlessly, and really turn on the charm, and Austin supposed they would both enjoy it.

"Sorry," said Millie. "Didn't mean to crash your night out."

"We're more than capable of taking care of ourselves. If we didn't want you to join us, we would've had you thrown out of the bar."

"Yeah," said Cassidy. "We're not afraid of a fight. I'm Cassidy, by the way."

"Millie," she said.

"I know," said Cassidy. "You're the librarian that everybody says Austin has gone soft about."

Millie looked up at him, her eyes wide, and he, who would never hit a lady, was about to drop-kick his little sister back up to the ranch. Right through that same window he'd broken once all those years ago. He wasn't afraid to do it again.

"I'm not soft," he said.

So much for standing firm in his outlaw reputation.

"Oh, I have no doubt," said Millie.

Cassidy held back a snort and walked toward the table.

"Sorry about her," said Austin. "Sisters."

"I'm an only child," said Millie.

"Wow. What's that like?"

"I don't know. What was having a lot of siblings like?"

"Loud. Annoying. Pretty great."

He introduced Millie to the rest of the group, even though he was reasonably sure she knew well enough who everyone was. As soon as they had sat down, Carson got up, making a beeline to the door to grab Perry, who had just come in, her blond hair piled up on her head, looking every inch the sweet, angelic soul she was.

Carson led her over to the table, then stood behind her like a bodyguard. Austin had never really been able to sort their relationship out. It was obvious Carson was almost afraid of being a bad influence on her by exposing her to things like this bar, and himself, and yet he was with her most of the time.

He was glad Carson had Perry, but he couldn't imagine befriending a soft little woman like that.

He looked back at Millie and felt something tug hard on his chest.

What a fucking annoyance.

"That's Carson's friend, Perry," he said, his teeth gritted.

"I know Perry. She's the florist. I mean, she was going to do the flowers for my . . . you know, the thing that didn't happen."

He grunted. "Oh. Right."

"She talks about your brother a fair amount," Millie said.

"Really? I was unaware the people in town talked about the Wilders in ways other than hushed tones of disgust."

"No. But then. . . ."

"Yeah. I know. If anybody was going to be a hero, it was going to be Carson."

"You said it, not me," said Millie.

Well, of course she knew Perry. Perry might be friends with Carson, but she was one of the good ones about town. She wasn't an outlaw.

Though, in fairness, Carson existed in the margins now too. When he'd joined the army, it had been like a baptism as far as the town was concerned. He was a born-again all-American hero.

He tried not to think about just how easy it was to fall into conversation with Millie.

He took another sip of his beer as the house band made its way out to the stage, the guys taking their positions behind their instruments.

Blame it all on my roots, I showed up in boots. . . .

The whole bar seemed to swell.

This was the theme song of every damned person in this place. He didn't need to know them to know that.

I got friends in low places. . . .

Millie seemed to shrink into herself, while Heather lifted her arms up and began to dance in place.

Flynn had the good sense not to ask a married woman to dance, then went and found himself a dance partner who at least didn't have a visible wedding ring, or a husband in town.

Dalton found a partner too. Perry sat, drinking her beer, and Carson did the same, as did Cassidy, resolutely keeping their seats.

Austin felt a hand on his shoulder and he turned and saw a pretty woman with long red hair looking down at him. "Care to dance, cowboy?"

"Sure," he said.

Because he had gone out, after all, and what was going out if you didn't have at least one dance with a pretty stranger?

But as he began to stand up, his eyes landed on Millie, and he found himself faltering. Wishing he was back in the library, actually, having a conversation about books.

He pushed that notion to the side, and went out onto the dance floor. It was a fast-paced song, followed by another one, and that suited him just fine.

"What's your name?" he shouted across the space.

She wrapped her arm around his neck. "Valerie," she said against his ear.

"Nice to meet you," he returned.

But there was something missing from the moment.

He was a fan of casual hookups. They had always been the only option for him. Much as he didn't believe in family *curses*, per se, there was definitely something happening with his family.

Whether it was the sins of the father being visited upon the sons or something else, longevity had historically eluded the Wilders.

So why plan for the future?

There were enough things in life that were hard, so he liked his hookups easy. This would've been one. On another night. But he had no doubt that tonight wasn't going to be one of those nights. So he took one more dance with Valerie, then thanked her, and went back to sit at the table.

Next to Millie.

"I don't mind if you dance," she said.

"I didn't come back to the table for your benefit," he said.

"I didn't mean . . . I just. . . ."

She *did* mind. That was why she'd said something. Because she did mind. It bothered her.

Maybe she was even a little bit jealous.

He could understand that. If another man came over here right now. . . . It wasn't that he. . . . It was just that she was sitting with him. It was just that he felt responsible for her. This bar was not her scene, clearly. She wasn't the kind of woman who came out to places like this. She had just gotten her heart broken.

He would be damned if he'd let some asshole start something with her and take advantage of her vulnerable state.

That was all.

She was a Talbot.

The evening wore on, and somehow, he spent it sitting next to Millie.

"We have to go," Millie said, when it was creeping up on midnight. She reached across the table to touch Heather's arm, and Heather broke away from her conversation with Perry. "I have been designated to drive you home."

"All right." Heather thanked everyone profusely for a great evening, and Austin couldn't help but think she wasn't going to have half as great a morning when her hangover came knocking.

"I'll walk you out," Austin said, standing. He wasn't going to leave them to the mean streets of Rustler Mountain.

He was well aware that most people thought he *was* the mean streets of Rustler Mountain. But no matter.

Millie looked at him as if she was going to protest politely. "Don't even think about it," he said.

He tilted his head toward the door, and Heather and Millie followed him outside. Heather swayed slightly. "Just a second," she said, "I need to run back inside and use the bathroom."

Which left him and Millie standing out on the sidewalk.

"I'll give you a call tomorrow," he said. "Set up a time to go over this Gold Rush Days thing."

"Oh," she said. "Right."

"You don't like me, do you?"

She jolted. "What makes you say that?"

"You seem genuinely distressed to be in my presence most of the time."

She shook her head. "I'm not. I . . . I have been imposing on you since the first moment I went up the mountain to ask you for help. I just feel a little bit self-conscious about that."

"Is that all? It's not because I'm a dangerous man who will never amount to anything?"

"You own a successful cattle ranch. And you've never hurt anyone."

"No, I haven't, but are you telling me that's not my reputation in town?"

"People don't actually talk about you all the time, Austin."

That made him smile. In spite of himself.

He didn't know why he wanted to push her. She was. . . .

He actually couldn't quite figure it out. Because he had an idea of what a Talbot was. But then, there was also her mother. There was Millie. She had always been kind when she was at the library. And not shy, really. She had been confident in what she was doing, whether it was giving recommendations or . . . scanning the barcode.

But seeing her in a different environment, seeing her out of context, it was strange, and he couldn't quite gauge her reaction to him. Whether it was that moment earlier when she had reacted with what seemed a little bit like jealousy, or the never-ending discomfort she seemed to feel in his presence.

"What did your mother think of me?" he asked.

She blinked. "I don't know specifically. But I would guess that she liked you. Because you were at the library. She didn't think that kids read enough anymore. You did, though."

He felt he had passed some kind of test, and that was ridiculous.

"Yeah, but I was also getting into trou—"

"Sorry," Heather said, pushing the door open and letting it close loudly behind her. "I feel better now."

"Great," he said. "Where are you parked?"

"Across the street," Millie said. "Just there."

She gestured to a sleek, blue car that was nestled against the curb.

"I bet you can make it just fine," he said.

"Yes," she said. "I'm sure we will."

"Well, sometimes there are shootouts in the streets," he said, deadpan.

"We would be the two that would be having a shootout," she said.

He realized that was true. Because she was the last of the Talbots.

"Well, then I guess we'll just keep our weapons holstered."

"I guess so."

"I'll talk to you tomorrow."

She nodded. "Yes. Talk to you tomorrow."

Then he turned on his heel and went back inside. Maybe he would change his mind about Valerie. Just maybe.

At least it would be in character, whereas the rest of this whole week had been decidedly out of it.

Chapter 7

A long time ago I imagined taking a wife. Most men do. But somewhere along the way I lost that dream. Until I met her. It would be better for her if we hadn't met at all.

—Austin Wilder's journal, September 14, 1855

When she arrived at the library the next day, there were ten crates filled with costumes stacked outside the door. Julie had told her that she was going to bring some things from the historical society by, but Millie hadn't thought she was just going to leave them, and she also hadn't thought there would be . . . *this* much.

She began to rifle through the items. Prairie dresses and chaps and spurs. A vest with the sheriff's star. She plucked up a pair of handcuffs and let them dangle from her finger before shoving them back down into the crate.

"Goodness," she said, as she unlocked the door and pushed past all the detritus.

Then she dragged each bin inside, stacking them behind the reference desk before flicking on all the lights and turning the CLOSED sign.

Nobody was busting down the library door today, which meant she had time to get out her planner and start making a list of things she needed to do to get ready for Gold Rush Days. She knew that Austin was going to call soon. . . .

She sat for a moment. She tried and failed to stop herself from playing last night through like a movie.

She had felt out of sorts the entire evening, from the moment Heather had dragged her into the saloon.

As if on cue, her phone screen lit up with her friend's name.

I come in peace. And with chai.

The door's open.

Heather came in a minute later. She had two cups in her hands, and she looked exhausted. "Thankfully, I am working remotely today," she said. "I got you your favorite." She set the pale blue cup in front of Millie, and Millie took a moment to take inventory of which animals had made it onto today's cup. Scallywag's Coffee Company served her very favorite drinks in town. And the cups had sketches of different animals on them. Her present one showed an elk, a raccoon, and a family of weasels.

"Thank you," she said, picking up the cup and taking a sip of the sweet, spicy liquid.

"Are you mad?"

Millie considered the question for a minute. She was surprised that Heather was even aware enough of the mood she'd been in last night to ask. Not because Heather wasn't considerate, she was. It was just that whatever had been going on last night was so subtextual, Millie didn't even have a definition for it. Or a way to articulate it.

She looked down at the top of her cup, then back up at her friend. "I'm not mad."

"I didn't mean to embarrass you. I just . . . I'm fascinated by him."

"I didn't realize that you were," Millie said.

"Come on. Who was more legendary—ever—than Austin Wilder? And yes, we were a little ridiculous about him when we were younger—"

Millie narrowed her eyes. "Not *we*."

"Okay, fine. You were immune. You made that position abundantly clear even then."

"Did I?"

"Yes. Every time someone at a slumber party would mention having fantasies about kissing a Wilder, you'd say they were bad news."

Millie frowned. "I don't think I was quite that—"

"You were. And it's fine. You're you. I love that you're you and that you never compromised."

But not everyone had loved her. Maybe that was why the only time she'd ever been invited to a slumber party was at Heather's house, where everyone else had to suffer her grim presence.

"You never wanted to stare down danger and see what might happen," Heather said, lifting a shoulder. "But it's not an uncommon thing to be a little bit fascinated by something—or someone—who might be bad for you."

Millie grimaced. "You seemed a little bit too excited about *Flynn* Wilder flirting with you."

"I have a two-year-old and a four-year-old," Heather said. "And most days only the top half of me is dressed, just what's visible in the Zoom meeting. I love my husband, he's amazing, but I expect that he's going to love me and think I'm attractive. After all, my body is like this because of his children. So yes, I was a little bit flattered to get attention from a different man."

Millie was tired of herself right then. Tired of the relentless catalogue of rules in her own head. Tired of the way she'd tried so hard to live up to the Talbot name—even in her own mind—so much so that even as a teenage girl, when everyone had been sighing over the Wilder Bad Boys, she'd been rigid in her adherence to rules and her admiration of people who liked said rules as much as she did.

"I can understand that," Millie said, suddenly feeling the burn of Michael's betrayal. No one had flirted with *her* last night.

Instantly a vision of Austin's face went before her eyes. She shouldn't be thinking of him and flirting, not in the same sentence or context.

"Actually though, I just wanted to observe the Wilders in their natural habitat. I'm fascinated by how Austin just . . . came and threw himself into all of this."

"I don't think it's that random. He has a vested interest in the history of the town."

"He's never had one before," Heather pointed out.

"That's not entirely true. You know he comes in here all the time." She gestured around the bright, well-organized room, at all the packed shelves of books.

Heather blinked. "Really. You haven't mentioned that."

"Well, it's not new. He's been coming into the library since before you and I were friends."

"We've *always* been friends."

"That isn't true. You used to be friends with Bonnie McElroy. And she didn't like me. So you didn't like me either."

"I always liked you," said Heather. "I just didn't know it. I had to aggressively friend you on the merry-go-round in fourth grade because you didn't respond to my casual hallway waving."

Millie scowled. "I thought you were waving at someone behind me."

"This is one of your problems, you know. You still act like everyone who's nice to you might be waving at someone behind you."

"I. . . ." Her mouth dropped open, then shut again.

It had been true, though, with Michael. There *had* been someone behind her. Getting rid of that feeling wasn't so easy when it had been reinforced at different times over the years. She'd known Danielle since middle school, but the woman had still betrayed Millie with Michael, which meant she must not have ever liked her either.

She realized that she was getting lost in the weeds of her own brain, and she fought her way back out. She cleared her throat. "Anyway. The subject of Austin and the library never came up because it wasn't as if he just started coming. He came in when my mom was the librarian. Every week. Sometimes two or three times a week. He was always here when I was here."

"Oh, he knows you."

Millie shook her head. "He doesn't *know* me."

"He kind of does. Is that why he jumped in to bail you out?"

"I have no idea."

"It just seemed like last night there was . . . I don't know. I wasn't as conscious of it as I should've been at the time, because I was more than a little bit tipsy, but I was afraid that I pushed too hard. You know . . . do you. . . ?"

With creeping horror, Millie began to anticipate what her friend was going to say, and she couldn't imagine anything worse. Not a single thing. "I do *not* have a crush on him," she said. "You know how I feel about the Wilder family."

"You asked him for help!" Heather said. "You don't think of him the way you did when we were teenagers."

"Well. No. But we are generationally sworn enemies."

"That's ridiculous. You are *not* generationally sworn enemies."

"Yes, we are. The issues between our families are enshrined on a plaque at the head of Main Street. We are the history of this town."

"It's fitting, then, that the two of you are running Gold Rush Days, I guess."

"I guess. I really didn't think it was going to include crashing his night out at the bar."

"I just thought that maybe you were mad because he danced with that other woman."

"I'm not mad about that," she said, ignoring the stinging heat in her cheeks. "I was going to get married two months ago. And he . . . he has always been around. Austin has. I've never. . . . *You* had a crush on him."

"Yes, I did," said Heather. "Because everyone did."

"*Everyone* didn't," said Millie. "I have never understood the bad boy thing."

Heather grimaced. "Aren't they better than fake nice guys?"

"I don't even know if you can call Michael a fake nice guy. He seemed normal. And now I'm worried that what he did is normal. Which I hate. I don't want to be worried about that. I don't want to . . . I don't know how I'm supposed to just trust somebody again."

Which was ridiculous. How had talking about Austin led to this? Because even if she did decide to trust somebody else again, it wasn't going to be the baddest man in town.

Well. That wasn't fair. He hadn't been the baddest man in town for a while, she supposed.

Though that was just because he wasn't causing trouble in the streets, not because there was anyone badder. There wasn't.

"Anyway," she said. "I don't care who he dances with. That isn't the point. He and I are going to be working together on history stuff. And I can give you all the juicy details about what I learn about him, but I suspect that what you'll find is he's just a normal guy. He actually isn't an outlaw."

"I do know that," said Heather. "Doesn't mean he isn't good-looking, though."

"So is your husband."

"Don't worry," said Heather, waving her hand. "I'm well aware of how hot my husband is. This is not a cry for help."

Millie felt tension rising in her chest that she worried might actually be a cry for help on her end.

"Good." She took another sip of her drink. "Thank you so much for this. Really."

"What do you have behind the desk?"

"Costumes," she said.

"Fun," said Heather. "I'm sorry, but if you don't dress up as the schoolmarm with him dressed up as the outlaw. . . ."

"*Heather.*"

"I just want to see you having fun. Whatever shape that takes."

"Rest assured, I will be dressing up and having fun—in the context of the historical event only."

"Sometimes dressing up in other contexts is fun."

Millie blinked. "Yes."

"I mean that sexually."

"*Heather!* I can't . . . have that kind of fun with . . . I don't even know how to finish that sentence. I see him all the time. And I'm not. . . ."

"I know," Heather said. "You're sweet and romantic, and I love that about you."

Millie grimaced. "I'm not romantic."

"You aren't?"

"No. I'm not. Why would that be your take?"

"You've just always been so careful about dating. I thought it was because you were waiting for that big love, and then you found it with Michael. And now I'm devastated he hurt you, and I just want to punch him in the face."

Heather had been so careful around the subject of Michael, and Millie just hadn't known how to talk about it. She hadn't realized what her friend was thinking.

It made her feel smaller. Sadder.

"I wasn't in love with him." She said the words out loud, into the sacred stillness of the library, and felt them resonate in her soul.

Heather went slack-jawed. "Then why were you marrying him?"

"I *thought* I was. I didn't have anything to compare it to. And then I caught him with her, and I have never been so angry in all my life. I have never wanted to hurt someone so badly. But it wasn't because I was heartbroken. It was because I felt pathetic. It was because I felt like I did in high school. Little Millie Mouse, who no one took seriously or even liked all that much. And I'd been stupid enough to think this man really loved me. It was hurt pride, not a broken heart, and that was actually a horrifying thing to realize. It didn't hit me like a lightning bolt but I . . . I really wish I was a romantic. I just wanted to marry the right person."

Heather frowned. "Meaning what?"

"Someone who would make my dad proud. And I wanted to give him grandchildren and. . . ." A lump formed in her throat. "I didn't get to do that. I'm the only one left."

Heather reached over the reference desk and pulled Millie in for a hug. "I am so sorry you've been feeling this way."

"I don't always walk around feeling this way. Mostly I feel . . . I don't even know." She pulled away and wiped at some stray tears that had gathered at the corners of her eyes. "I almost married him. I almost married him because I was so dedicated to this vision of . . . sometimes I think I live in a fantasy world. And not a fun one. Like I'm caught in this nostalgia for the past because my dad cared about it so much, and it colored my relationship with him in real life, colored my image of myself."

"There's a lot of expectation on your family."

"I guess. But it feels silly to be upset about that. Austin's family is treated like a pack of black sheep. Your family was cheated and discriminated against. It feels stupid for me to complain."

"Expectations are hard," Heather said. "I don't care where they come from. If they come from a hundred and fifty years ago or they come from . . . your parents. Or even if they just come from yourself. You had an expectation for your life, and why wouldn't you? It isn't a bad thing that you wanted to be in love, that you wanted to get married."

"But I wasn't. And I very nearly married him. That's actually why I feel . . . unmoored. Messed up. Like I can't trust myself, like I don't know my own mind. Because I was so sure. I had this version of how everything was going to be cemented so firmly in my head. I was wrong. About everything. About him, and about what I wanted. I feel like a failure. I feel like I can't fix it."

"Because you can't give your dad what you wanted to give him. But he had *you*, Millie."

She wished she could believe that was enough. That she was enough.

"I know. I . . . it's just hard."

"Bless you," Heather said. "You poor thing."

"I'm not poor."

"You kind of are," she said, and frowned deeply at Millie. "Very poorly. But you aren't alone. Remember that. My family is your family. We love you."

"I do know that," she said, her throat getting tight again.

"I really didn't mean to be pushy last night."

Millie frowned. "You just wanted to go to the bar. Because you wanted to see them."

"Well, and I was a little bit hoping you might decide to do something wild."

"I already told you," said Millie. "I couldn't. Also, it's laughable."

"It really isn't. Because he showed up and did all that for you. Most people would assume that a man would only do that when he wants a woman."

"He doesn't want me," Millie said, pushing that thought as far out to sea as possible. She wasn't even going to entertain it. Because it was ridiculous. She had *never* had a crush on Austin Wilder. He had been dangerous. She'd been furious at her friends for sighing over him, when she heard over dinner every night about the kinds of trouble the Wilder boys were causing about town.

He had *certainly* never had a crush on her. They were opposites. Kind of. Except maybe they weren't.

"I think you might have an inflated idea of me," Millie said, looking at her friend and embracing wholly the sadness inside her heart. "You thought I was involved in some kind of great love when really I just wanted security. I wanted to nail down this really specific future while my dad was still around to see it, with the kind of man he would've approved of. You thought it was a big wild romantic thing and it just wasn't. And this isn't me being brave."

"Maybe it should be. Maybe it would do you good to learn how to be an outlaw, Millie Talbot."

For a moment, it was tempting to envision herself as the gunslinger. Wearing all black.

"You said it yourself," she said. "I would be the schoolmarm."

"Wasn't Austin Wilder, the original, married to a schoolmarm?"

"Yes," Millie said, her cheeks getting hot, and most certainly red. "But what does that have to do with anything?"

"I guess I just think any woman who was married to an outlaw must have been stronger than she seemed."

"Well, I am not a schoolmarm. And I'm not related to anyone like that. My family were the law-abiding citizens. My family were the ones that kept the peace."

"And you disturbed it. When you crashed that meeting. When you wrangled Austin Wilder, the second one, down from the mountain so that he would come and vote your way. I see it in you. I always have. Little bits of sparkle here and there. Don't get me wrong.

I love you no matter what. But I wish there was just a little more fired-up Millie sometimes. For your sake."

She didn't feel particularly strong or fired up. She felt destabilized. She felt . . . lost. Her identity had been so set in stone from the moment she was born, but she had never quite lived up to it. And her efforts at being what was expected of her hadn't worked. Maybe she would just be a spinster. Maybe the Talbot line would end with her. She didn't hate the idea. Because it sounded safe.

She would never disappoint anyone again. There was no one left to disappoint.

"Thank you for the chai," she said.

"Of course. I just wanted to make sure that everything was okay."

"It really is. It was probably good for me to go to the saloon. I've never done that."

"I guess it's unbecoming for the sheriff's daughter to be seen in a house of ill repute," Heather said, reaching over the counter and picking up a fan, then wiggling it next to her chin. "It will be gossip all through church."

"Never," she said, snatching the fan back. "Because I have never done a gossip-worthy thing in my life. I was the designated driver, remember?"

"Oh, it's one of the things that I do remember from last night." Heather sighed. "I have to go. Are you all right?"

"Yes. I'm all right. You don't need to baby me." But it was nice that she had.

And now Millie just had to push all these revelations away and wait for Austin to text her. Easy.

Nothing could be easier.

Chapter 8

There's no life for a good woman with a bad man.

—Austin Wilder's journal, September 18, 1855

The box of papers he had taken from the museum was a hot mess of miscellaneous items. Order sheets and invoices, mine claims. There were some personal letters, but most of them were from family members who had lived on the East Coast, writing to the Talbots in Oregon.

None of it provided the insight he was looking for.

Austin pinched the bridge of his nose and opened up his manuscript. It was deeply uncomfortable for him, putting words on the page. Trying to articulate the feelings he had every time he opened up Austin Wilder's journal. Because there were a lot of them. And he couldn't say that he was especially articulate about matters of the heart.

He never had been.

But he had done a lot of reading. He knew what he wanted out of a story. He knew what he would want to know. What he would want to feel. He was trying to convey that.

It was like therapy in a way he hadn't quite imagined it would be. Which made him a little bit resentful. Especially writing about the love that Austin had shared with his wife. . . . Yeah. That was way outside his scope of emotion.

He turned away from the computer again and went back to the box.

He pushed through a few more papers and then paused. Because right there was something he hadn't expected to see. Not even in his wildest fantasies.

It was a receipt. Neatly made out to Lee Talbot from Butch Hancock.

Holy shit. He couldn't believe what he was staring at. This was so beyond anything. . . . Well, that wasn't true. He'd wanted a journal entry. He'd wanted a mustache-twirling, tied-to-the-railroad-tracks, maniacal-villain confession. Something that indicated a deal had been struck allowing Butch Hancock to get away, that the Wilders had been double-crossed. That they had been implicated for murder even though they hadn't actually committed it.

But this proved that Lee Talbot and Butch had had contact. It proved that money had changed hands. Butch had given money to the honorable sheriff, in fact. Money that was likely to have been stolen.

The front door to the house opened, and he stumbled out of his office.

"Carson," he said. "This is fucking crazy."

"We might have different definitions of crazy," Carson said.

"I don't really care." He shoved the receipt at his brother.

"What is this?"

"Why are you here?" he said, looking at Carson.

"I just . . . I didn't want to be alone. I figured that you were probably done working for the day."

"Yeah. I am."

Concern for his brother suddenly overshadowed everything. "What's up?"

"Usual sad-sack bullshit," Carson said.

"No, *what*." He wasn't going to let his brother do this. Deflect and stew in his own misery. Because Carson might not think he was on the path to an early grave, but Austin wasn't so certain.

"It's my wedding anniversary."

"Shit," Austin said. "I mean, shit. I'm sorry. I didn't remember."

"Why should you?"

"Because. I'm your brother. And I should."

"You barely remember your own damned birthday, Austin."

"That's not true. I actually know everybody's birthdays. I just don't always know what today is." Unless he had a library book due. And then he would check.

"Anyway, it's not that tragic. I don't need to be talked off a ledge. I'm just waiting for Perry to get off work."

"You're going out with Perry?"

Carson grimaced. "Well, don't say it like that."

"I didn't say it like anything."

"Everybody says it like *something*."

"No. That is in your head, little brother. But considering what a cesspool I imagine your head is on any given day, I'm willing to let it slide."

"Gee, thanks," said Carson. "Can we go back to whatever thing you were excited about, because it's more interesting than my old demons."

"I can talk about your demons all day."

"You can't cast them out. So. I find talking brings diminishing returns. My wife is dead. It sucks. I'm fucking sad. About . . . well, a lot of things. Someday maybe I won't be sad. It just feels pointless and terrible and I don't have a clue how to reconcile with it. First, I'd have to figure out a way to picture a different future. I haven't done that yet. So."

Austin understood that difficulty. It hit him, right in the pit of his gut. The challenge of picturing a new future, a different future. That was some pretty miraculous shit. It certainly wasn't anything that he'd mastered. Not yet. He was working on it. Because there was a future now up-and-coming, something other than an early grave. Most likely. But he still didn't have a clear image of it. He was working on that.

"Truth is," Carson said, "I'm not sure we'd still be married if she'd lived."

This was the first time Austin had heard his brother say anything along those lines. "What? You were happy."

"Mostly. But . . . you know, at this point in my life it feels like nothing I do goes like I want it to. Why would that?" He sighed heavily.

"I understand," he said. "And I mean that. Not in a flippant way."

"Yeah."

"We ought to be dead," Austin said.

"Not me," said Carson. "Not yet. But you already know that when Alyssa died, I figured. . . ."

"An early death would be a favor you weren't getting."

Carson looked away. "Damn straight."

Austin sighed. "Life is a trip."

He stared at his brother for a long moment and their shared history stretched between them. All the dumb stuff they'd done when they were kids. All the trouble they'd caused as young adults.

He could remember Carson putting a cherry bomb inside a trash can one time, just to make a loud bang in the public park and cause some mayhem.

Austin had laughed his ass off.

And now here they were. Men. Carson's face was lined with grief and Austin . . . wanted something different. Wanted something to change.

It was easier to be a young, angry kid, actually. When you'd never had something precious and lost it, like Carson. When you never wanted anything but to cause mayhem, like Austin. Because now he wanted more, and it made him aware of all the things he couldn't know, all the things he couldn't control.

"Tell me what this thing is," Carson said. "Because I meant it when I said I really don't need to go through all my bullshit."

He decided to honor Carson's request.

"Okay. So I found this receipt. It looks like Butch Hancock paid Lee Talbot two hundred and fifty dollars. That is a lot of money. You know, adjusted for inflation and the time period."

"Wow," Carson said. "But what does that even mean?"

"It points to what I think probably happened."

"I don't really understand what you think this discovery is going to get you, Austin. Because the bottom line is, the Wilders were criminals. And if the Talbots were dirty too, what difference does it make?"

"It changes things. Aren't you tired of everybody seeing you as that kid you were? Or even dumber, seeing you as a reincarnation of your ancestors, or a carbon copy of Dad?"

"I was. I was tired of it, and that's why I left. That's why I joined the military, because I could put *hero* on. It was a uniform. And people really are that simple. If the United States military says I'm good, then I'm good. Plus, I found a woman, away from here, who said that I was good. And. . . . Yeah, Austin, I get it. But I didn't sit down trying to sift through the past to make people think I was good enough."

"Is that what you think this is? That's what you think I'm doing? I'm just . . . sitting down? I have done plenty of stuff, Carson. I lived my entire life in this town not being a criminal. I work this land. I . . . I didn't sit down and. . . ."

"I'm not insulting you," said Carson. "Sorry if it came out that way. I'm an asshole. At least these days. But what I really meant was that it just. . . . Yeah, I get it. Maybe nobody gets it more than me. Flynn thinks it's all a joke. He thinks it's fucking hilarious, doesn't he? And Cassidy doesn't care. She's . . . I dunno, it's different for her, moving into all this when she was nine. I think she still finds it romantic or wild or something. She likes that she's with the outlaws. Because we kept her safe, didn't we?"

"Yeah. And all Flynn really cares about is that he gets laid."

"I wish I could care about that." Carson shook his head. "That was never enough for me."

It wasn't enough for Austin either. There had been times in his life when he would've said it was. Times in his life when he hadn't thought about the future. Maybe it was why books had always been more comfortable than the world around him. And if he could disappear into somebody else's life for a while, then he could live differently. Be different. Maybe it was why he was trying to write Austin Wilder's book. Because it was giving him a chance to look at himself from a different angle. His legacy, his family. To see something other than what the townspeople did, other than what his father always claimed.

"I don't think that the original Austin Wilder was innocent," he said. "But I think that's the point. I think that he was in some ways a good man. Who did some bad things. But I don't think he was a murderer, and I really do think that's an important distinction. I think he was shot in the street for no reason except that the sheriff wanted to bolster his legacy. He has this whole town, six generations on, believing that the Talbots are the best of everything and the Wilders are the worst. Congratulations to him. But I have to wonder how it would've been different, for you, for me, if that wasn't our legacy. What if Dad wasn't born thinking something was wrong with him? What if we weren't?"

"I have bad news for you. Dad was a selfish prick. I don't think *history* played a role in that."

"I do. You just said it all right here, didn't you? You went and put on a military uniform to turn yourself into a hero. Because somebody made you feel like you weren't one. You went and found a certain kind of life and—"

"I loved my wife," Carson said softly.

"Sorry. That's not what I meant. It's just . . . it put you on the path. The past matters. It echoes into the future. And the present."

"I just realized," Carson said, looking at him as if he'd grown another head. "You're a romantic."

Austin recoiled. "What the fuck is romantic about that?"

"I don't know. It just seems romantic. This idea that everything is connected. The idea that the past matters."

"It does. It's true what they say—and I really do mean it—if you can't learn from history, you are doomed to repeat it. Our family is an example of that."

"Are you trying to learn from history, or are you trying to change it?"

"I want the record set straight. Because we have to be learning from the truth, don't we?"

"So you think you're gonna prove that the Talbot family doesn't deserve the praise they've gotten all this time. But they did a lot of good over these past decades. You can't erase that."

"I don't want to do that." He thought of Millie. Of the fact that she was the only one left. Of the fact that this little bit of truth might actually hurt her. But she loved history. He knew that much. And she would care about the truth. He was pretty damn certain of that too.

"What is it you do want?"

"To introduce some complexity to the narrative, to our thinking about the past?"

"Wow," Carson said, laughing. "You have actually amused me today, and that was a tall order."

"What?"

"You're not going to get complexity of thought here. Small minds."

He thought of Millie again. "That isn't true. You have a pretty dim view of humanity."

"You have a weirdly optimistic one."

"We stayed here for a reason," he said. "And you came back for a reason."

"Yeah. I did. Because there was land. I wanted to buy a piece from you. Because I was supposed to start a family. Sorry. I just brought the room down again."

"Well, I want to fix this. For the family you will have eventually."

His brother laughed. "Please. I'm done with that. I'm never doing that again. Ever. I don't know much, but I do know that. I can't take it. I cannot fucking take it. Not ever again."

"I don't blame you."

"Legacy," he said. "That's the real mindfuck, man. If you live long enough, you can't escape that pull toward making yourself into something more. We might disagree on how, and who should care. But I tried it with marriage, with the military, and you're doing the same with your book."

"Eventually it's going to get Flynn too. And probably Cassidy. Whether she believes it or not."

"Maybe your book will change my mind. Maybe I'll read about Austin Wilder, his life and great loves, and I'll suddenly see the light."

"Just maybe," Austin said.

Carson's phone buzzed. "Oh. Perry's off work. She's cooking me dinner."

"Well. That sounds nice. As nice as a shitty day can be."

"True enough."

Austin clutched the receipt in his hand, and replayed the conversation with his brother after Carson left. He decided not to think about it too much, and took his phone out to tap in Millie's number. It was still saved in his call list from when he had dialed himself from her phone. She answered immediately. "Hello?"

It was strange to hear her voice on the other end of the line. "Hi. I have some information that I want to share with you. Some historical stuff that I discovered."

"Oh. What?"

"I'd like to meet up. Anyway, we were going to discuss the Gold Rush Days."

"Sure, would you like to go get coffee?"

"No," he said. "I'll meet you at the library. When you're closing up. I think it would be better if we speak in private."

"We close at four today."

"That's just fine," he said.

Austin hung up and let out a long breath. This was the victory he had been waiting for. It didn't feel as good as he had expected it to.

Not for the first time, he thought that he was stuck in a pretty useless space.

Not an outlaw, and definitely not a hero.

At least when he was a kid, he hadn't cared what anybody thought. He never would've worried about preserving Millie Talbot's feelings.

He thought about her mother, about the library, and for a moment, he questioned whether he'd ever really been so tough.

The problem was, he might have been a troublemaker in his youth, but he had never been without feeling.

Would've been nice.

All his acting out had come from a place of anger. None of it had been for the maniacal joy of it. He might've told himself that sometimes. Might have said that he got off on being a completely uncontrollable element. But the truth was, he had just been an angry kid. With a dad who had put too much weight on his shoulders, a town that hadn't seen him as anything but trouble, and a mother who hadn't wanted him at all.

His discovery was vindication, in some ways. He was going to cling to that belief.

Because he didn't need any more guilt.

Chapter 9

Went to see Jasmine's girls at the saloon and left feeling worse than when I rolled in. It's a hell of a thing to have your pick of any woman you want, and to wish you were with the one you can't have.

—Austin Wilder's journal, September 25, 1855

Alice was checking out, but slowly, and Millie felt a little bit overcharged knowing that Austin was going to come in soon. Because he had a historical revelation to share that necessitated a private, in-person meeting.

That was all.

"Do you read romance, dear?" Alice asked.

Millie blinked. "No."

"You should," Alice said.

"Alice," Millie said. "My wedding just got called off a couple of months ago."

"I know. That's why you should be reading it. Because let me tell you, that Michael Hall could never have been a romance hero."

In spite of herself, Millie was intrigued.

"Why?"

"It's hard to explain if you don't read the books. But I always thought there was something about him. And I was right, considering his behavior."

Millie couldn't argue with Alice.

"I tried to read one," Millie said. "I found . . . certain scenes. . . . They were just terribly unrealistic." She felt her face getting hot. Just mentioning *those* scenes made her feel missish.

Alice's eyebrows shot upward. "Did you really? Well. That is sad.

I don't find them unrealistic at all." A sly smile creased her wrinkled face, and as she touched her cheek, her wedding ring, which had been firmly on her finger for fifty years, twinkled. Millie knew a moment of envy for this woman, who was beautiful and happy and lived in her skin with ease. She had known a lifetime of love, and did not find the sex in romance novels unrealistic.

"Maybe I'll try them again," she said, the words coming out in a rush.

"I have a list of recommendations for you," Alice said. "When you're ready."

She patted the counter and then took her stack of books and walked out the door. Millie was left feeling uncertain what to do while she processed that information and waited for her next inter-action, which was not going to do anything to settle her.

The door swung open again, and in came Austin. Black on black on black, and looking like an outlaw without ever pulling any cos-tume pieces out of her crates. He had a folder in his hand.

"I guess you're the first one to show up with a folder," she said, smiling weakly.

He looked down at his hand. "What?"

"You were excited about folders earlier. Because I said I had some that would help with our planning."

"Oh."

She had just let him know that she remembered every word of every conversation they'd ever had. While he clearly didn't. That was maybe not the best thing.

No. Maybe not.

"I thought it was funny." She forced out a nervous laugh. It sounded worse. More desperate.

"There's no one else in here, is there?"

"No."

She stood up and slowly made her way around the reference desk, very conscious of the fact that she had thought of it as a barrier between herself and Austin on more than one occasion. Now, she didn't have it, and they were here alone.

She opened up the door and turned the sign. Then she turned the lock on the door. Now they were locked in.

"Officially closed," she said, moving past him and making her way toward a table in the center of the room.

"You can sit down with me here. It's a good place to. . . ." She realized that she had left all of her things behind the desk. "Just . . . just a second. You can sit down." She went back to the desk, collected her planner, and on a whim, grabbed a sheriff's star from the costume boxes. Then she went back to the table.

"Okay. Now I have all of my things, and we can discuss Gold Rush Days, and your . . . your revelation."

"Which do you want to do first?"

"I want to know what you found."

He opened up the folder and pushed it across the table.

She frowned, looking at the slip of paper inside.

"Butch Hancock paid Lee Talbot for . . . services? Something?"

"Something. Take a look at the date stamp on it," he said, pressing his forefinger to the date.

It was two days before Austin Wilder had been killed.

"I don't understand," she said.

"I can't prove it, but I think Butch gave up the gang, then paid Lee to look the other way so that he could get away. I've always thought that. I wasn't sure how it happened, or who approached who, but this definitely suggests that Butch wanted to get free of the gang, and he was willing to pay for it."

"But . . . so you think that Lee Talbot just let a notorious criminal escape?"

"I do. I've always thought so. Butch Hancock the Traitor. . . . His name is mud as far as we Wilders are concerned."

"Is that why you hate the Hancocks?" she asked.

The reason for the long-standing feud had never occurred to her. It should have, she supposed, since this whole town was powered on grudges that seemed to be as old as the dirt.

"Yes," he said easily. "I mean, also because the Hancocks haven't changed—a bunch of lousy, no-good, untrustworthy. . . ."

"You're exactly like everybody you don't like," she said brusquely. The conflicting feelings rattling around inside her made her tone firmer than she would have used otherwise.

"*Pardon?*"

"You're so angry at everybody in the town for clinging to the past, but you do the same. You're angry at the Hancocks, you're angry at me—"

"It's not just the past," he said. "I was born being told that I was bad news. I was a ten-year-old boy who walked into the library and wasn't welcome. And yes, I did my part to earn the reputation I had been given on day one, but you tell me this, Millie, do you think that I would've had a hope of maybe turning out just a little bit differently if people hadn't told me who I was before I ever knew?"

This was the truth of him. This deep, unrelenting anger. And as she stared down at the papers, trying to grasp the full implications of what this receipt meant, she had to wonder how much of what he said was true of her.

She had spent her whole life trying to measure up to an ideal. A level of bravery, of goodness, brilliance, that might not be real.

The town was divided. Lawmen and outlaws.

But what if the past had never been so clear-cut?

What if the lawman hadn't been trustworthy? What if she had built her entire life on a foundation of shifting sand?

It would mean. . . .

Freedom. The realization, the feeling, took her by surprise. She felt overwhelmed all at once by a total and complete rush of adrenaline, of relief.

And yes, there was grief too, but she was so familiar with grief at this point. With loss. The loss of a legend could never compare to the loss of a human being. She had lost both of her parents.

But slowly, she felt pain start to creep in. All the stories she had heard on her grandfather's knee about the largesse of the Talbot family just weren't real.

Because of course they couldn't be.

Because no bloodline could be all bad or all good.

But people wanted narratives to be simple and straightforward.

Because they didn't want to get into the complexity of people.

It was why the telling of history could be so contentious. Why people resisted looking beyond tales of bravery, looking at the ways their heroes had hurt people to get what they wanted.

This was just another example.

To ensure the legacy her family had benefited from all these years, there had been bribery. There had been betrayal.

Worst of all, if what Austin had said earlier was true, that there was no mention of murder in his namesake's journals, then that would make her ancestor a murderer. Because it would mean the Wilder brothers had been wrongfully executed. Criminals they might've been, but it was possible they had never spilled blood.

And suddenly the celebration of the death of Austin Wilder, of his bleeding out in the street, seemed a horrendous thing.

Heroes were enshrined. Made larger than life. More than human.

Villains were somehow made less.

In the end they were all just men, and that was the hardest thing for people to accept.

She knew it, and it was hard for her too.

"I'm sorry," she said. "And sorry I reacted that way. I can't pretend that it isn't . . . that it isn't entirely likely you're right."

"Well, it must be disturbing for you. Taking away the legacy that you trade on for Gold Rush Days."

"Yes," she said. "It is. It's taking away the easy story. Now what we have is a historical mystery. And, actually, that is pretty interesting."

She tried to push away the personal implications. She wasn't going to cry over her own ancestor being less than she'd always been told. Not when the Wilders were the ones who'd truly been harmed.

She was caught somewhere between elation and horror, and there really was no way to sit there in front of this man, with his blue eyes that were far too keen, without feeling as if she wanted to slide through the floor.

"Well, I'm going to work on getting more information," he said. "Somehow. I'll dig through everything in that museum basement if need be."

"You didn't tell me what made you think Austin was betrayed in the first place."

He had alluded to it, but he hadn't said.

"There's an entry in the journal. Where Austin says that he suspects Butch is planning to make a run for it. They had just done a bank job, and there was a lot of money. Austin wanted to make a change. His kids were getting older, he had been writing a lot about what he was going to tell his sons. He didn't want them to be outlaws. Neither did Austin's wife. And whatever you might think about him, I can tell you for certain that he loved that woman. He was willing to do anything for her. He wanted to give her a good life. Something she could be proud of. He was obsessed with her."

For some reason, hearing him say that made her profoundly sad. She had been dimly aware of the original Austin's wife and children, but not his feelings. Because it had never occurred to her to attribute feelings to him. "That he was married and had kids is a footnote in the historical record," she said.

"It wasn't a footnote in his life. It was everything to him. And I know, you would think in that case he would've stopped robbing, but I don't think it was that easy. It was the only way he knew how to provide."

"It would be nice if everybody had access to that journal."

"Not enough people read. You and I both know that."

"But some do. And if it's a compelling story, then maybe people will be more interested in it. Maybe they'll understand."

She realized that for Austin, the past was more real than it had ever been to her, because he had that journal. He had a full, complete picture of the man he was named for, and she didn't have that with Lee. She had dry historical record, she had paperwork that you could piece together, like that receipt Austin had brought. But it didn't fill in the substance of who the man was. Didn't give an idea of his inner thoughts, or the voice that he used to speak.

Austin knew his forebears in a way that she couldn't.

"Until we have more information," Austin said, "I don't know that there's any point marinating on this too much."

She narrowed her eyes. "I have a feeling that you'll be marinating on it plenty."

"I'm still investigating."

"Maybe I'd like to help."

"Maybe I don't trust you," he said, leveling his gaze at her.

Her heart rate started to pick up. There was something exhilarating about this, but she couldn't quite pinpoint it. "Well, I guess maybe we have to start over. If we can't rely on our legends."

"I know you plenty well enough."

"Does that mean I know you?" she asked.

"You do know what I read."

"That is true. And that means I know a fair amount about you. But I'm sure there are things I don't know."

He lifted a brow. "You know my arrest record."

He was throwing that out like a hand grenade. Trying to be provocative. To see what she'd do. She could feel it. That anger simmering beneath the surface. "True. I do. Is that who you are, though?"

She'd never bantered like this before so she hadn't known she could do it. But here she was. Firing right back at him, as if she might have something wild in her blood too.

She had never talked to a man like this before. Gone back and forth, felt the exhilaration of a challenge.

It was. . . . Maybe it was almost flirting, except it felt a little too sharp for that, and when she breathed in deep it hurt a bit.

Very Good Girl Millie Talbot would never.

But the Millie Talbot who had mysterious danger in her background? Who knew. Who could say at all.

"Does it make you feel better to think so?" he asked.

"I've always found it hard to figure you out," she admitted. "Not that I spent a whole lot of time trying."

"Really? I'm so complex that you can't figure me out? You, who read as many books as I do, can't sort through who I might be?"

He looked way too pleased by that.

"I said I didn't *try*."

"Yes, but I don't believe you."

Damn him. She felt hot and itchy now.

"I used to get very angry at the girls I knew, because they all thought you and your brothers were so . . . dangerous. And handsome."

She shivered when she said those words, because they felt too close to a truth she was trying not to delve into.

"*Did* they?" He leaned forward, clasping his hands and looking at her far too intently.

There was something dangerous about him *right now*. Not just in the past.

He was angry, but it wasn't the kind of anger that made her scared he'd hurt her. It was intense. Pitched his voice lower, made his eyes go sharp. She could feel his voice resonate inside her. She could feel the intensity of his gaze.

The feeling was more powerful than being touched all over by Michael, and that realization had her wishing she'd worn a string of pearls for the express purpose of clutching them now.

"Yes," she said. "They did." She put the emphasis on *did*. "But I knew that I didn't want anything to do with somebody who had broken the law."

"Then you don't want anything to do with your own bloodline, now do you?"

She swallowed hard.

"Apparently," she said.

She felt *warm*.

"It seems to me," he said, "that we really do need to work on dispensing with some of the narratives around this place. Because the founding families kind of suck, and they're resting on legends filled with half-truths to justify their place in town."

"Well," she said. "That is true."

"And, I would argue that it's pretty obvious your ex-fiancé is one of the worst."

"I can't argue with that." She didn't even want to.

"And frankly, it makes him an even worse person that after he left you for somebody else, he's also actively participating in undermining something that's important to you."

"Well, he's aligning himself with the woman that he. . . . With her."

"Sure. But don't you deserve some loyalty for all your years with him? How long were you with him, anyway?"

She did not like this question, because she didn't like the answer to it. "Six years," she said. "I can be glad at least that it wasn't a lifetime."

"I'm surprised you were with him that long without marrying him. Doesn't seem like a very good-girl thing to do."

"This isn't 1950," she said. "Or 1850, regardless of how the town might occasionally feel."

"True, true."

"Anyway, I only lived with him for a couple of years before we decided to . . . before the engagement."

She really didn't want to talk to him about this. It felt sticky. Oddly intimate in some way, but maybe that was weird of her.

"Wow. You were even living with him."

"Yes. Though thankfully I had actually moved out to start getting our house ready, and I really should've seen that as a red flag. That he didn't want to come with me immediately, but it made sense, because our lease wasn't up, and I was busy with the renovations. It turned out, he just wanted to stay in his own place because it gave him more opportunity to cheat."

"What ended up happening to the house?"

"Well, it was my dad's house. So, it's mine now. I'm very thankful for that. Thankful that I hadn't gone to the trouble of adding Michael to the deed. I was going to, after we got married."

That Michael had almost walked away with part of her inheritance made her heart beat faster. Not in a good way.

"Outlaws are everywhere," Austin said.

"Yeah. No kidding."

"So, about the Gold Rush Days."

"Well, I think we have to start planning it without any reenactments. You know, of the shoot-out. Because until we know all the details. . . ."

"Yeah. Actually, I don't want to have one no matter what we learn."

"I understand," she confirmed. "But we might."

She pushed the sheriff star forward on the table. "I have costumes."

"Costumes." He pressed down on the edge of the star and picked it up, turning it over and examining it. "Well, I'll be."

"I definitely want to do some living history. Covered wagon rides. That would be amazing."

"Well," Austin said slowly, still hanging on to the star. "As it happens, we have a wagon."

"You do?"

"Yeah. I mean, we have the base of a wagon. It doesn't have the big covered part on it anymore, but that would be easy enough to fix."

"You're not telling me that it's an original Conestoga wagon."

"It actually is. It's been on the property for a long time, in one of the barns. Carson and I got a hankering to do some restoration on it maybe ten years back. He'd be the last one to tell you this, but Carson is actually a brilliant woodworker. He can make any sort of furniture, or restore old things. He's done a lot of repairs on family heirlooms for people willing to trust a Wilder. But the wagon was maybe the start of that. We worked on it when he was on leave, and it's in pretty good shape now."

"I would love it if you would drive a covered wagon for the kids."

He flipped the star from between his thumb and forefinger, to rest between his forefinger and middle finger, then stopped. "I don't know about being the driver, but I'll consider it. My sister would probably love it."

"Does she know how to drive a horse team?"

He flipped the star back. "Cassidy knows how to do just about everything. If you wanted somebody to be your Annie Oakley, she would be your girl."

"Well, Annie Oakley isn't really connected to the history of Rustler Mountain."

"I know," he said dryly as he put the star back down on the table.

Her face got hot, and she was very afraid that she was blushing.

She put her hand out to grab the sheriff's star, but he reached out at the same time and took hold of it, and as he did, his fingertips brushed hers.

It was like being struck with a lit match.

Her whole body lit up.

And suddenly she understood something. As her stomach leapt into her throat and her heart sped up, as she felt an ache between her thighs that began to expand. She began to understand that scene she'd read in the romance novel all those years ago that she'd dismissed as unrealistic.

Michael wasn't a romance hero. . . .

She swallowed hard. Austin Wilder wasn't one either—how could he be?

You're my hero.

She'd said those words to him, but she hadn't meant them like that.

She hadn't.

She could actually feel sweat beading on her forehead, and she was afraid he'd be able to see it. Was afraid she was telegraphing her feelings all over her face. That he could read her right now the way he could one of his books. She wanted him.

She really did want him, right then.

Maybe what Heather had suggested wasn't so out of the question, maybe she could be an outlaw.

Maybe she didn't have to be so good.

What had being a good girl gotten her anyway?

Six years wasted on a man who hadn't really loved her. Who she hadn't really loved.

What was love anyway?

She'd been certain she knew. She'd been certain she wanted it, yet now she really had no idea. What had she actually been after? Security, knowing she'd done something to continue her family legacy. The Halls had always been well-respected, but Austin was right. They actually did suck, and there was extensive documentation of their misdeeds, but they had started the first bank and so there was an air of respectability about them that they weren't entitled to.

But all these stories were so entrenched in town lore, even when they were challenged, it didn't seem to change much.

Michael felt entitled to his good name in the same way Millie felt pressured by hers and Austin felt stained by his bad one.

Finding common ground with Austin Wilder had not been her goal. But she had found it. Here in the disruption of her many losses. It had taken an earthquake. It had taken cracking the ground she was standing on, but here she was.

She looked up at him, and their eyes clashed, and she felt something tremble inside her. Another earthquake. Another seismic shift.

Did she only think that something was changing because she found him attractive?

Just letting herself think that she found him attractive, rather than merely acknowledging his general handsomeness, was like ringing a gong inside her soul.

She breathed out, shaky, unsteady.

"I think it's a great idea. The covered wagon, I mean. I would love to . . . to come up and see it."

"Sure. You're free to come up anytime. We're there most of the time. And if I'm not home, Cassidy could show you around."

The idea that it didn't matter to him whether or not he was there when she came was a jolting one. An injection of reality. Of course he didn't care.

She shouldn't either. He had mentioned that Cassidy might want to participate in the Gold Rush Days, so honestly, she should try to connect with Cassidy. It would be better than filtering everything through Austin, that was for sure.

"I want to put together a children's program," she said. "So that I can contact the elementary schools and try to arrange field trips."

"Sounds good," he said.

She looked at him. "Do you really think so?"

"It's a polite thing to say."

"I think it really will be good," she said.

She suddenly felt desperate to get him to understand. Because she felt buoyed by their common experience, and she wanted to extend it.

"Especially if we get all this new information about what actually happened."

"Yeah, you really think that people are going to be interested in that?"

"Yes. I do."

"Well, I hope so, considering I'm writing a book on it."

She shook her head. "I don't know why it surprises me that you're writing. Of course you are. You love books."

"Because even you can't quite believe that I'm not a big idiot?"

His question scraped against her skin, because she had just been castigating herself for that very thing.

"No. I don't think you're an idiot. I never have. But I admit that I find you confusing."

"So you said. And also that you didn't care to try to figure me out."

Her ears went hot. "It wasn't that I . . . I didn't think I should try to figure you out."

"But rather that you shouldn't think about me at all?" He lifted a brow, his expression provocative now. But that didn't seem possible. That he'd bother to provoke her. "Even thinking about me was forbidden, wasn't it?"

His voice was pitched low and her heart started to beat faster.

"I . . . I . . . well, you were bad. I mean . . . you did bad things. You did all that stuff when you were younger. The things that you're accused of." She sounded unconvincing and ridiculous.

"I was angry. If you were a kid just trying to make your way around this town and you were told you weren't welcome by half the adults, wouldn't you be angry?"

Yes. She would've been.

She had never really been angry a day in her life, that was the thing. She had never pushed back or rebelled against her role in Rustler Mountain. She had just tried to live up to it. No matter how difficult it seemed. It had felt like an important thing to do, because her family was so revered. And now . . . now she felt a slight simmering of anger. Or something adjacent to it. Because all her life she hadn't felt quite good enough.

She had never really fit the image of a Talbot.

And now she wondered if that image was a lie. If the beautiful portrait that had been painted of her family was a counterfeit.

She had seen a documentary once about art thieves who painted over famous portraits to conceal their worth. She wondered if the real piece was buried beneath a reproduction. She wondered if she had been living a lie, and she felt an echo of the same anger that must've dogged Austin since birth.

"I don't blame you for being angry," she said. "I guess you aren't actually confusing. I think I just didn't know enough. About life. Because I was so insulated. It's just that sometimes insulation can suffocate you."

"Suffocate you right into a relationship with an asshole," he said.

She bit the inside of her cheek. To keep from laughing, actually, because Michael really was an asshole. "I can't argue with that."

"The older I get," he said, "and getting older is kind of a surprise to me considering my family history, the more I realize everyone has a story. Reading was sort of the foundation of that realization, I guess. I always liked redemption stories. Where somebody starts out low and ends up somewhere good. It was what I could relate to. But everybody has a story, no matter how bad they are, even Michael. I assume he's the product of a lifetime of indulgence. Of getting his way. Of never thinking that perhaps he doesn't get to treat people however he wants."

"Don't make him a sympathetic character," Millie said.

"Oh, I don't find him sympathetic. It's just that when you understand everyone has an origin story, they're less confusing."

"What do you think mine is?"

She realized her mistake as soon as the words exited her mouth. But it was too late.

His blue eyes raked her up and down, and she felt it like a physical touch. As if he had popped a button on her blouse, and then another. As if he had pushed the fabric away and looked *through* her skin. Not at it, but straight into her.

Her soft, vulnerable heart. Her frailties. Her imperfections.

The deep fear that she was nothing.

Not good, not bad. Just nothing. A bland, beige smudge on her family tree. A branch that would end right where it stopped growing.

He stood up and she felt that something was slipping through her grasp. That he was drawing a line under this moment, and she didn't want him to.

She wanted to keep talking to him.

She wanted him to stay.

In the library, the only place where a Talbot had ever been able to meet a Wilder without handcuffs or bloodshed.

She stood, feeling dizzy, and wasn't quite sure why.

He picked up the sheriff's star again and began to walk toward her.

"You've been trying too hard from day one," he said. "All that effort, it's invisible to you because it's all you know. I can see it because I never tried at all."

He took a step closer to her and then another, and she thought her heart might beat straight through her chest.

He opened up the pin on the back of the star, his big hands sure and quick. Then he reached out and plucked at the fabric of her dress, not touching anything but the garment. But he was close, so close. She could hear him breathing, she could smell his skin. The soap he used, the hay from his horses.

Then he pushed the pin straight through the fabric and fastened it, his knuckle brushing against her and releasing something in her knees that made them buckle, just enough to make her wobble but not fall.

And there that star sat, pinned to her chest.

She looked up at him, and she felt the color flood her cheeks like a tide as her heart throbbed painfully and her palms went sweaty.

She saw something then, in those electric-blue eyes, that she'd never seen before. It sent her mind careening down paths she'd never explored but suddenly. . . .

What if he moved closer?

What if he touched her?

What if?

He lowered his head and her breath caught.

"Keep trying, Sheriff," he said, his voice a husky whisper. "You'll be all right."

Then he straightened and moved away from her, and it was as if a bubble had been popped. Whatever had been there a moment before was just gone, evaporated into the air.

"Come up tomorrow and check out that wagon," he said.

"S-sure." Her mouth wasn't working. Her brain wasn't working.

"See you later."

"Yeah." She nodded and followed him to the door, closing it behind him and relocking it. Then she pressed her hand over the star, over her heart, and waited for it to calm down.

Chapter 10

She sees something in me I don't see in myself.

—Austin Wilder's journal, December 14, 1855

Austin knew he shouldn't be playing with fire. Because when a Wilder picked up matches, it turned the world into a whole conflagration.

Now, a week ago he wouldn't have said that Millie had the ability to generate a spark.

Hell.

He'd been incorrect.

And he knew that if he reached down into the darkest places inside himself, it wasn't actually a big surprise that he was intrigued by her.

Any psychologist would have a field day. She was the daughter of the man who had arrested him. You could put all the generational stuff to bed and just focus on that.

If her dad were still alive, he would be tempted to assume that he found her interesting because she was completely off-limits.

Hell, he supposed it didn't really matter that the other man was dead. Fucking his daughter would be worse than dancing on his grave.

Lord.

He braced his hand against the frame of the barn door. He was waiting for her to arrive, and he shouldn't be thinking things like that. Not when they had the power to gut-punch him in a way sexual thoughts never really did.

He was pragmatic about sex. It was a drive, like anything else, and he honored his drives. When he wanted something, he made sure to satiate the need.

In a healthy way, he liked to think. Because he wasn't reckless in the way that his father had been. Not these days.

Which was why he had a preference for hooking up with women who were from out of town, or getting himself out of town in order to do the hooking up. He didn't like planting landmines on the streets he had to walk, thank you very much.

He had enough problems without causing more for himself. Again, a mindset he had adopted more recently, but still.

So it shouldn't really surprise him, he supposed, that there was a . . . fascination with Millie. A temptation.

Because temptation wasn't really something he had a lot of experience with.

When he was younger, he had just done whatever the hell he wanted. Older, he had found a place to put everything.

Ironically, that mousy little woman aroused something wild in him that very little else did.

He shouldn't have played around with her yesterday. Shouldn't have let himself get close enough to smell her. Vanilla and some sweet flower, mingled with paper and ink, and there was little else half as erotic to him.

He groaned and started walking over to the stables. He needed to get the horses fed before Millie came up.

But that meant running into his siblings, which was something he wasn't in the mood for.

Or maybe it was. Because they were his reason, after all. His reason for not being a total degenerate. His reason for giving a damn about much of anything.

Assholes.

Like everything else on the Wilder Ranch, the stables were rustic. But serviceable.

They were clean because if there was one thing that they all had in common, it was an obsessive focus on keeping the ranch healthy.

Carson had his own parcel of land, but they worked the ranch together. Flynn had his own place, but his land wasn't working land. And as for Cassidy, this was still her home base.

Carson and Flynn had been driving cattle down from one pasture to the other today, and he wasn't sure where Cassidy was occupying herself. He didn't micromanage them. Nobody was in charge.

And that suited him just fine. They were all good at anticipating where the work needed to be done, and they did it.

He didn't have the energy to tell all of them what to do, not on top of everything else. He didn't want to be a manager.

Especially not of that motley crew.

He walked into the stable right as Carson and Flynn came riding up, hats on their heads, horses breathing hard.

"Howdy, big brother," said Flynn, dismounting, his boots landing hard on the ground.

He grinned, and Austin felt . . . something tugging at his chest. He wasn't even sure quite what.

Flynn was still so quick with a smile. He seemed to take everything in stride. None of the cares brought on by years or loss seemed to impact him in quite the way they did himself and Carson.

Carson had been gut-punched by grief, like cannon fire in the center of his chest, while Austin just felt old sometimes.

Maybe Flynn's sunny outlook came from having more family around. Being not just a Wilder, but also a Hunter. His mom's family was a factor, even if he wasn't close to his mother.

And that was something that none of the rest of them could claim.

Maybe it was just enough to make being a Wilder more enjoyable. Or maybe Flynn was just Flynn.

"Doing great," Austin said. "I think I might have gotten the ranch tangled up in Gold Rush Days."

Carson looked down at Flynn, and they exchanged a glance. Then Carson dismounted. "Is that so?" He crossed his arms and gave Austin a hard look.

"It is so," Austin said, staring his brother down in turn, daring him to say something about Millie.

"And how did that come about?" Flynn asked.

"I met with the librarian yesterday."

"The little librarian who seems to have you tied up in knots?" Carson asked.

So he was doing it. Starting a fight.

That bastard.

Austin guffawed. And then decided on denial. "No woman has ever had me in knots."

"And yet," Flynn said, "you seem to be doing whatever she wants you to do."

Oh, good, Flynn was hopping in.

"She has information I want. And, as you both pointed out, potentially the key to altering some of our family reputation. You know how much I want that, to be something other than bad Austin Wilder."

"Right," Carson said. "So you can find a wife and build a new legacy. She in the running?"

He couldn't quite articulate his reaction. It was like an explosion in his chest. Not a pleasant one.

"She's a Talbot," he gritted out.

"Yeah," Flynn said. "Pretty famously, but it's not keeping you from associating with her."

"Associating on this level is different from . . . whatever the hell you're talking about. Anyway. All that stuff is in the future."

"Right."

"I'm going to. . . ." He didn't want to get into all of it with his brothers.

And just then, Cassidy rode up on her horse, dark hair tangling in the wind behind her. She was like hell on hooves, and she skidded to a stop next to Carson, a devilish grin on her face. "Howdy boys," she said.

"Where have you been, Cass?"

She shrugged the shoulder. "Here and there."

"Do you think you might be interested in giving wagon rides for Gold Rush Days?"

Her eyebrows shot up, then knit together and lowered. "For what?"

"You heard me. You don't need it repeated."

"Austin is volunteering us," Carson said. "Well, that is something."

"I didn't volunteer *you*. You'd scare the children."

Flynn laughed. "True."

Austin turned to Cassidy. "I didn't volunteer you either. Yet."

"Why me?" Cassidy asked.

"Because you're a great wagon driver. And I thought you might enjoy it."

She looked irritated, mostly because he was right, and he imagined that she hated that.

"But I'm mean and untamed," she said, lifting her hands and making claws out of them. "Don't you think *I* would scare the children?"

"I think you're the sort of strong female role model the kids need to see," Austin said.

Cassidy gripped the brim of her hat and pulled it down low over her eyes. "Flattery will get you . . . more than I wish it would. Okay. Sounds interesting."

"Great. I'll keep you apprised of the details."

"Why do I get the feeling that means you're going to present me with a schedule and tell me where to go and what to do?"

"Probably because I will."

"You're lucky I love you," she said.

He found himself grappling with uncomfortable feelings yet again. Because Cassidy had been responsible for the biggest shift in his life. He was ten years older than her. Not old enough to be her dad, and yet, in many ways, that was the role he filled. All three brothers had come together to take care of her in some way or another, but her coming had changed Austin profoundly. Cassidy had single-handedly put him on the straight and narrow. After their dad had died, he could've gone either way. Entirely off the deep end and into an early grave, or right to where he was now. With hope and a future. With a book half written and a mystery to solve.

"You too," he grumbled.

Not because he didn't mean it. But because he meant it a little bit too much, and if he wasn't careful, his throat was going to get tight.

"I have some venison I need to use," Carson said. "I figured I would grill burgers tonight. I'm going to ask Perry to come up. She's going to bring rolls and salad. Dalton said he would bring some ribs."

Austin was pleasantly surprised that Carson was organizing a get-together, but he wondered how much of it was Perry's influence. If she had actually suggested the plan. But whatever. As long as Carson wasn't disappearing into his own sadness.

"Sounds good."

"Maybe I have plans," Cassidy said, sniffing.

"Do you?" Carson asked.

"No," she groused.

"Sounds good to me," said Flynn. "Free food is always a draw."

"Great. I figure we can use your place, Austin?"

"My house is . . . literally the house you grew up in. So sure."

"See you all later, then," Carson said, urging his horse along. "I have some chores to finish out at my homestead."

"Great," Austin said, waving him off.

He was feeling kind of antsy to get rid of Cassidy and Flynn also. Mainly because he knew that Millie was going to roll up any minute, and he didn't really want an audience.

Right. You don't want them to notice that you're hot for her.

No. He didn't. He didn't want anyone to notice. He could only hope that she was just a shade too innocent to have any idea of what he was thinking.

Sure, she had lived with Michael Hall. But Michael Hall was one of those guys. Two-pump chump.

He could identify them from a mile away.

The kind of guy that thought he deserved sex, but didn't do

anything to make a good time for his partner. And Danielle LeFevre wouldn't give a shit, because she was all about having something that someone else had.

He wondered if Millie understood that.

That Michael had wanted something illicit, and Danielle had just wanted to win. That they were a very basic set of characters. No surprises. And no change for the better on the horizon.

In his mind, you had to want a redemption arc to get one. You didn't just stumble into it.

They could go to hell as far as he was concerned. They were boring. That was maybe their biggest sin.

But whatever, he didn't need an audience.

"Flynn," Cassidy said. "I'm trying to clear some bullshit out of the north pasture. Do you think you could come help me? There's some heavy stuff."

"Are you saying you're not strong enough?"

"I am but a frail woman," she said, lifting her hands and showing her slim but quite strong arms.

Flynn rolled his eyes. "If you're feeling lazy, Cassidy, just say so."

"I'm feeble," she said, sniffling as she got back on her horse.

"Whatever," Flynn said, getting back on his own. "See you for dinner," he said to Austin.

Cassidy grinned as they went off, and Austin really couldn't have scripted that better. So maybe things were going to go according to some kind of plan today.

He did his chores, and let his mind go blessedly blank. He gave himself over to the physicality of the work and took a break from thinking about *her*. Then he headed back toward the house, just in time to see Millie's car roll up the gravel drive.

He ignored the tension in his gut, in his groin. Because what the hell was the point of focusing on that?

She looked at him through the windshield, and it seemed to him, took a little bit of extra time turning the engine off. Then she got out of the car, slowly.

Almost as if she was delaying the moment of their reunion. Almost as if she had picked up on what was bubbling between them when he had left her at the library. He should never have touched her.

Technically, he hadn't. Other than the accidental brush of their fingers. He had only made contact with the fabric when he'd pinned that sheriff's star to her chest.

But it had been a risky move, and he hadn't fully realized it until after he was committed to it. "Hey," he said, aware that his voice sounded a little bit gruff.

"Hi," she said.

She was so small. He had forgotten. In the hours since he had seen her yesterday, he had intentionally made his view of her a little bit blurry.

But there she was, wearing one of those prim little floral dresses that shouldn't do a damn thing to rouse his interest, but managed to.

Her figure was neat, petite. And the tiny little buttons on the dress fueled his imagination in a way they shouldn't.

Was this what a midlife crisis looked like when you had already made your rounds as a hellion? He didn't care for it.

Besides, he was too young for a midlife crisis. And speaking as a Wilder, for most of them it would've been an end-of-life crisis. But he had survived. He was here.

He did not need this.

"I brought . . . I brought my binder," she said, holding up a very large folder.

"Yes, you did," he said.

He knew he was being a dick, but he was having trouble rerouting himself. Because he was afraid that if he got closer to her, then he might do something they would both regret.

Lord Almighty.

"Great. We can talk about it . . . after we go see the wagon."

She trailed behind him as he took long strides, heading out toward the old barn that housed the covered wagon.

She was moving at a decent clip, but doing nothing to make him think of her as anything other than a mouse.

He flicked a glance at her. A cute mouse.

Dammit.

He muscled open the door, and her eyes widened.

"We don't go in here that often. Truth be told, the thing might've fallen into a state of disrepair. Hopefully not, but I'm not sure how seaworthy the roof is."

She laughed.

"What?" he asked.

"Seaworthy. That's funny. Because it's not a boat. It's a roof. But you mean . . . water. . . . Anyway."

"I do know what I meant," he said.

Their eyes caught and held for a long moment.

He cleared his throat. Then he turned around and walked into the barn.

It smelled clean and dry inside, which would suggest there was nothing much to worry about.

And there it stood, the big old wagon, including the large white covering that he and Carson had fashioned out of heavy canvas all those years ago.

Before Carson had been wounded so badly. Before he had fallen in love.

Before things had gotten so complicated.

It had been a strange moment in time.

Carson had been away in the military, which had been a little bit of a bummer, but he was determined to become a hero.

Flynn and Cassidy had been doing all right in school, and not giving him too much hell. His dad wasn't around to make things difficult. It had been a rare moment of quiet in his life.

It was when he had discovered the journal.

It was when he had started really digging into the past. And while he had felt his own mortality looming in front of him, he'd been sure he had a little bit of control.

He'd been an idiot.

But still, he remembered working on this wagon with Carson, and it was a strange, good memory among all the bad ones.

"Family heirloom."

"It's amazing," she said, circling the wagon. "And this is really the wagon the Wilders used on the Oregon Trail?"

"As far as I know. I can't think of another reason it would've been here. Unless Austin Wilder stole it. Which is possible. But he didn't really start taking things until after they arrived in the Willamette Valley."

"Really?"

"Yes. Their father died when they got to Fort Stevens. After that, they were pretty desperate. They made their way down south on their own for a piece. They started with stealing food. It wasn't until they met up with Butch Hancock that they aimed for bigger fish. Though to be fair, from Austin's own writing, he got a little bit of a kick out of robbery. Changing his own circumstances using his wits. Especially if he thought the people who had what he wanted possessed an excess of things. He was angry."

"Like you," she said.

He gritted his teeth. "Yeah. A little bit like me. Their mother died when they were small. They just had their dad. I think the family was pretty normal until the boys ended up left to their own devices."

"So Austin Wilder was the first outlaw."

"That he was."

Silence stretched between them. "Anyway, Cassidy said that she'd be happy to drive the wagon."

"Oh," she said. "That's . . . that's good."

"Yeah. I don't think you want me driving the wagon."

"I don't," she said. "Because I've been thinking. Actually, I was wondering if you would consider leading a walking tour."

"What?"

"You know the history of Rustler Mountain. I mean, in a really vivid way. Even if we don't figure out the exact truth of what happened . . . I think it would be impactful to have you give the tour."

"Why me?"

"You're Austin Wilder. You're named for him. Imagine the impact of having you standing there telling everybody the story. Imagine the kids . . . when they find out that you're the descendant of an outlaw."

"I'm not sure we want to be glorifying outlaws."

"I'm not sure that we want to be glorifying my ancestor either. But maybe there's a benefit to really personalizing the legend."

"We'll discuss it."

"Maybe we could both do it. We could wear costumes. I have the sheriff's star after all."

She looked up at him, and there was a sort of fierce light in her eye that made him pause. "You do."

She looked away again. And then she took a step toward him, and he could see the intent in her eyes. The near comedic determination. And what he really wanted to do was reach out and grab her. What he really wanted to do was finish it for her. Close the space between them. Taste her mouth.

Damn. What would it be like?

He couldn't remember ever wondering what it would be like to taste a specific woman.

To kiss a Talbot. To have her mouth under his.

But not just a Talbot. Millie. Whom he had known since she was a girl.

Who was the only person who really understood him in some ways.

That realization, the idea of what they might be opening up, almost sent him running in the other direction. For her own sake.

Because her mother had been the kindest person he'd ever known.

Had been the mother figure his own had never been. Hell, had been more to him than even his own father.

And if she were here, she would want Millie to be protected. He didn't give a shit about her dad. Yet he'd had that thought earlier. That it would be akin to dancing on his grave to touch the man's innocent daughter.

But he wouldn't take any joy in that transgression. Not any fucking joy at all, because of Millie's mother. Because of Millie herself. Because of the ways he already knew that she had been hurt.

Because she wanted to get married.

She wanted to have a house and a life. And yes, someday maybe he would have those things. But he was never going to fall in love. Not the way she would want to.

There were just certain bridges that couldn't be crossed, and this was one of them.

That was just the truth.

So he did the merciful thing. He wrapped his hand around her wrists and he pushed her back, just slightly.

"Don't do that," he said.

Her cheeks turned bright red. "What?"

"Don't look at me like that, little mouse. Because you're gonna get yourself in a whole lot of trouble if you do."

"I . . . I wasn't. . . ."

"You were. Don't think you can tame me. Don't think you can handle all this. You can't."

"You don't know me," she said, her voice quiet. "You don't know what I can handle."

"I've known you your whole life. I'm pretty sure I know what you can handle."

"That's bullshit." She bit her lip as soon as she uttered the expletive, as if it was a shock to her. Hell, it was a little bit of a shock to him. Though he was never going to let her know that. "You know some things about me, but you don't know me."

"I know you well enough," he said. "And believe me when I tell you, you don't need to be getting yourself mixed up in this. You don't need to be getting yourself mixed up in me."

"I just wanted. . . ."

He shook his head. "You don't know what you want."

"Stop. I am so desperately tired of people telling me who I am. I would've thought that you of all people could understand that."

"Let me guess, you've been with one man."

Her mouth dropped open. "I. . . ."

"And you're mad. Because that one man turned out to be an absolute dick. And I'm sorry about that. I'm sorry he did that to you, but you're not going to make yourself feel better by taking revenge on him and fucking me. Also, I'm not really here for that."

Her eyes went glassy, and she blinked. "I didn't say I wanted that. I didn't even do anything. You're making assumptions. Maybe you're the . . . maybe you're the dick. Did you ever think about that?"

"I am quite certain I'm a dick. Just a different brand than he is. A kind that you don't know how to handle." He gritted his teeth against the very regrettable choice of words. Against the hurt in her face, against the need tightening his gut.

God Almighty. He could go out and have sex whenever he felt like it. Finding a willing and enthusiastic partner was like breathing for him. Why was he letting himself get involved with Millie? Why wasn't he just shutting it down, cutting it off, and feeling nothing?

"I. . . ."

He heard the sound of horses' hooves, then boots hitting the dirt.

"Fuck. It's my sister."

He knew it was. Because only Cassidy had timing this awkward.

She came striding into the barn, hanging on to her horse's lead rope. "Oh hi," she said. "I didn't know you would be here, Millie."

"I came to look at the wagon."

"Austin said you'd like me to drive it. I'm a good wagon driver. What did you have in mind?"

"Well, what do you think?" Millie asked, her voice still trembling slightly. She looked at him, and her expression was . . . fierce. For the first time he wondered if he actually had underestimated her.

"I don't know. There are some wagon trails up here, but of course, I'm not sure that anybody wants to take the drive. We could drive through town, but then there would have to be a lot of blocked-off traffic, and since we already have the town council riled up, it might not be the best thing to go asking for blockades."

"Some blockades are going to be inevitable," Millie said. "In more ways than one, I imagine."

"Sure," Cassidy said. "I have a couple of different ideas. I can draw you some maps. You should stay for dinner. We're eating in just about twenty minutes or so."

"Oh," Millie said.

"The whole gang," Cassidy continued.

He shot his sister a hard look, but she didn't see it. Or if she did, she chose not to acknowledge it.

But Millie would say no. She would. Because what had just happened between them was too uncomfortable. She would scurry back to her little mouse hole.

It was as if she heard him think. Because her head swiveled around to look at him, and there was a challenge in her eyes.

"I would love to," Millie said. "In fact, I have my whole folder with me, all kinds of plans for the event. Really looking forward to it."

"Great. Why don't you come on into the house. We're just going to be getting things ready. My brother is bringing over burger patties. Well, it's venison. So you ought to be warned. It has a different flavor."

"Oh, my dad was a pretty avid deer hunter," Millie said. "I'm familiar."

"Great. So it's nothing you can't handle."

"No," she said, her eyes resting defiantly on Austin. "It's nothing I can't handle."

Chapter 11

The honorable thing to do would be to marry her. But in my case, it would be a damned dishonor to her. I should have told her to walk away.

—Austin Wilder's journal, January 5, 1856

Millie was. . . . She felt like a cat that had run into an electric fence. She was angry, she was embarrassed, and she was outright refusing to show her reaction.

Because he didn't get to win this particular battle.

And yes, it had been impetuous of her to think that maybe she ought to kiss him. It had been foolish. Ludicrous, even. But he hadn't had to humiliate her in that way.

She felt so . . . small. So rebuffed. He had patronized her in a way that was just unforgivable.

It made her want to punch him in the gut. Because how dare he say what she could handle. How dare he?

Millie Talbot had never been a rebel—with or without a cause. She had never been one to make waves. What she did was dig into her principles and entrench. When she made up her mind about something, she didn't change it. Her burden to bear was that she was a people pleaser. But she was absolutely incapable of violating her own code of conduct. When she had decided something, she didn't change course.

And that stubbornness flowed through her veins now. That absolute unwillingness to move.

That trait, she thought, she had gotten from her mother.

The woman who had seen a waif the rest of the town had rejected and decided to make space for him.

Yes, that woman.

Her conviction galvanized her now. Of course, she doubted that her mother would approve of this particular *conviction*, since it was all about digging in to antagonize Austin now that he had wounded her.

She hadn't been certain she had pride. But she'd discovered a rich vein of it.

The thing that irked her the most was that she had been. . . . She was going to kiss him.

She had *wanted* to.

She had thought that maybe *he* wanted to, also, but then he had moved her away from him.

And she had felt so stupid. Because never, not once in all her life had she thought that a man wanted to kiss her. Michael had taken her entirely by surprise the first time he'd done it. She hadn't expected it at all. She had thought maybe they were friends, because most men saw her that way, and then he had utterly floored her by taking her hand and kissing her sweetly outside her dad's house.

Her very first kiss at twenty-four years old.

But now, with Austin, she had thought. . . . She had been convinced that she wasn't making the attraction up. There was heat arcing between them. She had thought about it all night last night. The way he had looked at her. Then when she had seen him today, it had been even more pronounced. Even more intense.

It hadn't felt risky. But it turned out . . . it was.

She surprised herself by digging in. She supposed it shouldn't have surprised her. Because she was the same girl who had lectured all her friends on their silliness regarding Austin. She was the same girl who had refused to skinny-dip in the creek, even though everyone had tried to convince her it would be fun.

When she dug in, she dug in hard.

And here she was, digging in, even though it was making her uncomfortable.

She was following Cassidy up to the house.

That very clean house she knew no one in town would imagine Austin living in. But she knew he did. Just as she knew the extensive list of all the things he'd read.

If only that had been more valuable ammunition.

Because apparently she had read the entire situation wrong.

Or maybe she hadn't. He hadn't said that he didn't want to kiss her. He had just told her it was a bad idea. It made her so angry. Because other people got to execute their bad ideas. But she was eternally protected. Even from the baddest man in town.

How fair was that?

He should want to corrupt her just by virtue of the fact that he was a wicked outlaw. He should tie her to the railroad tracks. Or to his bed.

Just thinking that made her heart rate increase. She was ridiculous. Maybe he had a point. Maybe she wouldn't be able to handle this. Whatever it was.

Nothing. Apparently, it was nothing.

She walked right into that well-ordered house, though, and then turned and said brightly to Cassidy, "What can I do to help?"

"Oh, you don't need to do anything," said Cassidy. "You want to be here?"

She wrinkled her nose. "Sure."

She hadn't planned to accept the dinner invitation, but she had found herself saying yes, simply because she wanted to surprise him. Maybe because she wanted to surprise everybody. Maybe she wanted to prove that nobody actually knew her. That they definitely couldn't tell her what to do.

An ice-cold bottle of beer was placed in her hand, and she nodded in affirmation. "Thank you, Cassidy."

"No problem." She grinned.

Cassidy was five years younger than Millie. At least she was reasonably sure that was the age difference between them.

She didn't know Cassidy personally at all. Austin's sister had been too far behind her in school. And she had been the subject of a lot of gossip, which had made Millie feel bad for her, but as a result she had kind of avoided her. Not because she felt averse to the scandal, but because she didn't want to make Cassidy feel uncomfortable. When she had been dropped off at Austin's house, the rumors about the abandoned Wilder child had been sensational.

Looking at Cassidy now, you would never think that she had practically been a foundling. She was confident, pretty, in an entirely unadorned way. Her clothing was simple, her hair loose and long. Halfway between curls and waves. Not styled in any particular way, beyond whatever the wind had done.

Her eyes were the same color blue as Austin's. It had to be said, all the Wilders were beautiful.

Austin was striding impatiently between the living room and the kitchen, seemingly doing nothing, but Millie would rather cut her own arm off than comment on him at this point.

And thankfully, she was saved when an entire cavalry arrived.

The door to the house burst open, and there was an immediate flood of loud conversation, laughter, and footsteps.

"And he was running like his boots were blazing and his ass was catching fire." A round of laughter followed. She wasn't sure who had delivered the punchline, until the troop rounded the corner.

Dalton Wade was the one talking, holding a large platter that was covered in tinfoil. She noticed how Cassidy's head whipped around, then immediately back. As though she was avoiding looking at Dalton for too terribly long.

Millie felt a slight twinge of sympathy.

One she didn't want to examine.

"I guess that's the last time he'll start a bar fight he can't finish." Millie was somewhat surprised to see that comment came from Perry Bramble. Her eyes met Perry's, and the other woman smiled. "Hi, Millie. What an unexpected and delightful surprise."

She was pretty sure Perry was being nice. She didn't know Perry that well. She had been ahead of Millie in school, and while Millie wasn't shy, she couldn't claim to be adept socially. Perry had actually been shy, something she didn't seem to be afflicted with anymore, given that she ran a shop on Main Street.

"Thank you," Millie said. "You too."

It was easy to just let the conversation wash around her. She noticed that Austin wasn't participating. He was . . . pouting. And if she said that to him she had a feeling he would absolutely pitch a fit.

"So what are the plans for Gold Rush Days?" Perry asked as she began to uncover different bowls and place them at the center of the table.

"Oh, we're still formulating them."

"I'm going to drive the wagon," Cassidy said, grinning.

"Off a cliff?" That question came from Dalton.

"Shut up, Dalton," Cassidy said. "I could drive a wagon in circles around you."

"I wouldn't want you to, though, because you'd be likely to run over my foot."

"On purpose," Cassidy said, smiling.

But the smile was sharp.

"I'm going to turn the hose on you two," Carson said.

"He's probably serious," Perry remarked.

"I have no doubt he is," Dalton said. "And it would be worth it. To take this one down a peg or two." He leaned over and messed up Cassidy's hair, and the condescending gesture made Millie die inside for Cassidy.

She wasn't an expert on the interplay between men and women, but she didn't think she had to be to identify what was happening here.

"I need a beer," said Flynn, jerking the fridge open. There was a round of requests, and he passed the bottles out.

And then it was time to serve up the venison burgers. It surprised Millie that there were so many chairs around the family table. It was crowded, in a way she had never quite expected the Wilder house to be.

How interesting that this family that was supposed to be comprised of misfits and outlaws gathered in a closer group than she ever had.

She thought of her own family table. Often stark and a little too quiet. Her mother, her father, and her. Back when she was little, her grandparents had joined them occasionally as well.

There had been love there. But it hadn't been like this.

This was noisy. And sometimes even raucous, when Cassidy flicked a pat of butter at Dalton, who responded in kind. And they cleaned up the mess without anyone getting angry.

She supposed they weren't children, so no one was going to scold them.

But at her house, behavior like that would've created a riot.

There was so much ease among all of them.

Carson was quieter than the rest, but that didn't really surprise her. She noticed the way Perry looked at him, as if she was always checking in with him. There was no doubt that they were connected. But she couldn't quite read the dynamic between them.

She wasn't even going to try. She had no idea what her dynamic was with anyone here, least of all the person she knew best, who was Austin. Right now she was . . . playing chicken with him? She wasn't sure if that was what you would call it. But she was absolutely certain it wasn't smart.

"The burgers are delicious," she said.

"Thanks," said Carson.

"And everything else too. Thank you so much for inviting me," she said, directing her words to Cassidy.

"I wasn't born in a barn," she said. "Just raised in one."

"*Next* to one," Austin said.

It was the first thing he had said the entire dinner. She wondered if it was normal for him to be moody and quiet. Because nobody seemed to notice. They were all busy entertaining themselves.

"I brought a cake," said Perry.

"Wow," Dalton said, looking at Perry. "You really know how to spoil a man."

And that earned sideways glances from both Cassidy and Carson. She filed away her observations in the memory bank where she was storing information about this family.

Perry returned a moment later with an absolutely beautiful cake, topped by fresh flowers set into buttercream frosting.

"I have to do something with the leftover flowers," she said.

"Well, you did something pretty damn spectacular," Carson said, shooting a look at Dalton.

Perry blushed prettily and cut the cake.

A plate was put into Millie's hands, and she was suddenly hit with a strange wave of emotion. It had been a really long time since she had sat around the dinner table with a family.

She had been so busy comparing and contrasting the Wilders to her own family, she hadn't really paused to think about how they were alike. How it felt. To be part of something like this again.

More often than not, she had dinner by herself. Most especially in the last couple of months. Michael had worked late a lot, which made perfect sense to her now, but hadn't at the time, and so they had only had dinner together a few nights a week. Even though they lived together. Even though they were supposed to be getting married.

She had eaten dinner with her dad almost every night until he died.

But she had slid into a void in which she'd ended up eating alone most of the time.

Tonight was so different.

"Thank you for having me," she said as she finished her last bite of cake. "I really mean it."

Her eyes met Austin's, and she looked away quickly.

"I have to go," she said. "I still have some things I need to finish putting together tonight. But I really do appreciate the invite. Really."

She was given an enthusiastic send-off, then was surprised when she heard footsteps behind her as she moved into the living room.

She turned and saw Austin.

"I'll walk you to the car."

"There's no need to do that," she said.

"I didn't ask you if you'd like me to walk you to the car, Millie. I said that I would."

"All right," she said.

"There might be a cougar out there. God knows."

She didn't turn around—she just opened up the door and walked outside. She continued down the steps, and then stopped.

"I'm fine," she said.

"I wanted to have a chance to talk to you," he said.

"Maybe I'm done talking to you."

"I want to explain," he said.

"You want to explain all the incredibly condescending things you said to me earlier?"

"Yeah. I do."

"Listen, if you don't want to kiss me . . . that's absolutely fine. Many, many men don't want to kiss me. *Most* men don't want to kiss me. Heck, Austin, the man I was supposed to marry didn't even want to kiss me that much it turned out, so that's not really what I'm mad about. The problem is that you're not treating me with respect."

"The hell I'm not," he said. "Not kissing you is a big fucking sign of respect, actually."

"It's not. You're protecting me. Because you think I'm not as strong as you are. I'm not as strong as other women."

"What makes you say that?"

"Because I don't think you're a monk," she said. "Have you taken a vow of celibacy?"

"You know good and well I haven't."

"So some women are fine for you to touch. And you're not worried about protecting them from you. But not me. Not me. *I'm* not okay for you to touch. It has to be something about me. And like I said, if it's just that you don't want me, then just say that. But don't you dare make it about—"

"It's not that I don't want you," he said, his voice rough. "But the reasons I want you are not good."

She didn't know what to say to that. It froze her completely, rooted her feet to the spot. She thought she might be getting pulled down into the earth.

"You want me?"

"Do you have any idea how many dirty fantasies I had about you when you looked up at me like that? Do you have any idea how easy it is for me to imagine it? But it would be a fine fucking mess, Millie Talbot. Because I don't have anything to offer you. Not the kind of thing you want."

"There you go again, assuming what I want. I just broke up with my fiancé, Austin. I don't want marriage again. I can't even imagine it. I hate that. Because I am thirty years old. And I wasted way too many years on a man who wasn't worth all that time. Someday, I need to find somebody else. I can't wait too terribly long, because biological clocks are a thing. Not for you. Because you're a man. Life isn't fair. I have to . . . move on at some point. But I'm not there right now. Right now, I am standing here grappling with the truth that my family might not be who I thought they were. I am dealing with the fact that the superiority complex that was injected into me at birth, that often just made me feel inferior, is . . . likely a lie. But everything is. Everything. And I don't want to be the person everyone thinks I am. Not anymore. Because what has it gotten me? Nothing. What am I protected from? Honestly, do you think the most dangerous thing in the world for me would be getting naked with you? My mother is dead. My father is dead. Someone that I trusted betrayed me. What I believed about my ancestry isn't even true. I know that you've been through a lot. But is that not a lot?"

She was breathing hard, and she felt ridiculous. She felt she might be on the verge of begging, which was just sad. Because she didn't want to be begging him for a kiss. And she definitely didn't want him to kiss her because he felt sorry for her. But honestly. He was acting as if she was a nun. As if she was sheltered. A hothouse flower to be protected. But that was just because he thought being revered as a Talbot meant she was sheltered from things.

But she had lost so much.

How was that being sheltered? She was just starting to be angry about everything she'd lost.

Finally.

Finally she was starting to get angry.

"All right," he said. "I can take some of that in. But you're right that I haven't taken a vow of celibacy. I have also never in my fucking life spent more than one night with a single woman. I don't do relationships. You have an ex, you've been betrayed. At least you've been with somebody. Really been with them. I've never even almost thought I was in love. At thirty-five years old. How about that? That should scare you. That is the biggest red flag. I've never been in a relationship. I've never even tried to be. I certainly wouldn't try with you. Because you might be grappling with what your family is, but I already know. And it would be a betrayal of my blood. . . ."

"But you invited me to dinner."

"My sister did."

His clarification stung.

"You didn't kick me out."

"I should have," he said, getting closer to her. Close enough that she could smell him again. Close enough that her heart started to beat faster. Close enough that it reminded her of being in the library yesterday. When he had pinned the badge onto her. "We have to work together. We have to live in this town together. And I don't want . . . I do not want to get involved. I don't even know how to get involved. Someday . . . someday maybe I will. But not with you. Not ever with you, do you understand me?"

She nodded. "I don't want to get involved with you like that either." The words left her in a rush. She was angry. She didn't mind that she was angry. It felt good.

There was something satisfying about it.

"Good," he said. "So we're in agreement on that."

He stared her down, and she looked back at him.

A showdown, right there in his driveway.

Her finger on a trigger she wasn't sure she had the guts to squeeze.

Maybe she was pushing him too far. Maybe she was miscalculating. She wanted to know what it would be like to kiss him because it would be something singular, different. Living out the bad-boy fantasy she'd never had. The one that was suddenly alive inside her, like a beast, something feral and wild that she didn't even recognize.

Yes. She wanted to kiss him.

But what kind of fantasy could she possibly arouse in him?

The timid little mousy librarian was hardly a fantasy.

And he had just admitted to her that all he'd ever had was a series of one-night stands.

Sex must be so boring to him.

So mundane.

And she wasn't even asking for sex.

She just wanted to kiss. She just wanted a window into something she hadn't been able to imagine when she was young. Something she hadn't ever allowed herself to want.

She wanted to shed her skin. She wanted to break out of a cocoon. She wanted . . . a better metaphor for whatever this was. For this feeling that what was growing inside her was too big to be contained in her body anymore.

This metamorphosis that she had been forced into.

Because she hadn't chosen to lose her mother. She hadn't chosen to lose her father.

She hadn't chosen to end up single and sad at thirty with a fiancé who had cheated on her. An infidelity that everyone in town knew about. That everyone whispered about. She hadn't chosen those things.

She never would have.

But they had happened to her. They were forcing this change. And she was so desperate to get something out of it. Something that felt good.

Life was forcing her into a different shape than what she had chosen, so why couldn't she be different? Just for a little bit.

She felt suffocated. By this prim dress, by her position as the librarian, by her last name.

By everything.

She took a step toward him, her breathing coming hard and fast. "I still want to kiss you, though. Just to see. Don't you want to know?"

"Oh, honey. You're going to wish you hadn't said that."

He grabbed her arm; he pulled her to him. He didn't look at her with tenderness. He didn't look at her at all. It wasn't slow. It wasn't a request.

It was an instant, immediate demand. When his mouth met hers, it was like a lit match had been struck between them, and they were both dry tinder.

He consumed her.

She had never been kissed like this. She had never known kisses like this existed outside of those books. The ones that she had flipped through sometimes before she shelved them. The ones she had just told Alice Adams were unrealistic.

This was one of those kisses. Deep and hard and bruising. Punishing the parts of herself that needed punishment. That had been demanding it, crying out for it. Because she needed instruction on how to change. Because she needed to learn how to be different.

He kissed her.

His mouth was a revelation.

A force.

And when his tongue swept across hers, she thought she was dying. The way her knees had gone weak yesterday had only been a taste of what was to come.

Had he not wrapped his arm around her waist as if he was anticipating how weak she would go with that slick glide of his tongue, she would've fallen to the gravel.

Austin Wilder was kissing her.

She couldn't think. She couldn't do anything but hang on to him.

"Kiss me back," he said against her lips. "You silly little mouse."

That was it. It galvanized her. She parted her lips, thrust her tongue against his, kissed him within inexpert rhythm, because even though she had been kissed, many times, it had never been this.

If this was a war, then she was going to fight it.

If it was a shootout, then she was going to take aim.

And maybe it would be wild and inexpert, but she would give everything she had.

Suddenly he released her, the rejection as brutal as the first, leaving her breathing hard, cold without his touch, and buzzing with sensation that she had never felt before. Her skin was alive.

She wanted . . . more. Everything. She had never felt like this before.

Hollow and aching and desperate for another person's touch.

Her mouth felt swollen, hot.

She had thought she knew all about kissing.

She had thought the women who wrote romance novels were making things up. That they were somehow ignorant of the topics they wrote about.

Exaggerating them. Or just plain wrong.

She was the one who was wrong.

Michael wasn't a romance hero.

That conviction echoed inside her. She looked up at Austin, full of questions.

"There," he said. "You got your kiss." His voice was like gravel.

"And that's it?"

"It has to be."

"But. . . ."

"No buts, Millie Mouse. It's a bad idea. We have to deal with each other. You know that."

"I didn't say that I wanted. . . ."

"But you would. Eventually. Because you're a nice girl. And that is what nice girls want. Even if they tell themselves it's not. They don't want a one-night stand, they want romance, and I can never give you that. I don't want to."

It wasn't the last shot that got her. It was the way he called her a nice girl. The way that even though she had asked him to stop, he continued to tell her who she was. She'd had quite enough of that. She wasn't going to be taking it from him too.

"Well," she said. "Thanks for the kiss." And she had no idea what possessed her. Except that she was furious. Except that she didn't want him to win. "If I have trouble sleeping tonight and I need to use my vibrator, I know exactly who I'll be thinking of. Just the lips, though. Not the personality."

On shaking legs, she got into her car, started the engine, and drove away. She refused to look at him in her rearview mirror.

Chapter 12

We couldn't get married in a church. It didn't feel right for me to step inside. She told me God was out there in the sunshine and mountains anyway. But that's how she is. She's good for me. I wish I was as good for her.

—Austin Wilder's journal, May 21, 1856

Austin stood there for two full minutes after her car was out of view. Her words were ringing in his head. Echoing in his blood. He couldn't remember the last time a woman had gotten the better of him like that. Hell, he couldn't remember the last time he had stood there and. . . .

Was this *pining*?

This wrenching, aching, horrible . . . *need*?

He had imagined that pining would be a little bit more emotional. What was happening right now was definitely sexual.

He remembered very clearly the first time he had ever read the original Austin Wilder's journal. He could remember the outlaw's description of seeing Katherine for the first time, wearing her prairie dress and standing outside the schoolhouse. He had just assumed that sexual attraction was different back then.

Because how the hell could you get excited about seeing a woman whose ankles you couldn't even catch a glimpse of?

He understood it now.

How a woman who was such a . . . study in contradiction could tie you up in knots.

He was standing in his driveway, boots in the gravel, fighting a raging hard-on. At thirty-five years old. He took a sharp breath, hoping the night air would cleanse his lungs, his soul, his dirty fucking mind.

As soon as he was calm enough, he turned around to walk back inside the house, because maybe he would find some sanity there.

Maybe.

He opened up the front door and cursed. Because he was face-to-face with his little sister. Who was looking up at him as if he had grown another head.

"Can I help you?" he growled.

"What are you *doing*?" she asked.

"Cassidy. . . ."

"I was watching you out the window."

"You nosy little varmint."

"I was curious. Because you walked her outside, like you're a gentleman or something. But you are not a gentleman, Austin Wilder. I saw *that*."

"You listen here, you little termagant, I will wear you to a frazzle if you don't watch yourself. This is none of your business."

"The hell it's not," Cassidy said, crossing her arms. "Millie Talbot seems like a nice girl."

"A nice girl," he said. "Do you hear yourself?" He realized it was a bit rich to get mad at Cassidy for referring to Millie in that way when he had just used the exact same words to shut down what had happened between them, but it was unflattering and insulting to have them lobbed back at him.

"I'm not as sheltered as she is," Cassidy said. "She's *sweet*. At least every interaction I've had with her has led me to believe she is. And you and I both know that we are not sweet."

"When I get in the mood to take dating advice from a twenty-five-year-old virgin, I'll let you know. Until then, why don't you keep your opinions to yourself."

He started to move past Cassidy, but she was gasping like a flopping fish on a dock. "You don't know that I'm a virgin," she said.

He paused and looked at her. She was right, he didn't know that for sure. It wasn't his business—Cassidy could do whatever she wanted. But the simple truth was the antics of their parents had messed them all up in a variety of delightful and interesting ways.

And to his knowledge, Cassidy had never had a connection to a man, so he'd made assumptions.

The idea that his assumptions could be wrong disturbed him in a way he didn't want to examine.

"You *don't* know," she said, crossing her arms and leaning forward. "I have my own life."

"Do you?"

"Yes. And anyway, this isn't about my life. It's about *yours*. And Millie's. Everybody knows that her fiancé just stood her up. . . ."

"I turned her down," he said.

Cassidy blanched. "You did?"

"What did you think I was doing? Standing out there playing the Big Bad Wolf, sharpening my teeth on unsuspecting Little Red Riding Hood? No. I told Little Red to run away. Why? Because I'm actually not the giant villain even you seem to think I am."

Thankfully, there was still raucous conversation going on in the other room so they hadn't been overheard.

He could only be thankful that his entire family hadn't shown up to watch him kiss Millie.

That would be a nightmare.

"Don't say anything to anybody," he said.

"I . . . I won't." She looked offended.

"I'm serious. I told her no. You're right, she did just get dumped, and she's upset." The words did a little something to calm the roaring in his blood. But just a little.

Millie wasn't herself. She was acting out of character, and there was something about that which didn't sit well with him. It probably did have to do with the outlaw in his blood, if he were honest.

"She is a nice girl," he said. "And I don't want to do anything to hurt her. So I told her to run the other way. She was mad at me."

"Well, I can see why," Cassidy said. "It's very condescending."

"Are you kidding me? You just lectured me about. . . . You just called her a *girl*."

"I'm just saying, if that was what a man said to me after I kissed him, I would be furious."

"She was furious," he said. "But it was for her own good."

"I'm sure it was," she said, sounding placating.

"You're infuriating, do you know that? I've got nothing to say to you on the subject. Keep it to yourself. Don't tell anybody what happened. She doesn't deserve to be embarrassed."

"You're the one who embarrassed her."

"What do you want from me, Cassidy?"

She stared up at him. "I don't know. I would like to go back in time and not see my older brother making out with a woman. But really. . . . Oh . . . Austin, you like her, don't you?"

"What the fuck kind of question is that? I'm not in high school."

"I mean it, though. Do you like her? Because if you do, then. . . . Actually, maybe you *should* do something about it, Austin."

"No," he said. "I don't *like* her," he said, something in his gut pushing back against that statement.

"It's just that I've never seen you actually kiss somebody. Or associate with a woman outside a . . . bar or a seedy online chat room, or whatever it is you do."

"Chat room? What the hell? How old do you think I am?"

She lifted her hands up. "I don't know how you relieve those needs. And I don't want to."

"I would like to never speak to you about this again."

He started to walk away.

"Austin," she said. "I . . . I'm sorry. I didn't realize you actually cared about her."

"I don't."

She ignored him again. "I really didn't mean to be mean. And I didn't mean—"

"Cassidy, there's no need to apologize, and there's nothing to figure out here. It's not anything." He really wasn't trying to be condescending to his sister, but he couldn't help it. "You might understand if you had some experience with this kind of thing. It's complicated, sometimes. And usually in those situations, it's definitely not worth it."

She looked scalded, but she let him go this time, and he went into his study and closed the door behind him. He rolled the chair over to the corner of his desk and picked up the journal.

He thumbed through it, until he got to the part where Austin was writing about marrying Katherine.

It wasn't a joyful moment for him. Not even close.

> *The honorable thing to do would be to marry her. But in my case, it would be a damned dishonor to her. I should have told her to walk away.*
>
> *I should never have touched her. But I did. I let my body get away from me, and my heart. Honestly, if it were only lust, that would be easier. I know how to say no, and I know how to say yes. I've never been attached before. Katherine is a good woman. An honest one. And she deserves the kind of man who can make an honest woman of her. I can't. Not even through marriage. An outlaw is never going to be able to give her what she wants. I'm never going to be able to give her a home, a life, a family. I want to. I've never been angry about life, or the choices I've made. I jumped into this life rather than suffer. Rather than having nothing, I decided to take matters into my own hands, and when I took the reins, I let go of everything else. Of the right to be in love.*
>
> *But now I've put my hands on her. She could be carrying a baby. Now I've well and truly ruined everything.*

He remembered reading all this when he was younger and realizing how little people had changed. He felt that truth even more profoundly now.

But he was going to learn something from the mistakes of the past. If you didn't learn from history, you were doomed to repeat it.

And so, he was determined not to get himself or Millie into an unwinnable situation.

He shoved the journal back and pushed his hands through his hair.

Here he was. Thirty-five years old, older than the Wilders who had come before him.

Losing his shit over a woman.

With age had not come wisdom. Or maybe it had.

He'd had the good sense to say no. Maybe he should just be grateful that he was a little better than the man whose name he carried.

Chapter 13

I thought I'd given up the right to joy, but it found me anyway.

—Austin Wilder's journal, May 30, 1856

Millie was *not well*. She went home and poured a glass of whiskey. She didn't drink whiskey. The bottle had been her father's.

But she could drink it now if she wanted to, and no one would blame her.

She stared at the amber liquid in the tumbler and wondered what had possessed her. She wondered a whole lot of things.

She clutched the cup and started to wander around the house, feeling restless and not at all interested in the whiskey. And then she decided to call Heather.

"Heather," she said. "This is your fault."

"What's my fault?"

"Sorry," she said. "Can you talk?"

"Kids are in bed, husband is playing video games. Yes."

She took a deep breath. "Austin kissed me."

"*No*," Heather said. "*No*. I mean, *yes*. Was it good? Is he hot? Is he a good kisser?"

"Yes, you already know he's hot, and yes. It was the best kiss I've ever had in my life." She didn't even have to pause to consider. It was just the truth. Unvarnished and real. "Until he pushed me away and told me that nothing was going to happen between us, and then I told him that I was going to go home and think about him while I used my vibrator. And *that* is your fault."

There was a stunned silence on the other end of the phone. It echoed inside Millie. Honestly, Heather probably thought she was lying, and she couldn't blame Heather for that.

Millie never lied. Ever.

She could hardly believe what she was saying now, and she'd been there. The words had come out of her own mouth. But what she'd said couldn't possibly be true. Because she was Millie Mouse.

The one who was so easily ignored. And yet, she'd always had this stubborn streak. An outright refusal to back down when she thought someone else was wrong. That was the problem, she realized. Austin was being dishonest with himself and with her. That was what had aroused the implacable part of her that simply couldn't accept lies.

"You . . . you *really* said that to him?" Heather finally asked. "And how is that my fault?"

"Because!" Millie looked at the whiskey and seriously considered a sip. "You're the one who gave me a vibrator as a joke gift."

There was another extended silence. "Oh. Millie, that was not a joke gift."

"It wasn't?"

"It cost almost two hundred dollars!"

"I . . . I didn't know they were that expensive."

"I don't go cheap on things that go *in* my body." Heather sighed. "I was being serious when I gave it to you. Based on conversations we'd had, I thought you probably really needed a vibrator."

"I had a boyfriend."

"Yeah. You did. Michael."

Millie stood, staring at the wall.

Had *everybody* else seen the truth that she hadn't?

She decided to put a pin in that and worry about it later.

"Well, if you hadn't given me the vibrator, I wouldn't have told him that I was going to use it and think about him. It never would have even occurred to me. I probably wouldn't have known what one looked like."

"I can't believe you *said that to him*. Did you rehearse it in your head first? I would have needed dress rehearsals to get that out of my mouth."

"No. I didn't think about it all. It wasn't premeditated. It was just . . . reckless. I don't even know who I am. *I* kissed *him*. I *kissed* him. I *kissed him*." She tried a different emphasis on every single word in that sentence to see if it changed the way she felt about it. To see if it helped anything make sense.

It did not.

Nothing made sense. She had been transformed into another creature.

An outlaw, maybe.

Wild West Mouse.

Right. All it took was finding out that her ancestor might actually have been a crooked lawman, and suddenly she was a vixen.

Well. She was not a vixen, because the man had turned her down, which meant that she wasn't irresistible and thus not really a vixen.

"I just wanted him to . . . I wanted him to suffer. Because he embarrassed me. And . . . I think he does want me."

"I'm sure he does. I cannot believe for one second that he doesn't, especially considering that he showed up to the town meeting and took your side like that. He had to have been interested in you. Men rarely show up for anything like that if they don't think sex is going to be involved."

"Is that true? Because we have other things in common. Historical things."

Still clutching the whiskey, she reached up and pulled the rope that hung from the ceiling in the hallway to tug down the attic opening. Then she reached up and grabbed the ladder, pulling it down. It made a large thunk.

"Are you okay?"

"Yes," she said as the whiskey sloshed over her hand. She didn't need to drink any of it. She was already acting drunk. She still felt completely bowled over by the kiss. Completely undone.

"Going in the attic to look at . . . things. To try to . . . make sense of myself and my life."

She climbed up the ladder, keeping the phone pressed to her ear, but discarded the whiskey on one of the steps.

Then she crawled into the attic, searching for the light.

"Millie, what are you doing?"

"I climbed into my attic."

"Go use your vibrator and stop climbing things."

It was a valid comment. "No," she said. "Because I can't . . . I will not fantasize about him, not after he did that."

"You can do a lot of things that aren't fantasizing about him but are also not scrabbling around an attic at nine p.m."

The single bulb barely illuminated the space. It was cramped, with a low ceiling, and stacks of boxes everywhere.

There were probably mice in here. Her kinfolk.

She curled her lip and made a face as she pushed around the boxes.

"I don't know what I'm thinking," she said. "I am trying to plan Gold Rush Days, I'm trying to open a museum. I got the funding for it, I have everything I want. And I decided to involve myself in kissing Austin Wilder? I have no idea what I was thinking. I have no idea . . . why am I doing so much? Why am I changing everything?"

"Because you aren't happy."

Heather's pragmatic, completely flat delivery set Millie back on her haunches. "I'm not?"

"No, Millie. You're not happy. Your wedding got called off. Your dad is dead. You're by yourself. Your life has changed in a thousand different ways that you didn't choose. Of course you want to do something that you're in control of. You've never rebelled in your life. It was bound to happen someday. And your rebellion is manifesting itself in this very *literal* way. He is like . . . the last man on earth you should touch. Your dad would've disapproved."

Millie huffed. "I know. He wouldn't have approved. And I wouldn't want my dad to disapprove of me. . . ."

"Or maybe you would. Maybe it makes you feel good. To push

back. To be different. To be doing something without permission. Something that you know is a little bit wrong."

"I never have."

"I know that. You have done nothing but the right thing, what you thought was the right thing, all your life, and where has it gotten you?"

Currently curled up in an attic feeling utterly humiliated.

"Nowhere," she said. "There's been no reward. Not a gold star. . . ." She pictured him pinning the sheriff's star to her chest again.

"Of course you're pushing back. And he . . . I'm sorry. I'm sorry he rejected you. That really sucks. I thought he liked you."

"I thought he did too," she said. She curled her knees up to her chest, and rested her cheek on her hand, and was a little bit devastated when a tear splashed down onto her knuckle. She didn't want to be that sad. "I don't know why I thought so. No guy ever paid any attention to me until Michael, and I couldn't hang on to him."

"He let go of you," Heather said. "Don't go blaming yourself for his nonsense."

"Thank you," Millie said. "I just feel ridiculous. And it felt so good to shock Austin. But almost immediately I just felt sick. I feel sick. It's like I took all my clothes off for him and showed him everything, and he's given me nothing. Absolutely nothing. I risked everything. I risked my pride . . . which I didn't even know I had until recently, and he walked all over it. And kissing me doesn't mean anything to him. He's kissed a thousand women."

"Did you ask him for a count?"

"No," she said. "I did not. But I just know he has. And he's only the second man that I've ever kissed. And it was . . . it was like a whole different thing."

"Do you want me to come over?"

She looked around the attic. "No. I'm too embarrassed. I can't face you."

"Okay. How about you face me tomorrow morning. I'll bring you a chai."

"Thank you."

"Just try to get some sleep. You didn't do anything wrong. This kind of thing happens. When you go out and you try to date. . . ."

"I'm not trying to date him. I just wanted to do something wild. And actually, I just wanted to kiss him. And I am so out of my depth here. I don't know what you do when you just want to touch a man—you don't want to date him."

"Ideally," Heather said, "you touch him. But tonight that didn't go your way."

"No," she said. "It didn't."

"Do I need to come over?" she repeated.

"No," she said. "I need to get out of my attic and get in the shower."

"That's a good idea. Everything makes more sense after a good shower rant. Yell at him beneath the warm spray. And text me when you're done. Let me know you're okay."

"I will."

She hung up the phone and looked around the attic. She didn't even know what she was looking for up here. She didn't know what she was looking for in general.

She moved the boxes around. Opened one up that had her grandmother's china in it. Maybe she would bring it down to the kitchen. Maybe she would use it every day, just because she could. Michael hadn't liked it, so it had been put away. But she liked it. So she was going to get it out. She would use it when she had a girl dinner, just collections of little bits and pieces of things. Cheese and pickles, and whatever else she wanted.

Because she didn't have to have a meat and a main to feed a man who was particular about what he wanted set on the table in front of him. As her dad had been, as Michael had been. There was more than one way to feel liberated, she supposed.

She moved the box out of the way and found a small one, wedged between two larger ones. An old shoebox, with a rubber band around it.

She slipped the rubber band off and opened the box up. Inside was a stack of papers. They looked like letters. And a slim book.

Her heart started to pound. She had never seen these.

She turned one of the letters over, and on the other side was spindly, neat writing.

The return address read: *Mister Butch Hancock.*

And it was addressed to Sheriff Lee Talbot.

Chapter 14

I haven't quite gotten the right of being a husband, and now I'm
going to be a father. I don't want my children knowing who I am,
or what I do. But if I don't continue to do it, I can't build a life
for them.

—Austin Wilder's journal, August 26, 1856

He was avoiding going to bed, because he wasn't in the mood to
deal with the fantasies that would surely dog him once he tried to lay
his head down. His phone rang.

He saw Millie's name flash across the screen and he froze.

"Dammit," he said, picking it up as quickly as possible. "Hello?"

"Austin," she said. "I need you."

Right then, he prayed to every saint, every sinner, and every
deity that he could think of. Because he was going to need some for-
giveness. He wasn't strong enough to say no. Not again. He couldn't
explain this. The connection he felt to her. The way he felt compelled to touch her.

He had tried. But if she was going to say she needed him. . . .

"I found a box."

"What?"

He wasn't tracking with her.

"I found a box of letters. Letters and a journal, and other things.
And I think you were right. Lee Talbot colluded with Butch Hancock."

The thrill that shot down his spine wasn't sexual, but he was still
feeling aroused, and everything inside him felt like a hot mess, so he
wasn't sure exactly what he was feeling.

"Are you serious?"

"I went up to the attic tonight . . . don't ask. I went up to the attic, and I was looking through some things, and I found a tiny shoebox that I hadn't seen before. It was wedged between my grandmother's plates and some old farm implements. Anyway. I've only looked at a couple of things, but you need to see this. And we can't do it in public."

"If this is a booty call, I need you to know, it's kind of a weird one."

Because he had to ask. Because he had to know.

"I promise you it's not," she said.

But there was tension in her voice, and that tension wound itself around him like a bronze thread. Pulling tight.

A lasso that secured him. Good and hard.

"I'll be there in a minute. I assume you want me to come to your place?"

"Yes. Do you know where it is?"

"You live in your dad's old place, right?"

There was a pause. "Yes."

"Then yeah, I know where it is."

He hung up the phone and stood. For a long moment. He grabbed his wallet off his nightstand, and then he stared at the furniture for just a moment. At the drawer.

Did it make him an outlaw or a hero if he grabbed a condom? He had told her no. And there were so many compelling reasons why it had to be no. But he was already opening the drawer.

Because his dad had not taught him a whole hell of a lot, but what he had taught him was not to be a fool.

You can't count on your best intentions seeing you through tough times, boy.

That had basically been his sex talk.

Be prepared. Always. Because your brain cells went out the motherfucking window when your dick was hard.

He was thirty-five years old. He was better than that.

He stuffed a condom in his wallet anyway. Then a second one.

It was practically chivalry.

He shoved the wallet in his back pocket, then grabbed his keys and headed toward the front door. Thank God he didn't have any siblings living in this house anymore. He didn't have the patience to be dealing with them right now.

His mind was a blank as he drove down the gravel drive, his headlights catching jackrabbits bounding into the ruts in front of him, then back out again.

Mangy little beasts.

He had to slam his brakes on to avoid a buck that leaped down off the side of a hill right in front of him and froze in his headlights.

"Out of the way," he grumbled, as the animal took its sweet time crossing the road. "I'll just run you over next time."

He was impatient. To hear about the history revelations. He didn't think about the condoms in his wallet.

When he pulled up to the old Victorian-style house, the thrill of the forbidden that rocked through him was unwelcome.

That wasn't why he was here. Provisional prophylactics notwithstanding.

He killed the engine and got out of the truck, very aware it loomed large in her driveway, extremely noticeable to any neighbors who might be setting their curtains twitching.

Then he walked up to the front door. He was about to knock when it opened.

And there she was, wearing the same prim little dress as when she had left his house a couple of hours earlier.

"Come in," she said, ushering him in quickly.

"I hate to break it to you," he said. "My truck is in your driveway, standing out like a sore thumb."

"Not everybody knows it's your truck."

"Oh, at this point, everybody knows."

"What do you mean by that?"

"We've caused a stir. I assume you know that."

"Unfortunately."

Her house was homey and warm. Nice. The furniture was old, and it was . . . just very her. Lace curtains, an oval rug on the floor. It might have been a portal to another time.

It wasn't as ruthlessly neat as his place. Probably because she didn't have the control issues he did. It was normal.

"I'm here for the letters," he said, ignoring the way his wallet seemed to be burning through his pocket.

"I thought we might as well go over all of it together. I haven't . . . looked at everything."

"So it could be a big nothing burger."

"Yeah. It could be. But I don't think it is. This was the first thing I found."

She took a letter out and handed it to him.

"Right." There it was. Plain as day. A letter from Butch Hancock to Lee Talbot. He opened it up.

> *Sheriff, I am prepared to give you the names and locations of the gang responsible for all the robberies up and down Oregon Territory. On the condition that I go free.*

"Oh, holy shit," he said.

"I know. I don't have Lee's response, obviously."

"Right. But we can assume that he accepted."

"I think we can assume that he accepted. And I don't think he wanted just information, but a cut of the money. It makes me think about those mining claims too. There was something to that. And the fact that it isn't well documented that my family filed for those claims. At least, it's not something that's been passed down."

"Right. So you think basically your ancestor was on the take. All around. Getting money where and when he could while pretending to be the savior of the town."

"That is what I think. I mean, there's nothing wrong with trying to make money outside of your job. That he had a mining claim isn't a problem in and of itself. But the other implications. . . ."

"Right."

"Come and sit down."

She ushered him into the dining room, and there in the center of a blond oak table was the shoebox. There was a small red leather book sitting in front of it.

"That's the journal," he guessed.

"Yes. Though I'm not sure it's a journal in the way that Austin's is." She shook her head. "It's weird to me now that he has your name."

"Imagine how I feel."

"Why did your father name you after him?"

"I don't know. My dad wasn't a terrible man, Millie, for all that he caused his fair share of trouble. For all that he wasn't the most responsible father. I think he cared quite a bit about us. About our family."

"I believe that," she said.

"I think he did it as some kind of gesture. Though sometimes I wonder. . . . Sometimes I wonder if it's because I'm the one who's supposed to fix this. Hell, I must be the one who survived for a reason."

"Because you lived longer than thirty-five?"

"Yeah. It's kind of a thing. For the oldest Wilder."

"Yeah, I get that."

She handed the red book to him. And he opened it up. Mostly, it was a ledger. And it was written out in a code that he imagined was lost in the mists of time. Abbreviations and initials that he would only be able to guess at.

"Yeah. There's definitely money stuff happening here."

"He certainly wasn't writing about his wife and children."

She sounded wistful. Sad.

"I think Austin was a pretty unique case for his time. Or maybe not. What else did people have back then but writing and reading to document things. To keep a record. He wrote everything out because nobody really knew him. I like to think that his wife did."

"I'm not sure if anybody knew Lee Talbot. This journal is coded in such a way that not even we could ever figure it out. I have to think there's something to that. If a man doesn't want to be known at all, there must be a reason for it."

"Do you think?"

"Yes, I do. I think there's probably a reason he didn't want any-one to know him. And there's probably a reason Austin Wilder did want someone to know. Someone, someday. He wanted us to know why he became an outlaw."

He nodded slowly. "I do believe that's true. I believe he wanted to keep track of his motivations, good and bad. Because he knew that there was a risk his legacy would be what it is."

"And Lee Talbot didn't want anyone to know there was more to him. Because the simple legend is the story he wanted told. I'm convinced of that now."

"Well, let's go through all this."

They found more letters. They sat there and pored over them. It wasn't just Butch Hancock. There were people Lee had extorted. Holding the threat of hanging over them if they didn't give up land rights, mining claims, money.

"He was like a crime lord," she said.

"Damn. This is . . . it's a lot bigger than I expected."

"Yeah. I thought maybe . . . I thought there was something to what you said, but I didn't expect this." She pressed her hand to her forehead. "Did my father know? My grandfather? Is that why all of this was tucked up in a shoebox, never donated to the museum, never brought out for any kind of viewing? They knew." The look in her eyes was suddenly wild. "They knew. And they let this same old narrative play out. This tired nonsense that painted your fam-ily in a bad light and my family in a glowing one. It's unnecessary. There's room for the truth. There is."

"I'm sorry," he said. "I really am."

"Why would you be? This absolves you. All of you Wilders. It proves that everyone was wrong. All this time."

"Not really. Lee Talbot can be a bad guy, and so can Austin Wilder. It's not really about absolution or condemnation."

"Well, it is to me," she said. "Because I was given a simple story all my life. And it isn't so much that the story isn't what I was always told, it's that the people telling it knew it was a lie. Because that means my own father had an investment in that lie. Even a dishonest one. That means he wasn't the man I thought he was."

"Unless you find records indicating that your own dad engaged in illegal activities, I don't think that's fair. He might've been entrusted with protecting the family legacy, and so he did. Family is complicated."

"Not mine," she said.

He looked at her, and he suddenly felt endless pity.

When you were the bad guy, you knew there was more to the story. Because you knew you were a full human being. But she had been sold a bill of goods. One that oversimplified all the people around her, one that oversimplified her family in a way that made her feel like the odd one out all her life, because she believed their story was the truth. The uncomplicated, unvarnished truth. And what a load of bullshit that was.

It had made her feel she wasn't enough. It had her trying to reach for a bar that wasn't obtainable because nobody before her had obtained it either.

He hadn't thought there would come a day when he would pity Millie Talbot. Right then he did.

For a split second.

Until he picked up the next letter.

If you will swear to me that you saw them commit murder, and provide a written statement, I'll be justified in hanging the lot of them. You can go on anonymously, live a decent life. You'll have your spoils, and I'll have mine.

This was it. Proof of the premeditated murder of Austin, Jesse, and William. Right here in black and white. It wasn't a vague log or coded transaction. Sheriff Talbot had asked Butch to lie. So that they would have evidence to hang the Wilders with no questions asked. So that shooting Austin in the street would be seen as a great act of bravery, and not a cowardly act of avarice.

"It was murder," he said, putting the letter down on the table. And in that moment, he couldn't care about Millie at all. Instead he saw red. As he looked across at a Talbot, who, even unwittingly, had been charged with keeping this false legacy alive.

"Your family were a bunch of criminals. Just criminals. No honor at all. Outlaws, at least, are supposed to keep the Code of the West. I'm not saying my family didn't do some despicable things, but they did it to survive."

"I don't think in the end they were robbing banks for their survival. Austin had a beautiful house in town, and you know that."

"Are you going to defend a murderer?"

"No. What the sheriff did is indefensible. But it doesn't make Austin a saint just because Lee Talbot was a sinner."

"Doesn't it? Because that's how it's been for my family all these years. Automatically bad while your family was blameless. The entire town is divided into sinners and saviors. Why do you get to do away with that rigid moral code when it suits you?"

"Because I've never—"

"You have. You believed in it plenty. That's why you have such a hard time believing that I read. That I write. Oh, but you don't have a hard time kissing me, do you? Because you're just like all the other girls, Millie, though you pretended you weren't. Even to yourself. You still want to ride a bad boy for a night and see where it takes you."

She was trembling, her cheeks scarlet, and he knew a moment of guilt. A moment of conscience that told him perhaps he should stop. That he was being unfair. That he was treating her poorly, because she was a victim too.

But he didn't want to consider the complex nature of their situation. What he wanted was to just savor this moment of being justified. Of being right. He'd believed all along that the Talbots weren't that good. That the man who had put him in handcuffs had known the whole time that the original Austin Wilder wasn't a murderer. That the original Lee Talbot had never been a hero.

"You want me bad when it suits you. Admit it."

"Don't," she said. "Don't bring the bad blood between our families into us."

"How can it not be? You don't think that's crossed my mind? Just how good it would be to have you? Knowing how much your dad would've hated it."

She drew back as if he had struck her. "That's not why I wanted you. It's not because I have some outlaw fantasy."

"No? Too damn bad. It probably could've gotten you off."

"Why are you being so horrible to me? I didn't do anything wrong."

"Make up your mind. I'm either innately horrible or I'm not."

"I never said you were," she said. "I never did. I was never your enemy."

"No. Just everybody else in your entire bloodline. And this whole town."

"I told you the truth. As soon as I found out, I told you the truth."

"Well, maybe the truth isn't going to fix anything. Maybe it's too late for me."

He looked at her across the table, and the need within him grew. The desire.

He had known why he'd come here the whole time. It didn't have sweet fuck all to do with historical documents. Not really. And this anger inside him—he wasn't even sure it had anything to do with the past.

He couldn't quite pinpoint what was driving him now. Except that she had always been out of his reach. He knew he shouldn't do anything with her because she was a better person than he was.

He hated that he was poisoned even against himself.

It was the kind of poison that could kill a man.

"This is a mess," she said, her eyes shining bright.

It was. It was such a big mess, there was no easy fixing it. They were going to have to present their findings and adjust the history of the town. The entire makeup of the place. And people wouldn't want that. They would resent it. They would resist it.

And then personally . . . he had said some things tonight that were pretty damned unforgivable. But Millie and he were still going to have to work together. Maybe.

So he decided it was time to do what he wanted.

He reached across the space between them and pulled her into his arms. "I'm going to kiss you," he said.

"Oh?"

"Hell yeah. Because I'm an outlaw. We take what we want."

Chapter 15

I never worried about being bad or being good. I worried about being alive.

—Austin Wilder's journal, May 25, 1857

Millie couldn't believe this was happening. Really, she couldn't believe any of the last hour had occurred.

And now Austin was kissing her again. But it was hotter, more dangerous than the kiss they had shared in his driveway.

She knew she could say no. Because he was angry and wild, and she wasn't much better.

But she didn't want to. Everything she had ever known about her life had just been dismantled neatly with one box of documents.

She would always be suspicious now. Of how much her family had known and hidden from her.

Of how calculated the legend was. To keep the Wilders in their place, while elevating the Talbots.

To keep this narrative as it was, rather than making room for the truth.

So maybe it was all right to just kiss him. Maybe it was all right to give in to the less rational part of herself. He had said it, and it had made her angry: that she wanted to know what it was like to ride an outlaw.

She never would've admitted that was true. But it was. Mostly because she wanted to tap into a part of herself that had been ignored all these years.

She wanted to feel something. If she couldn't feel good enough, then she wanted to feel exciting. She wanted to feel . . . pleasure. Need. She wanted to feel desired.

You're unhappy.

Heather's words echoed inside her.

She had a feeling Heather was right.

She was dismantling her life because she didn't like it.

And this . . . it was going to be a disaster. It was never going to be anything more than just this one night. And then they were going to have to contend with each other all the days afterward.

But she was already living a disaster, and none of it was of her own making.

Just as it wasn't his.

Not really.

Yes, they had made choices within the framework they had been given, but that framework had been so . . . set. From the beginning.

They hadn't had a say in that.

So now she wanted to make her own mistake, maybe.

To do something ill-advised.

Wasn't that her right?

Because she wasn't inherently good. And if she wasn't inherently good, then maybe she didn't have to work so damned hard.

So she kissed him back. Let him consume her. Let her need for him burn through her like a wildfire.

His touch was firm, almost brutal. And there was a desperation in it that was healing.

No man had ever touched her like this. His hand skimmed down her back, down to her rear, and he cupped her through the thin fabric of her dress, squeezing hard.

"Oh," she gasped.

"You want this?" He kissed her deep, dizzyingly. His tongue licked slowly against hers. And then he looked at her with those wild blue eyes, and her heart beat a rapid response.

"Yes," she said.

"You gotta be sure. Because I don't do things by halves. And this? This might burn us both to the ground."

"Good," she said, the word coming out a raspy whisper. "I am so tired. I'm so tired of being careful. I have been careful all my life, and what has it gotten me? Nothing. I don't want that. It didn't protect me. I want to feel something."

"Hang on then, Sheriff. Because I'm damn sure going to make you feel more than you ever have in your life."

He picked her right up off the ground, as if she weighed nothing. His kiss was like an all-consuming fire as he carried her out of the living room, up the stairs.

"Which bedroom?"

"I'm still in . . . I'm still in my old room."

It felt silly then. But she had never moved into her dad's room. Because that had seemed wrong. Austin carried her over to the bed and placed her in the center of the mattress. And he looked down at her. She couldn't believe this. She could not believe she was about to do this. But she wanted it. And she didn't want to do anything to break the spell. She didn't want to do anything to make him stop.

"Did you have sex with him here?"

His words shuddered through her, making her heart stop.

"I . . . what?"

"Michael. Did he have you in this bed?"

She looked away. "Yes."

"Good. Because I'm going to obliterate that memory. Next time I ask, you'll say no. Because sex with him isn't anything like sex with me. You understand?"

This was terrifying. Because then and there, she knew that he was going to ruin her for other men. Michael hadn't done that. She'd never worried he would. But now she was terrified. Because she knew that Austin was going to keep his promise. He was going to show her something so different from what she'd experienced before, it was going to shift her world on its axis. Everything about him was like that.

He challenged her on every front. Why should it be different in bed?

"Have you ever had sex with a woman in her own house?" She

didn't know where she found the boldness to ask that question; she didn't even know where it had come from.

"No," he said.

"Just hotel rooms."

"Yeah."

"So you won't have to walk by and wonder if she's still there. If she has another lover. But you'll have to do that with me. So maybe you should be a little bit worried about how tonight is going to change you too."

He leaned down over her. And her breath left her body. Hell, her soul just about left her body. He smelled so good, so intoxicating and wonderful. She wanted him. She had never felt like this before. She had felt the need to be close to somebody, and she had felt flattered by Michael's attention, but she hadn't felt desperate before.

"I'm not worried."

She didn't have time to ask him what he meant, because he was kissing her again. Carrying her off to another place and time.

She would've believed that he was an outlaw. Bad enough to rob a bank, a train, a stagecoach. He seemed that dangerous.

And if she wanted that, then what did that make her?

Definitely not the woman she'd believed she was her whole life. Definitely not.

"These buttons," he growled. "I've been thinking about these buttons for too damned long." He began to undo them, parting the fabric, and looking at her, bold and hard.

She had mostly had sex with the lights off. She didn't know what to do with this frankness. She also thought it was silly to protest. If you wanted someone's hands on you, wanted their mouth on you, wanted them inside you, how could you complain that they were looking at you?

He stripped her dress away from her body, leaving her in her simple white cotton bra and matching underwear.

He rested his forehead against hers, and he was breathing hard.

"What's wrong?"

"Trying to get it together."

His bravado broke then. That certainty he'd been trying to project that she wasn't going to do to him what he was doing to her.

Something about her extremely unsexy underwear was pushing him to his limit. She had seen it. He couldn't take that knowledge away from her.

Then he reached up and unclipped her bra, exposing her breasts to his hungry gaze.

They were small. Nothing to write home about, really, but he looked as if he was starting to compose a letter.

Then he grabbed the waistband of her underwear, tugged them down all the way to her ankles.

"Damn," he said, raking her with a fierce look. "You are . . . hiding under those dresses. Behind that library counter."

"I'm not really *hiding* behind the library counter. I'm doing my job behind it. It's just people assume things about librarians. . . ."

"Yeah, we're the kings and queens of assumptions around here."

"I want . . . I want to see you," she said.

"Just a minute."

He kissed her neck, down to the crest of her nipple, which he tugged into his mouth, wringing a hoarse cry from deep inside her. Then he kissed his way down her body, to the center of her thighs. He pushed them wide, and buried his face there, his lips and tongue stunning her, the move so definitive and bold, all she could do was cry out.

"Austin."

He held her still, clinging to her hips as he ate her. She had . . . she had read about this. In that romance novel. But she had never once experienced it. She had thought it sounded embarrassing. Wet and unsavory. And anyway, Michael had never offered to do it, and she was never going to ask.

But Austin was. . . . He was putting the illicit descriptions on those pages to shame. Each flick of his tongue was a revelation as he drove her closer and closer to the brink of something she couldn't quite reach.

"Yes," he growled, pushing two fingers deep inside her as he continued to taste her.

Her hips arced upward, shock lancing her.

And with two deep strokes of his fingers, she unraveled, crying out his name, her orgasm breaking so easy, so fast, she hadn't even seen it coming.

She had never . . . understood. Why people lost their minds over this, why somebody would wreck a relationship.

She had assumed it was just men. Men who got off easy, who liked variety, who could engage in this sort of thing without feeling deep intimacy.

But suddenly, it was as if blinders had been torn from her eyes.

I didn't buy you the vibrator as a joke. . . .

But she had thought so. Because she hadn't. . . . She just hadn't understood. She wasn't sure she did now. But she was . . . undone. Utterly and absolutely.

And then he moved away from her. She was still shaking and shuddering. He stood back and took his shirt off in one fluid motion, his body leaving her speechless.

He was entirely made of muscle, with tan skin stretched tight over the top of enticing ridges. Dark hair covered his chest, moving down his stomach in a line that left her mouth dry.

He undid his belt fluidly with one hand, demonstrating just how good he was at this. At this entire thing. She would maybe be jealous at some point, but not now. Now she was just grateful that she was benefiting from all his experience. From the fact that he knew how to put on a show, and also deliver.

Her body was buzzing with the aftereffects of the orgasm he had just given her.

Nothing like any of her previous experience.

She'd had orgasms. But they had been hard ones. Something she'd fought for with her eyes squeezed shut, something that she had taken control of in bed with Michael.

If she could be on top, if she could direct the movements, then she could make it happen. Having someone else wrench a climax from her when she hadn't even been trying, when she hadn't even expected it, well, that was something she hadn't known was possible.

She forgot to be insecure. Forgot to wonder what he thought about her.

The first time she ever had sex, she had been flattered. Grateful that Michael found her attractive enough. That he wanted to take on the difficulties of being saddled with a twenty-four-year-old virgin.

Because honestly, most men found it weird. Not that she had been close enough to any to really know how weird they found it, but she'd felt as if her virginity hung over her head, a great big scarlet V that followed her around and made her Teflon to men. They just sort of slid right off.

But Michael had said he liked that about her. That she had made it something special. Because she had waited.

She had never pushed back and said that she hadn't waited on purpose.

Instead, she had fallen into line. Had played into his idea of her. Maybe a little bit too much. She had difficulty being bold. Voicing her opinions. She had wanted to stay attractive to him. And he had indicated that he found her traditional values, his words, attractive.

So when he had gone and slept with somebody else, it had hurt in a very particular way. Because she had felt incapable of fulfilling his fantasy.

She didn't care about Austin's fantasies.

She wanted to laugh. She didn't care at all. He was her fantasy. And right now, that was all that mattered. Right now, she wanted to bask in that realization.

As he undid his jeans, she stared at him, shamelessly. She watched him get naked. And she bit her lip when she looked at that most masculine part of him. Thick and long, more than she had ever seen. More than she had ever imagined was possible.

Her internal muscles clenched tight in anticipation. She was aching already. She had never wanted it like this before. She had never wanted another person like this.

She had never had a fantasy that felt like this.

Before she could overthink it, she got up onto her knees, then moved to the edge of the bed. She put her hand out and touched his chest, a sensual shiver moving through her body. She kissed his jaw, and he made a deep, masculine sound that resonated in his chest.

Then she kissed his neck, down his chest, his stomach.

Her stomach tightened with a sense of dread and anticipation.

She had done this before. But it was a strange, uneasy sort of thing. Again, as if she was violating her Madonna image and straying too far into whore. Not that she thought there was anything wrong with it. It was just. . . .

She wanted to do it for Austin. Because he was beautiful. It was about her, not him. And that helped banish her trepidation. She leaned in, flicking her tongue over the broad head of his arousal. She shivered.

He tasted so good.

He growled, his hand moving back to grab her hair.

He guided her head down onto him, and there was no question about whether or not he was enjoying this. Whether or not he wanted it from her.

He wasn't subtle, Austin.

She found that she liked that about him.

She also liked the flavor of him, filling her mouth, the feel of him.

She was helplessly aroused by what she was doing. By her own boldness.

She didn't feel like a sad, insipid woman who ought to be grateful for a man's attention. She felt empowered.

She felt desired. And better still, she was desirous.

She felt she deserved it.

And she was going to have it.

He urged himself farther down her throat, and she accommodated him like a valiant soldier.

She had never thought this could be arousing. But she was helplessly turned on.

Suddenly, with just as much certainty as he had brought her to him, he moved her away.

"Fuck," he said. "I don't want to finish like that."

He bent down and grabbed his wallet.

She watched him with round eyes as he opened it up, took out a condom packet, and tore it open. He took out a second condom packet and threw it onto the nightstand. Then he rolled the latex over his long, hard length, his eyes never leaving her as he did.

It was so erotic she could barely breathe.

And she never would've said something so clinical could be sexy.

But it didn't feel clinical. Not with him. Not now.

"Are you ready for me?"

She nodded, words failing her.

"Lie back, spread your legs."

Heat rushed through her face. But she did exactly as he instructed. Because she wasn't going to flinch now.

He was an outlaw. And he was going to take what he wanted.

She was an outlaw. She was going to have what she wanted.

And right now, what she wanted was him. Filling her, buried deep. Thrusting inside her.

She was trembling with anticipation. There was no room for nervousness. No room for anything but need.

"Please," she said.

He moved to the bed, his blue eyes intense on hers as he captured her mouth, positioning himself at the entrance to her body. Then he moved his hand on her thigh and hooked her leg up over his lower back as he thrust deep.

She gasped.

He was so big. And it was so good. She let her head fall back against the pillow, arching her hips upward into his. Meeting him thrust for thrust.

Gratitude, she realized, put you in a passive position. All you could do was lie there, thankful for the attention. Trying to make sure you didn't disrupt the enjoyment of the other person.

This was about her own pleasure.

Her own need. And she was thankful, but not in that other way. Not in a way that rendered her an inert vessel for someone else's enjoyment.

She was wild.

She dug her nails into his shoulders, let them scrape down his back. She made sounds that she had never thought herself capable of. She didn't have time to be embarrassed, because that would require pausing to think. And she wasn't going to do that.

His thrusts became shorter, harder, his forehead resting against hers, his eyes blazing. He spoke dirty poetry against her lips, and she didn't know if she could ever read erotica after this, because how could it ever top his words?

"Come for me," he said.

A simple command. But so, so effective.

Because he wanted her pleasure. Her pleasure mattered.

It was enough to send her right over the edge, tumbling down into the abyss.

Then he froze above her, his own release coming on a hoarse cry.

And as they lay there, clinging to each other, their breath mingling, she understood something else she never had before.

People went out of their heads when they were turned on.

She had never understood that. She had never understood how much of a different person you could be when what you really, really wanted was to be touched. Possessed.

She had never understood how something that might otherwise shock you felt completely reasonable when you were in a deeply sexual haze. Because now she was just lying there. With this man who in some ways she had known all her life, and in other ways was a stranger.

Having just had a fight that had turned into sex.

He had been venting his anger, and she had been lost in the moment.

He had asked her to be sure. She had said that she was.

Because the Millie Talbot who had so badly wanted his hands

on her body had been willing to say anything, even if she wasn't totally certain. She had been willing to try anything. To do anything to have him.

And now she felt . . . small and scraped raw. Alone, even though he was literally still on top of her. Still inside her.

She felt foolish.

She felt as if she had been on some wild, destructive path all day. Longer than that.

Maybe Heather was right. She wasn't happy.

And she was doing things to try to disrupt her life. Trying to change it, to fix it.

She was still holding on to his shoulders.

It was a terrible moment. This in between. Waiting for what was going to happen next. But it was worse when he actually moved. Worse when he put distance between them.

"Bathroom is down the hall?" he asked.

"Yeah," she said, her voice scratchy.

She was lying there in the middle of the bed like a starfish as he left the room. Then she scrambled beneath the covers, her heart beating fast.

She felt fragile.

She didn't quite know what to do.

She had no idea what he was going to do.

It was a strange and terrible thing, being on the edge like this. Wonderful too, in a weird way. She had done things in the correct order before. She had been in a serious relationship before she ever let it get sexual. Tonight was the result of being with a man she just didn't know all that well.

Maybe he was halfway out the door now. Butt naked.

She stared at a spot on the ceiling and swallowed hard. Then she heard footsteps.

She didn't look at the doorway.

She kept on looking at the ceiling.

"Millie?"

"Yes?"

"Are you going to look at me?"

She did. She wished she hadn't. Because he was still gorgeous, and he was standing there completely naked. Broad shoulders, muscular chest, lean waist, thick thighs.

It was a bit much. He made her heart flutter. Made her feel an ache between her thighs again already. There was still another condom on the nightstand.

"It's getting very late," she said.

"Yes, it is."

"Your truck is in my driveway."

"Yeah."

"People are going to talk."

"They're already talking."

"I know," she said. "But until tonight they were wrong."

His mouth tipped up at the corner. "Were they?"

"Well, I . . . I guess not."

He stood there, his arms folded across that broad chest, and she had the terrible feeling that he was only still there because he was being nice to her. Because he believed she was too soft to handle what he would normally do. Which would be to leave her.

"I don't need you to stay."

They both looked over at the second condom. "I mean. . . ."

"Yeah." He took in a sharp breath, then went and began to collect his clothes. "I'm sure you don't." He tugged his pants on, then his shirt. "We need to go through all the rest of those papers," he said tonelessly.

She felt disconnected from their discovery now. What did the past matter when the present felt like this?

Too big, too confusing.

Spectacular and awful all at the same time.

"Well, not right now," she said.

He pulled his jeans on, and then sat down on the bed. Probably to put his boots on.

"Scoot over."

"Excuse me?"

"Unless you're desperate for me to leave because you don't want people to see my truck in the driveway."

"I. . . ." This debate felt unwinnable. Because she kind of didn't want people to see the truck in the driveway. But it wasn't because of him, it was because of her. Because she didn't want to explain the insanity that had just overtaken her when she couldn't even explain it to herself.

She didn't understand what was happening.

"I'll sleep on top of the covers. But I don't want to leave you. It doesn't feel right."

He sounded as if he was weighted down with the duty of staying with her.

But if she told him to leave, then it would seem as if she was ashamed of him.

And she wasn't.

She really wasn't. It was just that she wanted to hide from him. And herself.

"You don't have to worry about the second condom," he said. "I'm not going to ask anything of you."

She wasn't sure how she felt about that either.

"I thought that men notoriously didn't like talking after sex," she said finally.

"I usually like to be in the car headed home after sex," he said. "Maybe stopping at the Wendy's drive-through on my way."

"That . . . doesn't help me."

He cleared his throat. "Sorry."

She didn't like thinking about him with other women. But, of course, there had been a lot of them. He was a hookup guy, and he was staying with her because he felt sorry for her. She felt a little sorry for herself, though, so she wasn't really in the mood to kick him out. Even if she should.

"Well, Michael's the only man I've been with, so. . . ."

"Right," he said. "It doesn't make you a bad person because you wanted to have sex."

"We had sex for a bad reason," she said.

"I was angry," he said. "And I'm sorry. I'm sorry it started that way. I'm sorry I let it continue that way. There isn't an excuse for that. But I wanted you, make no mistake. It was just that being angry was what made it all right."

"I don't understand," she said.

"Not even a little? I just had to be thinking a little bit less clearly."

"That's not really flattering."

"That's not about you. It's about me."

"Oh."

"I don't want to hurt you," he said.

"So don't," she said.

Her voice sounded small and stubborn, and even she realized that what she was saying was ridiculous.

Because she felt sore right now. And who knew what else could be done to her. In the name of sex. In the name of change. Self-exploration. Exploration of a hot cowboy. . . .

"You know, my sister saw you kiss me."

"Oh," she said.

"And she was mad at me. Because she figured that you were a nice girl, and I was not a nice guy. She's not wrong, Millie. I have never had a relationship. I've never even wanted one. Until recently. I've started thinking about getting married, having kids. Leaving a legacy of some kind. But even so . . . it's not. . . ."

She didn't need him to explain further. He was talking about legacy, not romance. Not falling in love. She hated that she understood. That his goal was closer to her own journey than she would like to admit. And definitely one that she was never engaging in again.

"Do yourself a favor," she said, looking up at the ceiling. "Don't get married for legacy. I got engaged for it. I convinced myself it was love, because nobody wants to believe they're doing things for the wrong reason. I was. I didn't love Michael. I wanted to. I wanted to be good. I wanted to carry on the Talbot legacy. I wanted to do it while my dad was still alive, and I wanted to do it so badly that I was willing to be in the wrong relationship. To overlook everything that was wrong."

"I wouldn't need to believe I was in love."

The way he said that told her everything she needed to know about the differences between them.

The realization was stark. A little bit painful.

She was starting to get sleepy.

"Go to sleep," he said.

"So you can take off as soon as I close my eyes?"

"No. I'm not leaving."

She could ask him to go, and he would. She really didn't want him to. She didn't want to examine how much she longed for him to stay.

Chapter 16

*I worry about it now. I want my son to be good. I didn't realize it
mattered until I thought I might have to teach another person how
to live.*

—Austin Wilder's journal, May 25, 1857

When Austin woke up, he was cold. He wasn't wearing a shirt, he
was wearing jeans, and he was on top of the covers.

Shit.

He had spent the night.

He had said he would, but still, the creeping realization that not
only had he defiled Millie Talbot, but he had left his truck in the
driveway the whole damn night, washed over him fully now that the
haze of his orgasm wasn't blocking his brain cells.

He rolled out of bed and put his hands over his face. She was
still asleep.

It was early.

He texted Carson to let him know that he wasn't going to be up
to do the morning chores.

And braced himself for the third degree he knew would follow.

You spent the night somewhere?

Obviously.

With someone?

No, I took myself on a little self-care retreat.

Damn.

Don't read anything into it.

Out of town?

Not your business.

He left it at that. And ignored the other texts that started rolling in. He put his shirt on and went downstairs, figuring he ought to go ahead and make coffee for the two of them.

He stood there in her kitchen and looked out at his truck, a beacon in the driveway. He could leave. Before the neighbors got up. Before Millie and he created a stir.

But he didn't want to abandon Millie like that. He hadn't wanted to last night, and he didn't want to now. And it wasn't just because of the documents sitting on the kitchen table. It was because. . . .

The way he had acted. . . .

He had been every bit the bastard his ancestor was.

Taking what wasn't his. Taking what he didn't have the right to. What he didn't have the ability to care for.

He had seen it in black and white. A man could even fall in love with a good woman, but if he didn't know how to shape up, it didn't matter.

Austin Wilder had left Katherine Wilder with two small children and a life full of grief.

There was a lot of talk about the Wilder men, and how they died young.

The Wilder women, though, were the ones who really suffered.

The Wilder men got off easy at the end of the day. They peaced out and went to whatever afterlife awaited them.

He didn't want to do that to Millie. She deserved better.

He heard soft, tentative footsteps on the stairs.

"I'm still here," he called up.

The footsteps paused.

"Millie," he said.

The footsteps were resolutely still.

"Are you hiding from me?"

"No," came a muffled reply.

"What are you doing?"

"Examining a cobweb in the stairwell."

"I think you're lying."

"That's rude," she said, sniffing loudly.

"I'm pretty rude."

She came the rest of the way down the stairs then, looking rumpled. She was wearing a nightgown that covered her from her throat down to her toes.

"Wasn't I a gentleman all night?" he asked.

She blinked. "After all the sex."

He laughed. "Yeah. After the sex. I was a gentleman then."

"You were."

"So don't stand there clutching your pearls like you're afraid I'm going to ravish you."

She walked into the kitchen, her movements jerky.

"I'm making coffee."

"Oh. Well. That's nice. Thank you. For the coffee."

"You haven't tasted it yet. Don't thank me for coffee you haven't even tried."

Their words were so careful, and he didn't like it. He'd never had a morning after before.

"I'm sorry," he said. "I'm a mess. And I feel like I kind of dragged you into that."

She laughed. "*You're* sorry. I'm a mess. My wedding just got called off. I had no . . . had no business getting involved in something like this. It can't go anywhere."

"No." He frowned. "Well. Good."

"But there's sort of a. . . . There's sort of a poetry to it," she said slowly. "I mean, this isn't exactly how I saw putting the feud to bed. . . ."

He snorted. "No. Not really. But then, your dad and my dad were not going to solve the issues our families had like that."

Her eyebrows shot up so far they disappeared beneath her hairline. "Very much no."

"We're still working on this Gold Rush Days thing."

"Yeah," she said.

"I need to get my book written. I need to figure my shit out."

"I understand that you don't want a relationship with me."

"Well, don't say it like that." Except it was true. It was specific to her. Because it just wasn't going to work. Because she was all wrong for him. Well, she was her own thing. He was all wrong.

"I don't know another way to say it."

"It's about me," he said.

"Well, maybe it should be about me too." She lifted her chin. She was a stubborn little thing. Much more so than he would've previously believed.

"Okay, sweetie, it can be about you too."

"Don't say that. Don't call me sweetie like I could be any one of the women you've slept with. You're at my house."

"I don't call anyone sweetie." It was true. He didn't know why he'd called her that.

She sniffed. "Oh. Well. Okay. So, what now?"

"You wanted to make it about you. So you tell me."

She shook her head. "Like you don't have an opinion?"

Austin Wilder was a whole lot of things, but a coward wasn't one of them. If she wanted to play chicken with him until he decided to make a move . . . he was just going to make that move. "I want more."

"Oh."

"We ought to get through this Gold Rush Days stuff. All the papers on the table need to be gone through. It's just not realistic to think we aren't going to get together again."

"Do you think so?" With stiff shoulders she walked past him into the kitchen and went over to the coffee maker.

"Yes," he said, watching her shoulders get even straighter. "I do think so. Because that was damn good sex. I don't think either of us is going to be looking at each other without thinking about it."

"Maybe I'm indifferent," she said, reaching up and taking a coffee mug out of the cabinet. Her movements were precise and somehow prim. He would be lying if he said he didn't like it. She was entirely different from anyone he was used to.

Last night. . . .

He had done his level best not to think about it. Because he had been lying there on the covers being a damned gentleman while that other condom burned bright as a beacon on the nightstand. But last night had been a revelation.

He knew it had been one for her too.

He knew good and well he had blown her mind. As she had blown his.

And it didn't hurt his pride to let her know that. Acting a coward about it, acting like it hadn't been mind-blowing, that was something a man ought to be ashamed of.

"Last night was fucking incredible, and you know it."

She turned toward him, clutching her mug with both hands, her fingers looking like claws. "It was . . . fine."

"Millie," he said, his voice a warning. He closed the distance between them, and she set the cup on the counter hurriedly. Her wide eyes connected with his, and he backed her up against the counter. What he wanted to do was to press himself against her. Show her just how much she wanted him, but he didn't touch her. He just looked. "Your fiancé made you feel you need to protect yourself by not showing your cards. You're afraid to let me know how good it was, because you don't want me to use it against you. Or you're worried maybe that I might feel less than you. So let's get one thing out of the way. You've been with one man. I don't know how many women I've been with. I don't count. I don't care. Last night was as incredible for me as it was for you. Which means it's us. It's not about experience. It's not about anything other than this chemistry between us."

"Maybe it's about our ancestors being enemies."

"Maybe," he said. "And what the hell is wrong with that?"

"I don't . . . I don't know."

"Maybe it's the lure of the forbidden. God knows blessed little is forbidden in this world anymore. Takes the fun out of things."

"I . . . I. . . ."

"I want to kiss you," he said.

She nodded wordlessly, and he captured her mouth, tasting her thoroughly, deeply. "Go get your coffee," he said, moving away from her.

He noticed that her hands were shaking when she picked the mug up. When she grabbed the carafe and began to pour coffee into the mug.

"I'm scared," she said.

"Am I that intimidating?"

"Yes," she said. "I think I could get addicted to you."

"Well. Addicts can recover."

She huffed a laugh. "You're full of yourself."

"In certain areas."

She wrinkled her nose. "This is improbable."

"I agree. And remember, I'm the one that tried to warn you off, so why the hell you're pitching a little fit about it now, I don't know." Then he understood. "Be careful what you wish for—is that it?"

She looked down. "I didn't know."

"You didn't know what?"

"I didn't know sex could be like that."

"Back up," he said. "I'm going to get coffee too."

He did, grabbing the biggest mug she had and pouring the whole rest of the pot into it. "Come on," he said, gesturing for her to go into the dining room. He took his seat at the head of the table, set the coffee cup down in front of him, and looked at her expectantly. She shimmied into the seat two chairs away from his.

"All right," she said. "Are you calling a meeting?"

"No. I'm not calling a meeting. I want you to explain to me what that means."

"Sex has never been that intense for me before. It's never felt that good. I . . . this is so stupid. And it's embarrassing."

"Millie, I've had my face between your legs. You don't need to be embarrassed with me."

Her cheeks went bright red. "That's another thing. I've never done that before."

"Good God," he said. "Just when I think I couldn't disrespect that little weasel more. I have no patience for men who want to fuck women, but then act disgusted by them. Men who want women to service them, but don't take any real pleasure in the shape of a woman, in the way that she talks, in the way she is. But he did bow out already and make room for the rest of us."

She blinked at him, her eyes wide. He felt passionately about what he'd said. He was the kind of guy who did hookups, which meant he was part of that scene. He saw too many men who disrespected the women they were sleeping with. Who judged them easy for having one-night stands, but never judged themselves. He hated it, and what she was saying made him think Michael was exactly that kind of guy. Because Millie knew how to give a blowjob. So it was clear she had done it before. But that jackass had never gone down on her? It made him violent.

"There are a lot of guys out there like that, don't get me wrong. But it's a flaw. He was just useless. It's not you. He's an archetype."

"Do you still feel sympathetic toward him? Do you still want to know his backstory?"

"I never said I was sympathetic to him. What I said is that everybody has their reasons. And even more insidious, everybody has the story they tell themselves. That he's better than everybody else, than the other people in this town, than the rules. Than the woman he was engaged to. If I didn't have so much contempt for Danielle, I might feel sorry for her. Because she landed herself a lemon."

"Maybe he's better with her," Millie said. "Maybe it was the combination of the two of us."

"No. He wasn't punished for his bad behavior. And because of that, he'll just keep on with it. She's not getting anything better out of it than you did. The sad thing is, maybe she doesn't want better."

"I didn't want better. I didn't know to want better. I was just so grateful that he. . . ." She looked down at her cup. "That he wanted me."

Hell. He moved across the space between them and cupped her chin between his thumb and forefinger, looking her right in the eyes. "Millie, I want you to listen to me. I am fucking grateful that you let me into your bed last night. I should get down on my knees and give thanks."

"And this is why you scare me."

"Don't worry. I scare myself a little bit too."

He moved away from her, went back to his seat. His heart was pounding too hard, and he felt a surge of something moving through his veins. Maybe he was mad because of the politics of this damned town, but if that was true, then he should still be feeling a lot angrier at her than he did. It was that spike of anger that had driven him into her bed last night. But the truth was, anger was an excuse. He had used anger to get him there, because it had blotted out common sense. And he had needed that. So that he could just do what he wanted. And now he had to deal with the consequences.

"So you're proposing that we keep sleeping together?"

"I think it's inevitable," he said. "I didn't say I thought we *should* keep sleeping together, or that it was anything like a good idea. It's actually a terrible idea, I just think the ship sailed last night."

Thankfully, she didn't look offended. Instead, she sipped her coffee thoughtfully. "I can agree with that. It was maybe not the wisest decision but . . . but what's done is done."

"The horse has bolted."

"So to speak," she said, lifting her brows.

"So to speak," he said.

"I have to head to the library soon," she said.

He nodded. "Do you mind if I take some of this stuff to go through?"

"No," she said, looking down at her hands. "I think you should. Because if we are going to be sleeping together, then we need to also make ourselves useful."

"I make myself very useful in the bedroom."

Her face went scarlet again. "I know."

He chuckled. "You have to stop being so cute about it."

"Why is this cute?"

"I don't know. It's just . . . you're not like anybody I've ever been with."

"Well. Same."

"I should hope not."

"Do you have an outlaw outfit?"

It was his turn to look a little bit shocked. "You want to do some role-playing?"

"No! I only meant that . . . we're going to need costumes. For if you do the walking tour. And maybe I can dress like a sheriff. Or a schoolmarm. That would be more accurate to the period."

"Well. Whatever you decide. What does an outlaw costume entail?"

"I don't really know. Black, I would think. But I have some crates of things like that at the library."

"All right."

"We should meet up later."

"I'm counting on it."

She hightailed it out of the kitchen, going off to get ready, and he sat there staring into his cup of coffee, wondering how his life had gotten turned quite so upside down, and why he wasn't more upset about it.

Chapter 17

When I held my son in my arms for the first time, my world changed. I am caught between wanting to change myself, and wanting to be certain he never lacks for anything. My own bad road was paved by need. I never want him to go hungry.

—Austin Wilder's journal, July 5, 1857

Millie felt sore, and conspicuous as she slunk into the library and flicked on the lights.

She was a little bit early, but she knew that Heather was already out and about and would be stopping by. And unfortunately, she had a lot to talk to Heather about. Part of her wanted to keep last night a secret. But there would be no keeping something like this from Heather, and besides, she needed advice. Her insides felt completely messed up. Mangled.

Her body still felt electrified, and she was . . . not embarrassed, not really. It was just that he was so frank. About everything. She had wanted to minimize the intensity of her response; she hadn't wanted to let him know that he had completely upended her. Ruined her. That he had shown her pleasure she hadn't really believed could exist.

But he hadn't seemed embarrassed about any of it. His reaction had both reassured her and left her feeling wired.

Heather texted her to let her know she was close, and Millie unlocked the door for her. Heather handed a cup of chai straight to Millie. She didn't even look to see what animals were on it.

"Oh dear," Heather said, regarding her. "Are you okay?"

"I'm. . . ." She stared at the back wall, trying read some of the titles on the books, or just guess what they were. She ought to just know them all by heart.

"What happened?"

"Well, I went into the attic."

Heather's gaze was level. "I *do* know that."

"I found something up there."

"Okay."

She took a deep breath. "Something relating to Lee Talbot. And his not actually being a great guy."

Heather nodded. "Old white guy with power not actually that awesome. A deep shock."

Millie let the breath she'd just taken in out in one gust. "I know. I know. But you also know the weight given to my family name, and to the lore and to. . . ."

"I'm sorry," said Heather, putting her hand over Millie's arm. "I get that it's personal to you and not a generic unsurprising truth about humanity."

"It's just, that's my family history."

"I know."

"So anyway, I called Austin and told him he needed to come and see the documents I'd found."

Heather's eyes narrowed. "Oh, then you called Austin."

"Yes."

"And you had him come to your house?"

"I did."

"You're not upset about the thing with Lee Talbot."

"I'm a little upset about it."

"You slept with Austin, didn't you?"

Millie sighed. "Yes."

Heather stared at her for a long moment. "How do you feel?"

"I don't know. I mean, I really don't."

"Was the sex not good?"

"We're really not passing the Bechdel test right now, Heather."

Heather let out an exasperated sigh. "What is the biggest thing happening in your life right now, Millie Talbot?"

"I. . . ."

"I believe it's your entanglement with this man—historical

mystery notwithstanding. If we studiously avoided the conversation, just to pass a narrative test that applies to *fictional characters,* then we would be disingenuous, wouldn't we?"

Millie huffed. "I *want* to talk about it. I just don't know how to do it."

"That's fair." But she was staring expectantly.

"I've never done anything like this before."

"I'm aware."

"And I didn't really plan on doing anything like it. But I made that discovery, and he was angry. Oh, he was so angry. Then he kissed me."

"It was angry sex?"

"Yes."

"I didn't realize you had that in you."

"Apparently I do. I feel like a different person. I feel like maybe I'm losing my mind."

"Well, what are you going to do?"

"Do it again?"

Heather sipped her drink thoughtfully. "I'm a little worried about you."

"I'm a little bit worried about me too."

"That actually makes me feel significantly less worried. Because at least you're still thinking clearly enough to know that maybe you need to keep your guard up a little bit. Just have some self-awareness about what you're doing."

"I do. It's not like with Michael. I don't think I need to be in love to make it okay. I don't feel like I should thank him. Even though actually, I kind of want to thank him. Because that was. . . ."

"Millie, of course you don't need to thank him. A guy is not doing you a favor by being with you. I hate this town sometimes. Because everybody decides who you are, and you never got to leave. You never got to see who else you could have been with people who didn't know you from the time you were a child." She shook her head. "You didn't get to see who you would've been if people didn't think of you as Sheriff Talbot's daughter, or the librarian's daughter. I just don't think it's fair."

"I didn't want to leave," she said.

"I know you didn't. I understand why you didn't. I understand why your life went the way it did. But it makes me so angry that you. . . . You are one of the best people I have ever known. You care about this town. You care about fairness. You are sweet, and you are funnier than people realize. You're loyal. And that wet lettuce of a man made you feel like something was wrong with you. He made you feel he was condescending to have sex with you. To be with you, and that . . . I wish I could do something to make you realize how much you matter. Not because of your last name, and not even because of what you do for the town. Because of who you are. You are better than ten thousand mediocre men."

Tears stung Millie's eyes, tears that she hadn't realized were building. "Heather . . . I . . ." She knew that Heather liked her. Of course she did. They had been friends for so long. Heather had included her in everything, and Millie had always felt she didn't have enough to offer in return. Millie had always . . . worried that she was a pity friend. And she felt guilty for that immediately, because Heather had never done anything to make her feel that way. And now Heather had made the most beautiful declaration, and Millie didn't know how to respond.

"I just never felt good enough," she said.

"I know. But you are. And then some. If something was in your control, and you wanted it, you made sure you got it. Like becoming a librarian. Do you have any idea how impressive that is?"

"I know, but nobody thinks just having the same job your mother did is all that impressive."

"That's because they're idiots. Sorry. But it's true. If it's what you want, it doesn't need to be prestigious. It doesn't need to be impressive. What is the point of being impressive if at the end of the day you're just Danielle. She's the mayor, and I'm not impressed. Because everything she does is small, and it's for her own benefit. I mean, except for Michael. He's just small. I doubt he's benefiting her that much."

Millie blinked. "Well. I can now say with confidence that in comparison to Austin, he is in fact small."

A look of surprised delight crossed Heather's face. "I love this for you."

Millie shifted, ignoring the infusion of heat in her face, and the pulsing between her thighs. "Well. I sort of do too."

"You know, I'm sorry that I lead with concern. You can make your own choices. Because you're strong enough. Because you're not anybody's mascot, and you are not mousy. You're actually very brave. You have consistently stood up to the people around you when it was important to you. I don't know why that fact isn't recognized more. Maybe because as you said, people don't value what you're standing up for. They think that because you don't walk around strutting, you aren't bold. But you are. You're one of the boldest women I know."

"I think that's a quality people have always called annoying. Or prudish. Or rigid."

"So many fancy words to get around the fact that what you actually are is a woman with the courage of her convictions. Too bad if nobody wants to call it strong. Or certain. Or knowing your own mind."

"We might pass the Bechdel test now."

"I don't care. What I care about is that you understand your worth. And that you understand that Austin is a lucky man to get to sleep with you. However long it lasts."

"Right," Millie said.

"And you have some control over how long it lasts too."

She considered the idea.

They chatted for a while longer, about what was going on at Heather's job, and her daughter's upcoming second birthday party, which Millie would be attending. Later, Millie kept replaying their conversation, over and over as she saw to her duties for the rest of the day.

Alice came in to get more romance books near closing time,

and Millie almost wanted to tell her she didn't think they seemed so unrealistic now. But she didn't.

When the door to the library opened and Austin walked in, dressed in all black from his cowboy hat down to his boots, she wasn't the only one who froze.

Her mouth dropped open, and she openly stared at him.

Alice elbowed her. "*He* might be a romance hero."

And before Millie could respond, the older woman stepped aside.

Millie faced him, trying to remember what Heather had said earlier. That she was brave. That she had some control about what happened. That he wasn't doing her a favor.

"Hi," she said.

"Howdy, ma'am."

Lord. She had to clench her thighs together to keep from falling over.

"You're here."

"Yes. I have some things to discuss. You want to do a walking tour, and I have some things I want to talk about on that tour."

Oh great. He was armed with new historical information. That made him even sexier, honestly. He was one of the few people who took history as seriously as she did. Another way they were actually alike, and not all that different.

"I need to help Alice check out," she said.

She took the stack of books from Alice's arms and made her way behind the desk. Several of the books had cowboys on the cover, one depicted a shirtless man with a full sleeve of tattoos staring into the camera.

She glanced at Alice.

"I have a vivid imagination," said Alice. "Honestly, why live one life when you can live as many as you want?"

Well, she had always felt that was the magic of books. Though Alice clearly took that belief to a more enjoyable place than Millie ever had.

When Alice left, Millie locked the door behind her.

Austin raised a brow. "Alone?"

"Yes," she said. "We are."

"Lee Talbot was desperate to catch the Wilder brothers. He had begun to suspect that Austin was an outlaw. Based on the amount of money my ancestor had deposited in the bank. Talbot was watching him. He knew that his import business was just a front."

She nodded. "I know this much."

"But he didn't just want to arrest Austin, he wanted to put an end to the Wilder gang. He caught Butch Hancock burglarizing the general store, and Butch started talking. He was drunk, but the information was still valuable. From what I've gathered, Lee told him to sober up and they'd talk again later. Which was where the letters came in. But what Lee really wanted was trumped-up charges. He wanted to be able to execute them."

"There was no evidence of murder?"

"No. I don't believe there ever was. There was only Butch's testimony. Saying that he had witnessed the Wilder brothers executing a stagecoach driver."

"And that was all Lee Talbot needed?"

"It was all he needed. They raided Austin's house. They. . . . Now, this is all reading between the lines, but it sounds as if he believed Katherine's life was in danger. I think that's why he got his gun. Honestly, even if there was no explicit threat, they had broken into his home."

"Yes." She nodded. "Of course, he would do anything in his power to protect his wife and children."

"And that was when . . . it all went into the street, and they both had their guns drawn. Now, I do believe that Austin would've killed the sheriff. I believe that he would've done anything to get away. To protect his family."

"But Austin was fighting for his family," she said, her heart twisting. "Lee Talbot was fighting for his reputation. For his personal gain. And I understand that it's complicated. I understand that Austin was still an outlaw. That he stole money from people. I get that. The Wilders terrorized people as part of the robberies. But . . . at the end of the day, what he did. . . ."

"He did for his family. Always. From the beginning. He stole to keep his brothers from starving; he did it so that he could have a wife. So that he could build her a house. There are plenty of people who struggle and never steal a damn thing, Millie. He was an outlaw. I'm not erasing that."

"No. Of course not. But there were no heroes here."

"It turns out we were all outlaws. All along."

She let his conclusion sink in for a long moment, and he seemed happy to let the silence reign.

"We're going to have to bring this to the town council. Because this new information changes everything. We're going to have to get a new plaque."

He chuckled. "I love that you're worried about the plaque."

"I am. We need lots of updated plaques, actually. I love the history of this town. Loving history means accepting all of it. And that means the deep imperfections of the people who founded Rustler Mountain. It doesn't benefit anybody to make icons out of men. They were just people. At the end of the day, they were all flawed, some of them more than others, to be sure. But how are we ever supposed to learn something from history if we cling to outdated mythology? And that's what it is. This is *mythology*. It isn't history. And it needs to be corrected."

"That's what we'll do with Gold Rush Days—we're going to correct it. We are going to give honest tours. We'll do that until we can get the plaques updated."

"It doesn't give you back your life."

He shrugged. "We Wilders stayed for a reason."

"You were fighting for what you were owed. I understand."

"I'm glad you do. Because sometimes I feel like nobody in their right mind would."

She laughed. "I'm not convinced I'm in my right mind, Austin Wilder. Because here I am, learning the real truth of my family,

standing across from the man who was named after the man my
ancestor murdered in cold blood in the middle of the street, and . . .
I've seen you naked."

He laughed. And the grin that flashed across his face was almost
too beautiful for her to bear.

"I'm glad you think that's funny."

"I fucking do."

"You're just like an outlaw," she said.

"You wanted to know if I had a costume, so I dressed the part."

"There's a prairie dress in the box over there."

"Well, you're obligated to show that to me."

"Am I?"

"If you don't, I'll tie you to the train tracks."

A little erotic thrill shot through her, because she knew he
was kidding, but she heard an innuendo that was maybe a little bit
naughtier than he intended. Or maybe he did intend it.

She went back to the crate of costumes and picked out a blue
dress with pink flowers, then ducked into the bathroom. With shaking hands, she put the dress on. They should probably mull over the
truth of his revelations a bit longer. Before they went on to playing dress-up. Except . . . there was something intent gleaming in his
eyes, and she wanted to follow. Wherever it went.

The dress was tight, and it made her waist look tiny, the skirt
flaring out around her. She took her hair down, moved her fingers
through it, looked at her reflection in the mirror and found she didn't
recognize that woman. Because in this demure dress, she didn't look
like mousy Millie Talbot. Right now, she definitely looked like an
outlaw herself.

She walked out of the bathroom and closed the door behind
her firmly. And there he was, standing in one of the aisles with
two shelving units on either side of him. The long stretch of floor
between them looked a lot like the main street. And this felt like a
showdown once more.

The question was which one of them would pull the trigger first.

Because one of them would. There was no question about that.

"Well," he said. "You really do look the part."

Her heart was pounding hard. "So do you."

She went over to the costume crate again and rummaged until she found the black vest she'd been thinking of when they'd talked costumes this morning.

She held it up and he arched a brow, unmoving.

She held it out to him. "Complete the look?"

"Sure."

The way he looked at her made her feel electric. Made her feel like something so much bolder and edgier than she was. Her heart was hammering. She wondered if this was how Austin Wilder's wife had felt when she had first seen that dangerous man looking at her. It was hard to understand what he saw in her. She supposed it was just that he was a man. And men enjoyed sex. Whatever form it came in.

It didn't feel like that between them, though. He hadn't left last night. He had stayed.

And now he was here. He didn't have to be.

In his eyes, their shared history made them a unit, rather than pitting them against each other. He was pulling her over to his side. He didn't have to do that.

So maybe he felt the same things she did.

The connection. The common bond.

Maybe he didn't.

But it felt . . . possible.

He began moving toward her.

She started to walk toward him, the two of them obscured by tall bookshelves on either side. Nobody who walked by any of the windows would see a thing.

She reached out and handed him the vest, and he shrugged it on. It fit perfectly.

Then he turned his focus straight back to her, moving closer. "This is a fantasy I have."

"Surely not of me," she said.

"I don't know about that."

He cupped her cheek, leaning in and kissing her slowly, deliberately.

She gasped.

Being kissed in the library was tantamount to being kissed in church, she thought.

It was a sacred space.

It was hallowed.

But this didn't feel sacrilegious, not really.

It felt like a reckoning.

Millie and Austin, in the stacks, her in this prairie dress, him looking like a dangerous outlaw.

This was never how she'd thought the feud would be settled.

Who would've ever thought that?

She moved her hand up his chest. It was firm and hot, muscular.

And images of last night bombarded her.

They had been everything.

Perfect. They had been beautiful.

And this was. . . .

Everything.

It was indulgent, luxurious. He swept his tongue against hers, and she very nearly swooned. He moved his hand around to cup her head, and she was lost.

He was so strong. Perfect.

He nuzzled her neck, trailed kisses down to her collarbone, to where the very top of her dress met her skin.

"I didn't realize I had a schoolmarm fantasy. But it's been there. Buried."

"I'm not sure how to feel about that."

"Flattered," he said. "I'm kidding. Don't feel flattered. Just enjoy it. I know I am."

"I didn't know I had a bad-boy fantasy."

"You didn't. You said yourself, you were warning everybody off me."

She scowled. "I just wanted them to be careful."

"Oh, you didn't want me to get my rough outlaw hands all over them?"

The question made her shiver. "No. Because I didn't understand the benefit of rough hands at the time. I didn't understand the benefit of any hands."

"Oh, Millie," he said. "Not even your own?"

She wrinkled her nose. "That always seemed like more trouble than it was worth."

"Why? Why is something that makes you feel good more trouble than it's worth?"

She didn't have an answer to the question. It was a good one. She didn't know why it didn't seem worthwhile to bring herself pleasure. But then, she lived in an endless cycle of feeling that she was underachieving, and then feeling that she couldn't rest at the end of the day, because she had to do just a little bit more. A little bit of community outreach, a little bit of updating the historical records for the county. Something. Anything.

To make her feel useful. To make her feel . . . at this point, she wasn't even sure. She had been trying so hard . . . for what?

So maybe this was deep. The fulfillment of long-held fantasies that were meant to be. The burying of old hatchets. Or maybe it was just Austin getting his own.

And maybe it was just Millie getting hers.

She couldn't discount that possibility. Maybe, right now, they were the only ones who mattered. So she kissed him as if there was nothing beyond the two bookshelves they stood between. As if there was no history other than theirs.

He growled, and backed her up two steps, pressing her against the wall. She gasped.

She was on fire with anticipation. For what was to come.

For what might happen next. She just wanted him. Needed him. In a way she couldn't describe. Because pleasure, her own pleasure, had just never been this important, and now it was everything. It felt like he might be everything.

Which was ridiculous. That couldn't be right. They'd had a very reasonable discussion about all of that last night and this morning.

But. . . .

For once, don't think.

She let her mind go blessedly blank, and she focused on his hot mouth against her skin. His hands moving over her curves. In the library.

They couldn't have sex in the library.

Except she found that her hands were moving of their own volition, going to the buttons on his shirt, tugging wildly at the fabric. She shouldn't be undressing him. She should let him do it. So that she could claim she had been led into temptation. But no. She was happily doing the leading.

Straight past temptation, right into indulgence.

His growl of appreciation echoed through her. And he pushed her skirts up, bunching the fabric in his fist as he brought it up around her hips, then moved his other hand to touch her bare thighs, and then in between them.

He found her wet and ready for him, and she couldn't even feel embarrassed about it.

"This is the thing," he said against her mouth.

Her heart fluttered. "Is it?"

"Millie," he said, his tone low and indulgent.

And then, he was pushing a finger inside her, then another, working them in and out and driving her to madness.

She curled her toes tight in her shoes and held back a cry.

"Don't do that," he said, making his way to kiss her neck. "Let it out."

He was right. There was no one to hear.

No reason to hold back. She was just doing it to herself.

She imposed so much denial on herself.

She decided to take so little. And now she was going to have it all. She let the cry rise in her throat, escape her lips. She clung to his shoulders and rode his hand as he brought her to a screeching climax, right there.

"Hang on," he said.

He reached into his back pocket and took out his wallet, removed a condom. He undid the front of his jeans, and she watched, rapt, as he rolled the latex onto himself.

And then he lifted her right up off the ground and urged her to wrap her legs around him as he thrust deep inside of her, using the wall to brace them both.

"Well," she said. "I am more convinced than ever that size matters."

"I'll follow up on that when we're done," he said, kissing her, claiming her. She had never . . . in all her life.

She was looking at the spines of the books, looking at that black cowboy hat, the black shirt he was still wearing, and her pale hand up against the fabric. Until she had to close her eyes, because she couldn't do anything but feel the rush of pleasure anymore.

Until everything started to shatter.

She couldn't believe that she was about to come again. Not after she had already. . . .

But then she shattered, her nails digging into him, her cry echoing in these hallowed, silent halls.

And he roared his own completion only a moment later, pulsing inside her as he gave himself up to the need that arced between them.

He set her down slowly, but her legs gave way, and she simply slid down the wall, feet out straight in front of her. "Oh," she said.

"Are you okay?" he asked.

"Yes. I'm just going to need a minute to recover from that."

Or two weeks of bed rest.

"I'll be back."

He turned away from her and she assumed he was going into the bathroom to dispose of the condom. He returned a moment later, blue eyes far too sharp and searching for her liking.

"Now what do you mean about the size thing?"

She feigned a cough.

"Millie."

"You scold me quite a lot."

"You're naughty quite a lot."

She felt ridiculously pleased by that characterization.

"I only meant that, it did occur to me last night that perhaps it felt so good because the dimensions of things increased sensation."

"Go on."

"I also thought I might have been blinded by your overall skill level. That perhaps it wasn't fair to simply attribute the difference to. . . ."

"My cock?"

Her cheeks went flaming hot. "Indeed. But, after this, I'm just saying . . . overall . . . were you a shorter man, were you a less muscular man, you could not have pinned me so effectively to the wall and. . . ."

"Screwed you senseless?"

"Yes," she said, face going red all over again.

"The library," he said looking around. "This feels like a full-circle moment."

"It's definitely a weird bibliophile fantasy."

"I am into it," he said.

"We really do need to plan this event we're supposed to be planning."

"Is the event not this?"

She laughed. "No. It's not. I didn't know you were funny."

"You didn't know me at all."

His words made her sad. It wasn't anything she didn't know already. "I want to know you," she said.

She was aware the words were heavy. That they were potentially ill-advised.

"I'm not actually that hard to know."

"Hard enough."

"And you? You're really easy?"

"There isn't really anything to know. You know everything."

She realized that she was still sitting on the floor, legs spread out in front of her like a debauched ragdoll.

She pushed her skirts back into place. "I was born here. Just like you. I had very few friends growing up."

"Another thing we have in common," he said.

"People already thought they knew who I was because of my last name."

"Obviously," he said.

"You fascinated me," she said. "And I told myself that I didn't have a crush on you. And I warned everybody away from you. But I really do know what you check out from the library. Because I always thought it was so fascinating. And I wanted to know more. Why you were reading, what you were getting out of it. Because . . . I know why I love to read. It's because sometimes I don't have an easy time connecting with people. And the pictures in my head, the people in my head, stories that I can step into, they feel safer. Yes, I love reading history books. But I also love being carried into a story where I can imagine myself being brave. Where I can identify with the hero. That's what I love."

"You know, I didn't want to stay here when I was a kid," he said, walking over to her and sliding down the wall, sitting right beside her. "And my dad was always on about something. Some woman he had met, a poker game he was going to play. The injustice of being born a Wilder. I found it easier to tune him out if I was somewhere else. And he didn't understand books. He couldn't understand why I wanted to do something as dumb as read when there was TV. And when I was a teenager, he would always ask if I shouldn't be out having sex." She looked up at him. "I assure you I have figured out how to do both. I read a couple chapters in my new Jack Reacher book today."

She huffed a laugh. "Well. What a relief."

"I liked books because they gave me a secret world that no one else knew anything about. My dad didn't know that the things I was reading were actually interesting. That they had as much sex and mayhem as anything on TV. It was my secret. What I really liked was that I got to read about people who thought the way I did.

And also people who thought about things differently than I did. It taught me a whole lot about the world off that mountain. And eventually, I didn't feel like I wanted to leave anymore. Because I realized the story of our lives was too interesting. And if I really wanted to know the whole story, I was going to have to write it."

"And that's what you're doing."

"Trying to."

"So you really did have to show up to that town council meeting. Because if you hadn't. . . ." She blinked. "I even had to kiss you. It was what sent me up to the attic."

"I'd believe in fate if she wasn't such a bitch. In my experience."

"Fair," she said. "But I'm not sure fate is a bitch so much as the people in power have always been bastards."

He looked at her as if he was considering the truth of that. "Well. That is a good point."

"Lee Talbot wasn't a hero," she said.

"He probably *thought* he was. I mean, listen. All the money stuff, that was self-indulgent. I won't give him a pass on that. But deciding that he was going to take the Wilder brothers out. . . . Well, maybe he thought he was protecting the town."

She shook her head. "I can't be okay with murder."

"Mostly I'm with you. But just as Austin decided it was all right to steal from people because he needed it, I can sort of see how Lee Talbot thought he was justified in killing a man to remove a danger from the community."

"Has anybody ever told you that you're too empathetic?"

He looked as if she had clocked him upside the head. "No. No one has ever said that to me."

"I've never known somebody to think so much about what other people are feeling."

"Well. I found that life's not very much fun when nobody thinks about you at all. I've tried to be different."

"A lot of people wouldn't try to be better."

"I guess not. But what's the point of being worse?"

He reached across the bare expanse of floor between them and locked his hands with hers. "Okay," she said. "Now I feel like I know you."

"I should hope so."

"How about we present our new version of town history together. We'll work on it. We'll write it. We'll bring it to the town council. But I'm the one who's going to establish the museum. And we are the ones planning Gold Rush Days. So we can have the event with or without plaques. With or without permission. We know the truth."

"Sounds good to me."

They lingered like that for longer than they needed to.

"I need to spend the night at my place tonight," he said.

"Yeah. That's fine. Totally understandable."

"Once you get the schedule nailed down, do you want to come over for dinner and see if Cassidy can actually drive the wagon?"

"I'd love that. Hopefully, I'll have everything finalized tomorrow."

"Perfect. Then I'll see you tomorrow night."

Now he was having sex with her and leaving. He was kissing her goodbye. And she felt bereft. But she wasn't going to go after him. She wasn't going to be ridiculous.

She wasn't.

She waited until she heard the door close behind him. And she still sat there, curling her hands into fists. She could feel him. The impression of his body, all over hers.

She could feel him.

And worst of all, she missed him. Even though he had just been inside her.

Chapter 18

I had hoped the love of a good woman would change me. If I am honest, it did. It made me fierce and protective. It has not made me good, though.

—Austin Wilder's journal, August 18, 1857

He had been texting Millie off and on most of the day, and if Carson and Flynn noticed, they had decided to keep their comments to themselves, so far. Which was good.

The brothers had been out riding, checking the fence line and making sure everything was shipshape. They had a respectable operation, raising organic beef that they sold to local grocery stores, and at different farmers markets. The name of Wilder might be mud in Rustler Mountain, but beyond that? Wilder beef was a lucrative thing.

They had slid right into that niche, and it did well for them.

They'd achieved something their father had never been able to do. Something no Wilder before them had ever been able to do. Because they weren't trying to cheat anybody. They were putting in an honest day's work.

It made a difference.

I have the entire school district committed to coming to Gold Rush Days. Three districts, in fact.

That's amazing.

And that was when he heard it. His brothers. Grunting in a way that was actually designed to get his attention.

He looked up. "You got something to say?"

"No," Carson said. "Nothing."

"Liar. Say it."

"I've never known you to text like a teenage girl," Flynn said.

"I'm planning something."

"What exactly?"

"Millie is coming to dinner."

"Ah," said Carson.

"What?" he asked.

"I think you're sweet on her," said Flynn.

The word made him think of sugar. Which did not make him think of anything that had happened between him and Millie—that had been more hot than sweet. "Well, I think you're an asshole."

"So you're going to tell me that nothing is going on with her?" Austin gave them a hard glare. "Did Cassidy blab?"

Carson and Flynn looked at each other. As if they had just hit the jackpot. "Well, I didn't expect to be proven correct," Flynn nearly crowed.

"I will *wear you to a frazzle*," Austin gritted out.

"Why are you so resistant to it?" Carson asked.

"You. You're asking me that."

"Right. Granted. I can certainly list the downsides."

"And?"

"You're not like us," Flynn said. "You never have been. You think. You don't just act like G.I. Joe over here, who enlisted without giving it a second thought. And you aren't . . . all this." He waved his hand over himself.

Austin crossed his arms and glared at them both. "What am I, then?"

"The thinking man's cowboy," said Carson.

Austin snorted. "Oh, bullshit."

"You're writing a book," Flynn pointed out.

"Well, I *would be*, if I wasn't staying late at the library so often," Austin said.

"I would think that staying late in the library would help you get your book written. Unless you aren't reading in the library," Flynn said meaningfully.

"It's none of your business."

"Be that as it may. I'm intrigued. It's character development."

"Leave my character and its development out of this. She's coming over for dinner and to see Cassidy drive the wagon. She'll be here in thirty minutes. You have to behave yourselves. And maybe you should splash some water on your pits."

"So charming," said Carson.

"A gentleman," said Flynn.

"I never said I was. You all seem to be having some fantasy that I'm turning into another person."

"Would it be so bad?"

"It would be pointless. Because what is it gonna matter?"

"Maybe you could be happy. Maybe just living past thirty-five isn't the goal," Flynn said.

"Clean your own house, you little weasel." His brother was in fact neither little nor a weasel. He was an inch taller than Austin and all lean muscle.

"Boy, you are a cranky bastard."

He mock-kicked at his brother, and then they got back on their horses and rode up to the house. He followed his own advice and freshened up to the best of his ability, just in time for Millie's arrival. Cassidy was nearly vibrating with excitement.

"The other two guessed," he said to Cassidy as Millie got out of her car and began to walk up to the front door. "So I no longer require your discretion."

"I'm free!" She made a dramatic gesture around her head.

"What are you doing?"

"Taking my muzzle off. Now I can speak my mind."

"Please be civilized."

"Where's the fun in that?"

"*Cas.*"

"I'm kidding. I'll be good. I want to drive the wagon."

Cassidy all but tumbled out the door, greeting Millie before he had a chance to.

"This is going to be so fun," she said. "Do I get to drive it around town?"

"Yes. We're going to block off some of the streets. We'll make a route for you." Her eyes met Austin's, and he smiled. She smiled back.

She bit her lip, and he felt that gesture resonate deep inside him. Cassidy was still yammering, but he was only slightly aware of it.

"Obviously we're not going to load the wagons down with bullets and grain," she was saying, "so we can use a team of horses. And we have the old draft boys."

"The draft boys?" Millie asked.

"Yeah. A pair of Clydesdales. They're really old, but they can still pull. They used to be in parades and things. They were glue factory bound, and Austin saved them."

Millie looked at him, and he felt a twinge of discomfort as her eyes skimmed over him. "You did?"

He tried to keep his expression blank. "Once I found out about it, I couldn't let that happen. Couple of fine horses."

"What do you need draft horses for?" Millie asked him.

"*This*, apparently."

"Come on out to the barn. We can get them ready."

The wagon was already sitting out, ready to have the horses hitched up to it. "This will probably disappoint the kids," Cassidy said. "Since every small child knows it was oxen that made up a real wagon team. I mean, those kids have all played *Oregon Trail*."

"They should just be thankful they don't have to ford the mighty Columbia," Austin said.

Cassidy looked bemused. "You don't ford the Columbia. You have to raft it or all your shit will float away."

Millie smiled. "That's true."

All this togetherness between his sister and his . . . whatever she was, was making him itch. This was the problem. He wanted to keep his connection to Millie private. For one thing, he didn't know what the hell to call it. But there was too much throwing them together for them not to be involved with each other. He had spoken the truth when he'd said that they might as well keep going. So he had kept it going . . . in the library. In the library. It was shameful. Awesome, but shameful.

It also proved his point. If there was resistance to be found, neither of them had access to it right now.

Their eyes caught and held.

How had this happened?

He would've said . . . he and Millie could never be a thing.

But he thought of her. How he had seen her for all those years in the library. She had always stood out to him. Because he couldn't help but wonder what it was like to have all that Talbot privilege be your world, from the beginning.

And maybe he'd also wondered what it was like to be good. Born good. Rather than born bad.

Of course, also, her father had been his nemesis. It was complicated.

Yeah. Complicated.

He thought of everything they had uncovered in the past few days.

Everything was shifting and changing.

What he needed to do was write his book. Not worry about tours through the streets, or where he could next have her.

But he was thinking about both of those things.

Hell.

He followed Cassidy and Millie at a slight distance as they went into the barn, and Cassidy scrambled for the stalls. "Loco and Moco," she said. Then she opened the stalls up, grabbed the oversized bridles for the horses, and went on in.

"Don't do it by yourself," he said.

They were gentle beasts. They really were, but they were huge, and he didn't love the idea of his sister disappearing into the stall.

He brushed by Millie as he went inside, and she stood in the doorway, watching as he and Cassidy outfitted the bay horses.

"They're beautiful," Millie said. "Twins."

"Close enough to it," he said.

"I can't believe that those two beautiful animals were going to be destroyed."

"Human nature," he said. "When people can't make use of something in the way they want to, they're done with it."

"I didn't expect the horses to be a metaphor."

"I'm a writer. Everything is a goddamned metaphor."

Cassidy snickered. "You're so grumpy about it. Like you think creativity makes you less manly."

He shot his sister a look. "I'm not worried about my masculinity, thanks."

He wasn't. He never even gave it a thought. Only the insecure worried about such things. He just felt exposed by his desire to write. But Millie already knew. Knew that he overthought everything. That he tried to figure out the story behind everything and everyone.

His blessing and his curse, he supposed.

He helped Cassidy get the horses hitched up to the wagon. It was a grand sight. The stark black bridles, reins, and blinders on the tan-colored horses, the bells that jingled merrily to signal their coming. The wagon with its big, white canvas draped over the top in an arch. Inside were benches for kids to sit on. Nicer than what the settlers would've had in a wagon train. Where passengers would've been propped up on supplies.

"This is amazing," said Millie. "I want to go for a ride."

"All right. Cassidy, do you want to give us a test drive?"

"I definitely do."

He went around to the back of the wagon and put his foot up on the step. He extended his hand. "Ma'am."

She blushed as she took it, and he helped lift her up inside, following close behind. Once they were seated inside, he turned and hollered to Cassidy, "Get along now."

He heard the snap of the reins, and the jingle bells started to ring. Then the wagon rolled into action along the bumpy dirt road.

They pitched and rolled in the back, and Millie grabbed hold of his forearm. Her touch was like electricity. His gaze met hers, and he smiled. "You know, Austin wrote a bit about the Oregon Trail in his journal."

"When did they make the crossing?"

"Eighteen forty-eight to forty-nine. Their dad passed, and then they were on their own. Just before they made it to Oregon. They decided to head down this way because there was talk of gold. California gold rush. But they were starving."

"That's so sad. And their mother was already gone?"

"She died giving birth. Before they set out west. That left Austin to care for his brothers. I think that might be the only good part of the story, you know." He felt slightly emotional even thinking about it. Maybe because he had taken care of his own siblings. Maybe because he actually knew what that was like. "That he didn't know Jesse and William were hanged. I think that would've felt like the biggest failure to him. After he'd done so much to protect them. His wife and children were all right after he died. His widow never remarried. She always mourned him, I think. But they were okay. I think if he'd known his brothers' fate, though . . . that would've made it all feel pointless."

"That's horrendously sad."

"It is." He cleared his throat. The noise from the wheels and the jingle of the bells, combined with the clip-clop of the horse hooves kept Cassidy from hearing their conversation. "I get it. I know what it's like to just want to protect your siblings. More than anything. And to know that you can't. Not from life. Not from how hard it can be. From the way everybody treats you. I consider it a blessing that Flynn and Cassidy seem to be immune to the talk in town. They find it funny. But I worry sometimes. That with Cassidy it's all just bravado. Hell. I worry about it with Flynn. He seems to like the chip on his shoulder. At least, that's what he pretends. But I don't know that I buy it. Anyway, there's nothing I can do about it. Because they're adults. It's a hell of a thing. To wish that your family could somehow be better off than you are, when you don't even know what to do for yourself. How can I teach them better if I didn't know better?"

"I think you knew better enough," she said. "You all seem so happy. I was struck by that the other night at the Watering Hole. I don't know how I imagined that bar, but it wasn't . . . that. It was welcoming. And it was . . . it was its own kind of good. I was always told that couldn't be true. There was just one way to be. I'm so desperately sick of appearances being the most important thing.

"Because at the end of the day, that's my family legacy. Men who didn't care about really being good. About *really* having honor. It was all stolen valor, in a way. A sheriff's badge to cover up the fact that they ought to be in handcuffs." She looked at him. "I want you to tell me the truth. What was my dad like?"

Her eyes were keen, and she looked so sharply at him, it made his chest hurt. "He was *your* dad."

"But I didn't know him. Not like you did. You know that. I didn't know who he really was. He arrested you. He. . . ."

"Held me in contempt? I don't mean in the court sense."

"Yes," she said.

"He wasn't a bad man, Millie," he said, looking down at his hands. "He wasn't cruel. He wasn't *friendly*. He definitely seemed a bit weary of having to deal with Wilders. And you know, fair enough. My dad was a mainstay in the drunk tank. He *earned* that. And at the time, hell, I earned my stripes too. I made sure I did."

"Because you got so much crap that wasn't earned."

"But not from him," he said. "I think it's important for you to know that. Your dad didn't antagonize me. He didn't target me. I did what I did, and I paid the price for it. He followed the letter of the law."

"What a low bar we set for our heroes," she said softly.

"But the regular folks don't know that, do they?" He looked at her. He meant her.

"No," she said. "It makes you feel like you can't live up. But. . . ."

"Your dad was a decent man," he said. "Don't go confusing Lee Talbot with your father. Any more than you should be confused with your father, or I should be confused with Austin. We are our own selves."

"That's true," she said. "Thank you."

"Are you making out back there?"

He reached forward and thumped the back of Cassidy's seat. "If so then you just interrupted."

"I'm your little sister. That's my job."

"Get it together, you weasel."

When he looked at Millie, she was smiling. And it made him smile right back.

When Cassidy was done driving the wagon, she hopped out and scurried around to where Millie and Austin were sitting. "Austin," she said. "Have you shown Millie your sharpshooting?"

Millie turned to him, her eyes wide. "Sharpshooting?"

He scowled, irritation lancing him. "Don't bring the sharpshooting into this. We can't do that on Gold Rush Days."

"Who cares about that? It's just cool."

"You do . . . sharpshooting?"

"It's dumb stuff. It's Hancock stuff. Showmanship."

"Well," Millie said, "why do you do it then?"

"My dad thought it would pay to be a quick draw. But this isn't the Wild West. We were all pretty good, though. We could shoot playing cards out of the air from the time we were little."

Millie suddenly looked determined. "I want to see."

"Cassidy. . . ."

"You love me," she said.

"Yeah. Just barely."

But Millie had gotten such an interesting light in her eyes, and he wanted to impress her. He wanted to know more. To see more. He felt as if he was in high school, trying to impress a girl.

How had it come to this?

He didn't need to impress her. He'd screwed her senseless in the library.

Just the memory made his body get tight.

She was a real firecracker. This mouse.

Damn.

"Come on, then," he said. "Let's do some sharpshooting."

Chapter 19

How can she love an outlaw? I ask myself that at least once yearly. I have lived in a way that doesn't allow for fear. I fear asking her that question.

—Austin Wilder's journal, January 9, 1859

Millie found herself piled into the back of a pickup truck that Cassidy was driving, with Flynn sitting across from her and Austin. There was a grin on his face, and her heart was fluttering wildly. This felt like the kind of teenage stuff she had never done. Like something dangerous and sort of special. Hanging out with her boyfriend and. . . .

Not that he was her *boyfriend*.

The word *boyfriend* could never apply to Austin. It sounded juvenile and soft in a way he could never be. He was too much a man for a label like that.

When they had said sharpshooting, they weren't kidding. They had old-fashioned holsters, and pistols just like the ones back in the good old days.

"This is the pistol that ended the first Austin Wilder's life," Flynn said theatrically. "Well, it's the same kind anyway."

"Yeah, Dad figured we'd better learn how to shoot. Since we had a legacy of being shot at," Austin said.

She blinked. "But there are, of course, more modern guns."

"Our dad wasn't *practical*," Flynn said. "He was *dramatic*."

Millie couldn't help but think Flynn seemed to have inherited some of that flare for drama. He was very handsome and had an air of volatility about him that Austin just didn't possess. Women loved

Flynn, and she could see why, even though for her, Austin was definitely the prize.

But she could understand in that moment how their dad had managed to catch so many women. There was something intoxicating about the Wilder men.

"Oh," she said.

The shooting range was out in a distant part of their property, with a big pile of gravel backing the targets, and mountains beyond that.

"We want to know that the bullets stop if we miss the target. You don't want them flying past where you intend."

She nodded. She knew the basics of firearm safety, though she had never fired one herself.

The little shooting range was surprising. With bright-colored targets in different shapes. It was almost like an arcade. Some were classic bull's-eye targets in red and white, others the silhouette of an angry sheriff, and big grizzly bears.

She laughed. "This is . . . this is great."

"Cassidy and I built it," said Flynn. "Austin obviously thinks it's a little bit too silly."

Austin huffed. "Yeah, but I can outshoot all of you."

Cassidy parked the truck, and they clambered out, making their way over to the targets.

"Who taught Cassidy to shoot?" Millie asked.

"I did," said Austin.

"But you said it was silly."

Austin shrugged a shoulder. "But if we knew how to do it, then she had to know how to do it too."

Millie couldn't argue with that logic.

Austin lined everybody up. "Okay," he said. "Everybody get their ear protection out." Cassidy opened the box she was carrying, which held big, brightly covered ear protection. She handed one to Millie, and everybody put a set over their ears.

"You stand behind us," Austin said.

She scrambled back, moving to the bed of the truck. "No worries."

He chuckled. "I'm not really worried."

"All right," he said. "We quick draw, and we fire. Ten rounds. Points for whoever gets them unloaded fastest, and then points for accuracy. When I beat your asses, don't cry."

Millie sat, rapt.

Austin turned to look at her and tipped his black cowboy hat, and she very nearly swooned. If she was honest, she very nearly had an orgasm.

"Oh my," she said.

Then he turned his focus back to the targets.

She watched as they all did a quick draw from their holsters, extended their arms, and shot. Cocked the hammer again, shot. Austin's movements were swift. Precise. He was firing off shots in rapid succession, his muscles flexing.

She bit her lip, uncertain when this sort of display had become sexy to her. Who cared? She just thought it was sexy.

It was over before she knew it. But Austin finished first.

"Fastest," he said, when the sound of the shots had died down.

She took her ear protection off, and it pulled hair into her face. She fought to untangle herself as she spoke up on Austin's behalf. "He was."

Flynn looked at her. "You're just saying that because he's your boyfriend."

Her face went hot, and she waited for Austin to correct his brother. But he didn't.

He just gave him a withering look.

"He was fastest," Cassidy said, nodding. "I'm woman enough to admit it."

She followed them as they went to examine the different targets. Austin's bullets had all hit dead center.

"You're a sharpshooter," she said.

"Yeah. I'm not bad."

"Oh, for God's sake," said Flynn. "Get a room."

"Can't I appreciate good marksmanship without it being prurient?" she asked, turning on her best stereotypical librarian's voice.

Flynn straightened his shoulders. "Sorry."

She suppressed a smile, her eyes meeting Austin's.

It *was* prurient. She knew it. She was comfortable with it.

"You want a turn?"

"Oh, I couldn't," she said.

"I think you could."

Austin opened up the chamber of the pistol and reloaded it. She watched as he dropped each silver bullet inside. Then popped it back in place. "It's easy. And I won't let you get hurt."

She put her ear protection back on.

"Never aim at anything you don't intend to hit."

"I know," she said.

"Yeah. Well, knowing and doing are two different things. As I think you're well aware."

She shifted.

He came to stand beside behind her, his heat and strength enveloping her as he put the gun into her hand and showed her how to hold it. Then he had her raise her hands and aim directly at the target. "Now when you're ready, squeeze the trigger. Don't be shocked by the recoil. You saw how much power it had when I shot."

She nodded. "See that bead there in the notch? There you go. Now squeeze."

She took a deep breath, squeezed the trigger, and scooted back as the blast rang out. Austin braced her with his body, laughter rumbling through his chest. "That was a hell of a recoil."

"Goodness," she said.

"Go ahead. Take some more shots."

"I don't know."

"An outlaw would, Millie Talbot."

That did it. She raised her arms again, cocked the gun, and fired.

This time the recoil didn't surprise her so much. This time, she didn't nearly get knocked off her feet.

"Go on," he said.

So she did. She fired again. And then again. Power coursed through her veins. A kind of giddy heat. She had never done this before. But what would her life have been like if she had known that her ancestors weren't quite so perfect?

What if she had been free to be something a little bit wilder?

A little more *free*. What if she hadn't spent so much time trying to be good? Trying to be safe.

She fired again and again, only dimly aware that Austin was no longer standing right behind her. That he wasn't holding on to her.

She was lost in the exhilaration of it.

And when she was finished, she turned to him. "Thank you. I . . . I needed that.

She didn't even know how to articulate what he was giving her. This man. This man she had known all her life but hadn't known really.

"Are you feeling peckish?" Austin asked.

"A bit."

She wondered for a moment if it was a double entendre, but if so, the answer was still yes.

"Well, let's go back to the house for dinner. Perry and Carson are providing."

They drove back across the ranch in the old pickup truck, the wind whipping through Millie's hair.

Austin dropped his black cowboy hat right on her head. She smiled up at him.

"Outlaw," he said.

And she let his approval warm her all the way to her toes.

This time, when she came into the house for dinner, she wasn't sure if she felt more comfortable or less comfortable. She'd had sex with Austin twice. And as far as she knew, that made her the world record holder in repeat sex with Austin. He was much more experienced than she was, generally speaking. But she was a first for him too. And she clung to that. Cassidy and Flynn clearly knew what was happening between them, and they'd been. . . .

They'd been so nice to her today.

But there was also Carson. And there was Perry, and even Dalton, who seemed to be part of the package deal with the Wilders. It mattered so much to her that they approve of her.

At dinner, she marveled once more at how they all shared.

Dalton was there again, and so was Perry, who seemed to act as an emotional support companion for Carson. She hadn't yet witnessed any of Carson's moods, but the way people talked about him, the way they moved as if on eggshells around him, let her know there was a lot of pain there.

Her own family had been structured so differently. But what struck her about this crew was the way they took care of each other. She wondered if that was a side effect of being on the fringes of society.

They couldn't count on others' help, so they came together themselves.

It created a tight-knit feeling that she had never experienced between family members before.

Not that her family wasn't lovely. But . . . it wasn't this.

"The covered wagon ride was a rousing success," said Cassidy. "It's going to be so much fun taking wagonloads of kids around."

"Are parents going to have to sign a special permission slip?" Dalton asked. "Because I definitely would want to know who was driving my kids around."

"You'd have to know who all your kids were first, Dalton."

"Hey," he said. "I don't have any kids."

Cassidy looked at him meaningfully. "That you know of."

"I am a man who takes safety very seriously."

"Sure," she said. "Because accidents never happen."

"Can you not," Flynn said. "This kind of talk makes me nervous."

Carson chuckled quietly.

"What?" Flynn asked.

"Oh. You people. Like having a child would be a terrible thing. I forget how young you are." He shook his head and took a bite of his dinner roll.

"Feel free to go out and get some kids, Carson."

"I'm just saying. Having to grow up and deal with life wouldn't be the worst thing for any of you."

"I think Carson just advised me to go out and get knocked up," said Cassidy, looking directly at Austin.

"If that's what you heard just now, then you're beyond help. And not my problem."

Millie smiled softly as she listened to the conversation.

She had hoped to have a baby in the next year or so. That was part of why she and Michael had finally decided to get married.

She couldn't mourn the loss of a cheating future husband. But at thirty, her biological clock was beginning to tick, and the idea of having to start all over again. . . . She didn't want to wait until she'd have difficulty conceiving. She looked across the table at Austin and felt uncomfortable. She shouldn't have looked at him. Not when she was thinking about babies. The conversation moved on to less touchy subjects.

"Has Austin told all of you about our historical findings?" she asked.

The siblings exchanged glances.

"Yeah," said Flynn. "But the truth is, it matters the most to him. It's quite literally his name being cleared."

"Not cleared," Austin said. "It's . . . it's just knowing our ancestor wasn't as bad as he was made out to be."

"Definitely not."

"Has Austin shown you the journal yet?" Cassidy asked.

"No."

He flicked her a glance. "I'll show you after dinner."

They fell into chatter about Rustler Mountain and its history, its good guys and bad guys. High on the list of bad guys was Butch Hancock the Traitor.

"I mean the thing is," said Flynn, "the Wilders never expected anything from the Talbots. They've never been our friends. No offense. Butch Hancock was the one who got the Wilders into thieving. And then he gave them up. Like he wasn't the one leading the charge."

"If there can't be honor among thieves, where is there honor?" Cassidy asked.

"Plenty of places," Carson said. "I'm sure."

"You know what I mean," said Cassidy. "They were like a family, and Butch was supposed to have their back. But instead he stabbed it. We knew he did. We knew it. That's why I cross the street when I see Jessie Jane Hancock. And I refuse to get any of my horseshoeing done by her."

"You drive somewhere else to use a different farrier?" Millie asked.

"Yes," said everybody around the table.

"That's the thing I find so fascinating," Millie said. "You all participate in the blood feud. Even though you say it's not fair when it's being done to you."

"It's not about fair," Flynn said.

"Didn't anyone ever tell you that life's not fair?" Dalton asked.

"Yes. But I'm sort of interested in making it more fair if possible."

"I think it depends on the nature of the crime," Austin said. "We had a Talbot sit down to our table before we ever had a Hancock in this place."

"And we never will have a Hancock in this place," Flynn said. "Absolutely not.

"Well. I think Jessie Jane is interesting," Millie said.

"So do I," said Perry. "She's got style."

"She's a menace," Flynn said.

And he left it at that. But there was no explanation required. Jessie was a hard-drinking, knife-throwing, competitive black-smithing, Wild West–reenacting hellion. Her family exploited and monetized their outlaw connection. Butch Hancock's Wild West Show ran it all through the summer, with special events around Christmastime too. But it was definitely a sensationalized version of local history.

On a school tour of the East Coast, Millie had once gone to Salem, Massachusetts. There, she had learned very quickly that the town was divided into two camps: the sensationalized tours and the historical tours. One portrayed witches and magic, and the hysteria that had gripped the town as being real. While the other presented facts. She felt that was the difference between the Hancocks and what she was trying to do. She had a feeling the truth wouldn't dampen the Hancocks' version of events at all. It would just give them another villain. And the crowds loved a villain.

They finished dinner and enjoyed another one of Perry's delicious desserts before everyone bid Austin good night. She was thankful that he'd offered to show her the journal after dinner. Because she didn't have to question whether or not he wanted her to file out with everyone else.

Still, she felt an expanding tension in her midsection when she realized that they were alone in the house.

"Come on. I'll show you the journal."

She nodded and followed him into a precisely organized office space.

Everything was immaculate, which didn't surprise her. Because as she had come to realize, that was Austin.

He had a computer and a notepad on an otherwise completely clean desk. And then there were bookshelves filled with books. Of all varieties.

"I didn't know you also bought books," she said.

"Yeah," he said. "Anything I think I might need as a constant reference. Or favorites. You know how that is."

She walked over to the shelf and touched the spines of *Hatchet, Caddie Woodlawn, Lord of the Rings, Holes.*

"I liked that one when I was a kid," he said, gesturing to *Holes.* "Something about seeing the treatment of kids that are considered delinquents made so . . . literal. Sentencing them to dig a hole every day and claiming it builds character. Using them to accomplish a secret goal, while pretending the work they're doing doesn't matter. I don't know. It spoke to me."

"I never read that one."

"You should. It holds up."

"*The Legend of Jimmy Spoon*," she said. "That one I did read. And *Jimmy Spoon and the Pony Express.*"

"Favorites," he said.

"This is a library any child would love to—"

She looked at him, their eyes meeting, and then she looked away. "I mean, it's a shelf full of good memories."

"Yeah," he said. "I mean, that's the other great thing, isn't it? When you read, you can make memories anywhere. So, my dad could be drunk and stumbling about in the kitchen, and I could be going on an adventure in the Wild West. It made childhood memories for me that I wouldn't have had otherwise." He paused for a long moment. "Your mom meant a lot to me," he said. "Just so you know."

"Thank you." She didn't expect to get emotional then. But she could feel sorrow tightening her chest. "She was a really wonderful person. She made me who I am, more than anyone else. Even more than history."

"Yeah. I think that was part of my problem. There was nothing but a big hole where my mom used to be. So I had to fill it with something. The scorn of the town. That was kind of what ended up going in there."

"Why did your mom leave?"

"A question for the ages. No. I think the whole situation was too . . . it was too damn much for her. Why would she want to stay? Who wants to live like this?"

"You all chose it."

"Yeah. But we're committed to making something better out of it, and I don't know how much you remember my dad, but he just wasn't. In some ways, I think he was harder to live with than someone who's truly evil. He never thought past his nose. Never gave a shit about anybody but himself. He wanted to feel good and have fun. He could be a really fun dad, actually. Until you realized that you couldn't trust him. Because he wasn't doing what he needed to do to keep us safe. He wasn't taking care of us. Not really. And you internalize all that until nothing seems all that safe. I had to fight to make this place livable. For all of us."

"That's why you're so neat and clean," she said.

"Yes ma'am. Kind of control freak 101."

"I can't blame you."

"No."

He grabbed a small leather book off the shelf and extended his hand toward her. "This is it."

"Oh."

She had forgotten why they were here. The past. She was much more interested in him, right in that moment.

She opened up the book, staring at the neat handwriting she hadn't expected from an outlaw.

Each entry was long. They spoke of events, feelings. Fears.

Her heart stopped when she opened it up to a page where he talked about seeing Katherine for the first time, even though he didn't know her name. It was vivid. His description of his feelings. Of how the world seemed to stop. Of feeling he wasn't worthy of her.

She looked up at Austin. "It's beautiful writing."

"Yeah. It is. It's what made me think maybe I could write. Because he did. And if things had been different . . . who knows what all he would've written."

Not for the first time, she felt desperately sad about the waste. Of a life. Of a man.

It was easy to see the people of the past in terms of dry facts and sepia-toned, stern-faced portraits. But these journal entries were funny, sad, filthy.

They were a 3D portrait of a man she could never know.

"But you're not just compiling these entries in your book."

He shook his head. "No. I'm making a novel out of it. It's a Western, I guess. If I had to choose a genre."

"It can't be a romance," she said softly. "Because he dies at the end."

"Everybody dies at some point. They ended up together. Just not for as long as either of them wanted."

"True, but I think if you put the death in the book, it won't be considered a romance."

"Yeah. You may have a point."

"Can I read some of your book?"

He looked as if she had slapped him.

"Well, you want to publish it. So you want other people to read it. You've talked to a literary agent."

"Yeah," he said slowly. "But it's not finished."

"Please."

He hesitated, then sat down at his computer. He minimized one window and expanded another. Then scrolled up to chapter one.

"It's not going to entertain you," he said as he stood to make room for her.

"Do you feel honor bound to talk down your accomplishments?" she asked as she sat down in the office chair.

"No, it's just you already know the story, and also you read a lot, so you'll be able to see how workmanlike my prose is."

She laughed and spun around in the chair. "Oh no, workmanlike prose. How will I cope?"

Their eyes met and she could see the moment he thought about leaning in and kissing her. He didn't. She wished he had.

He straightened. "I mean, hey, if you want to bore yourself."

She swatted at him and then spun back around to the computer, leaning in.

Before she knew it, she had been swept away to a different time. To the eighteen hundreds, when a young boy named Austin Wilder had found himself orphaned, with two younger brothers to care for. The novel swept her through the story of how he chose to become an outlaw, the guilt he felt over enjoying winning when a take was particularly hard. And the initial conflict he felt about whether or not he was still a man his father would've been proud of. Whether or not he was good.

Austin walked out of the room and came back in no fewer than

three times, but she was caught up in his words. The way he captured feelings that were so complicated in his stark sentences.

She could see all the care he put into understanding every person that appeared on the page.

It was just like him. It was the way he thought about people.

She read every word hungrily, not just because it was a good
story, though it was, but because it felt like a window into who he
was that wouldn't have been opened to her otherwise.

And somehow, as the words filtered through her, she realized
she knew him better than she had ever known Michael. Not just because of the conversations they'd had, though they'd had some deep,
frank conversations, but because of his writing. And because of their
physical intimacy. It was a truly incredible realization.

He walked back into the room, and she looked up at him. "This
is amazing, Austin. It's beautifully written. I feel like I understand
him. Deeply and . . . it's so sad. But beautiful all the same time, because you've captured what our retelling of history has missed. His
complexity. You're right, he wasn't totally a good guy. Or a hero.
But anyone who thinks they might not have ended up in that same
position isn't being honest with themselves."

"You know, I wish we could learn more about Lee Talbot. I wish I
could know what he thought. If he thought he was a hero at the beginning. If taking money here and there started to get too enticing until
he was doing things he wasn't proud of, but couldn't stop. I wonder."

"Yes. But you have done a really beautiful job of showing people
how complicated Austin was. Plus, it's just a very good book."

And right then, he looked so pleased it was almost better than
sex. Almost.

"Well, I appreciate that."

"I'm not just saying it."

"I know. I bet you've never just said anything to keep the peace
a day in your life."

"You're right. I haven't."

She felt proud then that he understood her. In ways no one else
had ever tried to understand.

He moved to her and bent down to kiss her. She felt it all through her body.

Ask me to stay.

She hadn't brought anything with her, and it would be so impractical.

"Thank you," she said. "For earlier."

He nodded. "For dinner?"

"No. The shooting. For . . . you make me feel wild."

"That's weird, because you make me feel a little bit calmer."

They sat there and looked at each other, and she had the feeling that they had crossed some invisible line. She didn't know if they could ever go back.

Ask me to stay.

"Why don't you spend the night?" he said.

All the breath left her body. "Oh. I mean . . . I . . . okay."

She ought to protest. Even though she wanted to stay. She ought to say that she didn't have anything with her, and it wasn't the best idea. But she wanted to stay.

"Your family will probably see my car in your driveway," she said. Echoing the risk he had taken in spending the night at her place.

"They already know."

And it didn't make her feel embarrassed. It made her feel . . . special. Happy. It made her feel that maybe she mattered. He had let her read his book.

She had to mean something to him.

She wanted to stay. She wanted to be with him. So she let him sweep her up into his arms, let him drop his mouth down on hers for a devastating kiss. She let the heat explode between them. And she luxuriated in it. In the way she felt different, but also more herself.

That was what struck her hard in the chest as Austin lifted her up and cradled her against him. As he kissed her, walking down the hall into his bedroom. His bedroom!

This felt more real. More real than anything she had ever done. More hers.

Authentic. Not for performance. Not to get kudos. She just wanted to feel. This. Everything.

And she was in his bedroom.

She would never have thought she was the one who would end up there. Of all her friends. Of everyone she had ever known. She had been the one who'd warned them all against such a downfall. But she had been an idiot. Because nothing about Austin Wilder was a downfall.

He had lifted her up. Stitched together some old wounds that she hadn't even known were there. He had fixed so much in her. In so many ways.

Even as he had deconstructed the narrative around her family, he had set her free.

And it didn't matter if no one else could understand it.

It didn't even matter if it made sense. She knew it. She felt it.

She was free to be herself, to take what she wanted.

She would end stronger than she was before, even though the idea of her connection to Austin ever ending made her feel heart-broken.

She would be better for having loved him.

She wasn't even going to examine that thought. Wasn't going to tell herself that there was no way she could be in love with him so soon, so fast.

She had spent six years thinking she was in love with Michael.

She had never really known him. He had never known her, but how could he have? She hadn't really known herself.

She was just now stitching this version of herself, remaking it into a new design.

Austin was showing her how to be wild. More importantly, how to be her.

He set her down at the foot of his bed. "You really like picking me up," she said.

"You're very pickupable."

"What does that mean?"

"I think you can figure it out. You have a way with words."

"So do you. Though I'm not sure that's one of them."

She wasn't worried whether she was good enough. Whether he liked her. Right now, there were no barriers between them. No labels. She was just Millie. And he was just Austin. She felt as if she had read him when she had read that manuscript. As if the words were written on his heart and soul.

She was totally comfortable calling that love.

It was more than she'd ever had with any other man. More than she'd ever wanted. She also wasn't stupid enough to think that everything had suddenly changed for him, just because it had changed for her.

She didn't need it to. Right now, she just felt happy. That she loved somebody in a way that wasn't pathetic.

That wasn't about making herself good enough.

This was just about feeling something glorious for another person.

Seeing him. Being seen by him.

She hadn't understood how wonderful that could be.

Maybe because she hadn't really understood herself, much less what she actually wanted. From anything.

Somewhere inside herself, she had decided she needed to make her parents proud above all else. And she had decided that would look a certain way. Especially after her mother was gone.

Maybe it was trying to deal with her own sadness.

Maybe she had taken that seat at the library partly because she had missed her mother so much, and she had been so desperate to fill the empty space inside herself that she had filled the space in the library, thinking it might somehow be the same.

That mixed-up train of thought had taken her to a dead end where she hadn't been happy at all. Where she hadn't known who she was or what she wanted. Austin had freed her from that. Challenging everything she thought she knew about herself. Realizing high school Millie would be shocked and disappointed to see her in Austin's bedroom now made her feel good.

Because high school Millie had just been afraid. Afraid of doing the wrong thing. Afraid of disappointing people. Tonight, she wasn't scared of anything at all.

So she kissed him. Kissed him and let him take her clothes off with the lights on. Let him look at her as if she was a decadent treat.

She kissed him and stripped his clothes off, marveling at his masculine strength. At his beauty.

She moved her fingertips over his chest, down his ridged abdomen. "You are. . . ." She clenched her teeth together for a moment, gathering her courage. "You are the sexiest man I've ever seen."

A slow smile spread across his face. "You do things to me. I don't even understand what it is. Magic, maybe. I've been turning it over in my head all day. Trying to figure out why the hell I can't stop thinking about you. Because that's not me. I don't get hung up on anyone. It's not just women. I don't have a lot of connections. I have my family. That's pretty much it. And today . . . today I thought about you. All damn day. And I . . . you're right. I have a way with words. Most people don't know it. But I do. I've got a good vocabulary, but I can't find a word for this. You're beautiful, yes. I can't say that enough. Sexy. I'm drawn to you. But it's something deeper than beauty."

It wasn't a declaration of love. But why should it be? It was still something special. Something that made her feel new. Something that made her feel glorious and special.

He had made it clear they were going to end up together. She could deal with that. As long as she mattered.

As long as their time together changed him as it had changed her.

She had never really believed that sex could be transformative. Maybe because the sex she'd had wasn't. Not in any way.

But with Austin . . . it was different. They were different.

When they didn't have words, they found a new way to communicate with their bodies. It was electric.

It moved her.

To new places, new heights.

It wasn't just the ecstasy, but the intimacy.

And it was different, when you really knew a man.

She really knew this man.

He gathered her into his arms and kissed her. His skin was hot, his kiss was deep.

She arched against him, reveling in how beautiful she did feel.

She had always felt like a consolation prize. As if Michael was doing her a favor. As if he was the better-looking one in their pairing. She told herself her personality compensated for lack of beauty.

But Austin made her feel beautiful. Kindled a bright, warm spark in the center of her chest. He changed the way she felt. About herself, about the world.

With his touch. With his words.

With everything that he was.

He laid her down on the bed and made magic over her body. She arched against him, and he kissed her. Everywhere.

He made her see stars.

She clung to him as he created a storm between them. And she rode it out, with the two of them reaching the peak at the same time, holding each other as they trembled through the end.

"Stay," he said.

She did.

He turned to her through the night. There was something so perfect about it. Something so raw and honest.

And she felt stripped clean, exposed, in the very best way.

Warm and cozy in his bed, and with no desire to leave.

I love you welled up in her throat, but she didn't say it.

"You want to get up early with me and do chores?" he asked, whispering into the darkness.

It was already early. They had barely gotten any sleep.

"I would love to."

Because in the absence of being able to say *I love you*, that would have to do.

Chapter 20

There are three mouths to feed now. And it's a burden, no mistake. But what did I survive all this time for if not for this? At least now I have them.

—Austin Wilder's journal, August 10, 1862

She stayed all night at his place, and he didn't worry about his siblings seeing her car there. Didn't even worry when she sat at his table, sipping coffee, wearing the same clothes she'd been in the night before.

It was a Sunday, and the library wasn't open, which meant that he could have her all day if he wanted to.

"Care to ride along while I do my chores?" he asked.

"Sure."

The ranch was a cocoon. He wasn't foolish enough to think otherwise. There was an element of fantasy about it. Here there were no consequences to the two of them being openly together as there would be in town.

Together. Was that what this was?

He took her out in the truck and drove all over the property. Eventually, he met up with his brothers, and they tried to show her how to mend fence.

He smiled at her determination.

He couldn't say for sure whether he simply hadn't seen her accurately before, or whether she had changed in these last few days.

Maybe it was a little bit of both.

Maybe he could take a little bit of credit for her spark.

He pushed back at that.

Since when had he ever done anything positive for someone else?

Cassidy. Carson. Flynn. Are you really going to claim you did nothing for your own siblings?

That was weird. That internal voice insisting he take credit for something that anybody would do.

How could you ignore family who needed you?

Not even his dad had done that. He had tried. He had just been bad at it.

He hadn't sent them out to fend for themselves. Hadn't abandoned them outright the way their mother had. She had seen so little in each of them that she had just . . . given them up.

Millie had Carson's hat on and was pulling out a stubborn nail that was embedded deeply into a fence post. She yanked so hard that when it gave, she stumbled backward and fell on her rear. He was moving before he could even think about it, lifting her to her feet. "Careful now," he said, looking at her.

He understood now how an outlaw could find himself falling for a sweet little thing.

Could find himself wanting to rearrange himself, his life, to make space for this . . . breath of hope. It filled his lungs now.

What he wished he understood was how a woman like Millie could fall for an outlaw.

It didn't matter that he had done a lot of good with his life. He was trying. He was alive. And hell, that was several steps better than most of his fucking family. But it didn't change the way he felt inside, and that was the thing he didn't know how to fix. How to handle.

"Why don't we go drive some cattle?"

Her eyes brightened. "That sounds extremely Western."

"Yeehaw."

The day passed quickly, and once they were finished, they were all hot and dusty, Millie included.

Cassidy offered to loan her some clothes, which was how she

ended up freshly showered, wearing a white T-shirt and jeans, and making his heart do things he didn't know it could do.

"We need to go down to the bar," Cassidy said. "Celebrate Millie's first day as a cowgirl."

"I don't know if I passed for a cowgirl," Millie said, but she looked so pleased that she obviously wanted to.

"Sure you did," he said, lifting her up and pulling her to him. "Let's do this."

He knew what he was suggesting. He was suggesting that they take this relationship and bring it down to town. He didn't know where in the hell that was going to lead, didn't think it was smart at all, frankly. In fact, he would say it was a god-awful idea.

But he wanted it.

With a ferocity that surprised him. He couldn't remember ever wanting anything so much, and hell, there was just enough bad in his blood that he didn't know how to resist the urge either.

"Okay," she said. "I'd like that."

His siblings drove in one vehicle, he took his truck, and Millie drove in her car. Once she took the car back to her place, he had her get into his truck, and he drove them both to the bar.

When they walked inside, it was already packed.

Live music was playing, and there was dancing and several rowdy games of darts. The lighting was just dim enough to disguise the grime in the place, and as always, there was that hint of danger hanging in the air, that little edge that made the distinction between this bar and the one down the road where the tourists would feel welcome.

Jessie Jane Hancock was down at the end of the bar, pointing at people and filling out sheets of paper. Flynn bristled. "Oh, good. The bad element's here."

"We are all the bad element," said Carson.

"Hey, Wilders," Jessie said. "I'm taking bets."

"Gus," Austin shouted. "You're letting her be a bookie in here?"

"Like I'm in a position to play morality police," said Gus.

"Who do you like for the fight?" Jessie asked.

"What fight?" Millie whispered.

"Librarian," Jessie said. "You want to bet?"

"Oh." Millie shook her head. "No, thank you."

Austin put his arm around her and began to guide her confidently through the bar. Jessie Jane's eyebrows winged up. "Interesting choice, Wilder."

"Since when were you ever in a position to comment on someone else's choices," Flynn said as he walked by Jessie.

"A big fuck-you to you too, Flynn," she said. "I can comment on whatever I want. Even a hot mess is allowed to have opinions."

"Keep them to yourself," Flynn said.

The rest of his siblings ignored their banter.

"I'm kind of surprised she recognized me," said Millie.

"You don't look that different in jeans," said Austin.

"Well, it's not like she frequents the library."

Flynn snorted. "Unsurprising. I think she only learned to read so she could hustle people like this."

"Careful," Carson said. "It's beginning to sound like you're protesting too much, little brother."

"Please," he said. "There're plenty of good-looking women around. I have no need to get involved with one bearing the name of Hancock. Or, with her attitude, quite frankly."

"Right on," Carson said.

Carson was distracted, on his phone.

"Just go to Perry's place," Austin said.

"See you," said Carson, getting up and walking straight out of the bar.

"Are they. . . ? Is he. . . ?" Millie started.

"No," said Cassidy. "It's not like that."

"When his wife died it . . . it changed him," Flynn said. "And he was never an easygoing guy. He's military. Through and through. He can say whatever he wants about joining up to try to change the perception of him, but it was more than that. He met her, and he could finally see a way to some kind of life. Finally he'd found someone who wasn't all bound up in this outlaw thing. Someone who didn't know us. He brought her back here, and he was determined they'd have a happily ever after. And then she died."

"How?"

"It was a brain aneurysm. Fast and unexpected. Had no idea there were any issues."

Millie looked down. "I'm so sorry for him."

"We all are," said Austin. He couldn't say that he had ever felt close to his sister-in-law, but she had made Carson a certain kind of happy. Had given him the kind of life he had wanted. She had been what he needed.

"It just about broke him," Cassidy said.

There were unshed tears in her eyes. And Austin knew exactly why. Because they knew just how bad it was. Because they understood just how dark it had been.

"You don't think he could love anyone else?"

Austin shook his head slowly. "I don't think it's that. I think he won't. I think he took her death as the ultimate sign that it was never supposed to be in the first place."

He understood that despair deeply. The idea that somehow, by doing well, they were cheating fate. And it was going to come to collect eventually.

"Well, I'm glad he has Perry, anyway."

"We all are."

He wished they had Carson a little bit more sometimes. He was there, but Austin often felt he wasn't all there.

Flynn went to the bar with Cassidy, and they ordered a round, brought it to the tables.

Millie looked askance at the beer.

"I'm driving," Austin said.

She wrinkled her nose. "It's not a concern about inebriation."

"You don't like beer?"

"I don't think so."

"Have you never had a beer?" Cassidy asked, her eyes round.

"No," said Millie. "I don't think it smells very good."

"It doesn't!" Cassidy laughed. "It smells like horse piss. We're supposed to drink it anyway."

"I don't understand."

"You could acquire a taste for it," said Flynn.

Millie blinked. "But why would I?"

"Take a sip," said Austin. "If you don't like it, I'll finish it."

"*You* are driving," she said.

"Two beers aren't going to put me under the table," he said.

She leaned close to the bottle, and picked it up slowly, very gingerly lifting it to her lips and tilting it ever so slightly.

She blanched and set it down on the table.

Flynn laughed uproariously. "Hang tight, I'll get you a soda."

He went back to the bar and returned a minute later with a tall, clear glass with a straw in it.

"Thank you," Millie said.

The live band, the same one that had been playing when they were there last, started playing "Friends in Low Places." He remembered dancing with that redhead. He couldn't even remember her name anymore.

He couldn't remember why the hell he had danced with anybody but Millie.

"Care to dance?"

She looked up at him with an expression on her face he didn't think he deserved. "I'd love to."

He extended his hand and brought her out onto the dance floor. It was easy to make a spectacle with her here. Nobody here would judge her.

They might think it was funny, like Jessie Jane, but these people were like him.

Millie was the outsider. What would it be like if he stepped into one of the cute little boutiques in town with her? Or had coffee sitting across one of the pink tables at Scallywag's? Yeah. That was the question.

But he chose not to think about it as they moved together on the dance floor. Because this felt right. It felt good. When they were finished dancing, he pulled her close. "Would it be all right if I spent the night tonight?"

He knew what he was asking.

He was asking to leave his truck in her driveway again.

He was pushing things.

After he had told her it couldn't be forever.

But there was part of him that wondered now. Part of him that . . . wanted to cement their relationship, even though he wasn't sure if it was good for her.

She lowered her gaze, and he could see she was thinking. "Yes," she said, and then she looked up at him, her eyes certain. "Yes. I do want you to come back to my place."

"Great," he said.

They stayed a little while longer, to be polite. And then he bid Flynn and Cassidy farewell. "I'm going to take Millie home."

"Will you be back tonight?" Flynn asked.

"No," he said. "I'm staying in town."

And with that, he swept Millie out of the bar and onto the street.

And beneath the neon of the bar sign, he kissed her. Because it just felt like the right thing to do.

Chapter 21

It is always one more job. Then one more still. I am the dark cloud over my own family, and I don't know how to be different.

—Austin Wilder's journal, December 15, 1865

Millie felt as if she was drifting in a lavender haze over the next couple of weeks. She was planning things, doing the work that needed to be done to get Gold Rush Days up and running. She had decided to set up a board of directors and bring in a couple of long-standing members from the historical society, including Heather and her brother Jonathan, along with their friend Alana and her father Martin, a recognized historian of the Takelma people. She didn't want to repeat the same mistakes the town had made for over 150 years. She didn't want mythology. She wanted the truth.

And one thing she knew for certain: You couldn't have the truth as long as only one perspective was given on history.

Together they all worked on writing programs and informational plaques they would recommend as permanent installations in town.

They also discussed displays for the future museum.

It was definitely the most exciting time of her life.

She had never felt so complete.

Things were going well at the library, they were going well in town. . . . And then there was Austin.

Of course, rumors were starting to fly.

There was no hiding it. Every other night, his car was at her house.

It had gotten to the point where she had started getting sideways glances from people at the library.

The other day, after Alice had been staring at her for an hour, Millie had asked if the older woman had any romance novels to recommend. She didn't think she would find the scenes quite so unrealistic now.

Alice had lit up like a beacon and produced a stack of books that Millie read in bed beside Austin. While he was reading about explosions, she was reading about fireworks of a different variety. Usually after they had created their own.

But then they would set off some more.

She could never have imagined that she would find someone so compatible in . . . him.

When he wasn't working the ranch, or spending time with her, he was working on his book. And sifting through all the new information they had found out about Lee Talbot.

And that was when she was treated to the greatest privilege of all. He had finally produced his reading glasses in her presence.

"I only need them at night," he grumbled. "And when the text is this small and the writing is in cursive."

She hadn't been able to keep her hands off him. It was the hottest collision of tropes she could have imagined.

She had made him leave the glasses on while he took everything else off.

She would say she didn't know herself. But she did.

This was who she had always wanted to be. She felt more confident with every step she took. In every area of her life.

She didn't feel that she was just the sheriff's daughter. She didn't feel that she was just a Talbot. She felt like Millie.

And it was a triumph.

She was humming as Austin drove her home one morning, because she had to open the library before ten, even though part of her wished she could stay up on the ranch.

"Do you want to grab coffee?"

A little skitter of electricity went down her spine. "Yes. I would love to. We have time."

"Yep."

He didn't seem to be making a big deal out of it. But that was the thing. They spent every night together, but they had never addressed their feelings or the future or anything of the kind.

They never ran out of things to talk about. They talked about history, they talked about the ranch, they talked about books. They mutually worried about Carson. Austin worried quite a lot about Cassidy.

They talked about his book.

He had set a self-imposed deadline, and she was helping him stay on track.

Though sometimes staying on track turned into sexual games.

She couldn't complain.

Still, the future was beginning to loom, like a dark, low-hanging cloud. Could they go on like this forever?

She wanted to. She wanted to freeze time. She just wanted everything to be okay.

She was in love with him. She wasn't confused about that.

She knew what it was like to be with somebody and not be in love.

With Michael she had imagined a generic life. The sitcom version of happily ever after. With a generic sort of house and children. With Austin it wasn't like that. He was one of a kind.

She had never known anyone else like him. He was her friend. Someone she loved talking to. He cared about all the same things she did. And a great many things she had never cared about before. He had introduced her to new thoughts. And she liked to think she had done the same for him.

They had made each other bigger, more expansive people.

His guard was lower now. Maybe it always had been with his family, but it was with her now. He was still Austin Wilder. He still had that air of danger.

But he wasn't dangerous to her.

And now they were going to walk into the coffee shop together.

He parked his truck against the curb, and they both got out, heading into the adorable little building with the raccoon decal on the window. It was like a small house, at the end of the street. And inside was the best coffee and pastries the town had to offer—in her opinion.

"I just make my own coffee," he said as they approached the door.

"But they have pastries," she said.

He patted his rock-hard stomach. "I'm not the biggest fan."

"Well, this is the first thing you said that makes me think we might not work out."

She regretted those words the minute they came out of her mouth, and his smile faltered for a second, and then fixed itself firmly back in place. "If that's the first thing, I've been on disingenuously good behavior."

She let out a nervous laugh. "I think you're fine."

He reached down and took her hand in his. Then they walked into Scallywag's hand in hand.

It was packed, and every single face inside was familiar.

And all those familiar faces turned toward the two of them.

Heads turned away quickly—people were clearly trying not to be caught staring. But there was just so much to stare at.

She lifted her chin, keeping hold of his hand as she got in line. Right behind Danielle.

She realized that the sleek blond ponytail she was staring at belonged to her nemesis a beat too late.

She tightened her hold on his hand.

He looked at her, and there was concern in his eyes.

It was just awkward. She wasn't jealous of Danielle. Not even a little. Her betrayal didn't even have the power to hurt Millie anymore. She didn't feel like the same person.

It was just. . . . She didn't exactly want to run into this person who irritated her so much while she was getting coffee.

Austin shifted, let go of her hand, and put his arm around her waist.

She sank into him. They looked exactly like what they were. Lovers.

And she felt giddy, and a bit dangerous displaying their connection like this. In this bright, clean space that was very much her element. The bar had been his. They had danced there. He had brought her into his world, shown her that she was welcome there. She was determined now to do the same thing for him.

The teenager behind the counter looked up, recognized Austin, and her eyes went round. In response, Danielle turned around.

"Oh," she said, sounding as if she had spotted a roach in the corner. "This seems out of character."

Millie couldn't tell which of them Danielle's comment was directed to.

"In order for something to be out of character, you need to understand the character of a person. And I don't think you understand either of us," Millie retorted. How dare that woman?

"Settle down, Millie. It's just that some people have the good sense not to bring their bit of rough into public."

Bit of rough? Bit of *rough.* As if he was just some . . . hired penis or something. Not a human being. As if Danielle was some outraged Gilded Age lady and not a woman in the modern era acting like an outraged aristocrat.

It wasn't that Danielle was a hypocrite for judging Millie's affair when she was having her own illicit relationship with Michael. It was that she dared judge the sex Millie was having when Millie knew full well Michael was mediocre at best.

Danielle couldn't glare smugly at Millie as if she had a secret. There were no secrets here.

"What would you know about a bit of rough?" Millie asked, stepping forward. Austin was staring at her, not saying anything as she stared down Danielle. "I know exactly what you're getting, Danielle. And I'll tell you. I feel sorry for you. You can't act high and mighty with me. It must've been fun for you to steal my fiancé. But now that you have him, you're stuck with mediocre sex and a small penis. But far worse than either of those things is the personality that goes along with the skills and the anatomy. I should be thanking you. Because 'greener pastures' doesn't even begin to cover it."

"You're disgusting," said Danielle. "And you've forgotten how to behave."

"Maybe, but you never knew how to behave. All of you people in this town who pretend that you're the good guys, and the Wilders are the bad guys, while you do hideous things to the people you're supposed to care about. I don't have to talk about who's good and who's bad, because I know. I am well aware."

And she didn't storm out. She simply stood beside Austin, while he stood silent. And she made Danielle stew in it. She made her decide to get out of line and walk out of the coffee shop in a wave of rage.

"What the hell?" Austin asked.

"Nobody gets to talk about you that way. Nobody."

"Millie, I've been getting that kind of shit my whole life. Getting called a bit of rough by that woman doesn't bother me."

"It bothers me. Because somebody should say something, Austin. Because the whole town stood by when you were a little boy getting thrown out of places, getting treated like you were a second-class citizen. They all just stood there."

"Not your mother."

And suddenly, something filled her. A certainty, a glow. The nicest feeling she'd ever had.

She was her mother's daughter. Not just because she sat behind the desk at the library.

She was her mother's daughter.

The kindest woman Austin had ever known. And it wasn't weakness. It was strength. Kindness had the power to change lives. To get a little boy a library card, and to shape what he became, to give him a safe place to be. Her kindness had turned him into the man he was.

And she would do the same. She wasn't small or insignificant. Because kindness could be everything.

Her mother's kindness had led her to this moment. It had brought her this man.

That was how powerful it was.

Her father was seen as the hero. Her mother's position had been secondary. Millie had absorbed that judgment and applied it to herself.

But it wasn't true.

"What do you want to drink?" she said, fighting back tears. She didn't want to dissolve into tears now.

"Just a coffee," he said.

When they ordered, she got herself a chai, and pastries.

And defiantly took a seat at a pink table by the window.

"You didn't have to do all that," he said again.

"Can't you handle the attention?"

He chuckled. "It's not about the attention."

"I know. I . . . I just can't stand it. I can't do it anymore. All these people up on their high horses because of good deeds they didn't do. While they ignore all the bad things that happened. Because Michael is never going to take any ownership of the fact that his father charged extra interest for people of color to use his bank. They're never going to think they owe Native people their land back. They ride on this idea of reputation. But you cannot pretend to be good while you're actively doing terrible things to the people around you."

She took a sharp breath and took a sip of her chai.

"Agree with all of it. But they don't care. Because at the end of the day, they don't care if they're genuinely good people. That's actually the story of Lee Talbot, Millie. He cared that people thought he was good. He didn't care if he really was. And I know it doesn't make sense to you, because you do care. About doing the right thing. About helping people. About correcting the record. You care about honesty and truth, and not because it benefits you. You just do. There are other people like you. Just worry about them. Danielle is never going to see the error of her ways. She thinks she deserves all the good things she has, and that the bad things are unjust. She has to believe that I'm bad so that she can believe she's good."

"I just can't understand."

"I know you can't. That's why you didn't have friends in school."

"Hey," she said, looking up. "I had Heather."

"I know. But I mean . . . people were worried about appearances, and that was never you. You wanted the inside to match the outside. Even when you weren't a particular fan of mine . . . you were never unkind."

"It's not that I wasn't a fan," she said. "I think I was afraid of you because I was fascinated by you. Some could say I did have a crush on you."

Now that she said it, the truth clicked into place inside her, like a key turning in a lock. She took a deep breath. "I think I've been scared of myself this whole time. Because you're right. I'm not mousy. I was just desperate to conform. But at the same time, I also had to honor my convictions. And I have a lot of those."

"I like that about you," he said.

He couldn't have said anything better. He couldn't have said anything more wonderful.

"Thank you," she said.

"I don't need you to defend me, but it is really sweet that you did."

"I know you don't," she said. "That's the thing. But now that I've gotten to know your family, now that I've gotten to know you, I know that you are strong. In ways most people can only imagine. Part of me is sad that you had to be. I wish you'd been given more. More help, more care. I wish so many things, and I can't fix them. But I wanted to be the one to stand and defend you, because you deserve it, and you're worth it."

"You're always going to do that, aren't you, Mouse?"

"Yes," she said, feeling a shift in the name. Feeling a shift inside herself. "I always will."

"God help anybody that ever stands in your way."

"I'm formidable."

She smiled, because she was sort of joking.

But he looked at her, long and steady. "That you are. That you are."

Chapter 22

When I die, if someone remembers me, I hope it's for how I loved Katherine. It is the one good thing I've done.

—Austin Wilder's journal, October 12, 1866

It was finally time for the inaugural day of the Gold Rush Days Festival.

Austin had spent the night down at Millie's, and she was running around in a prairie dress with the back open. He was sort of trying not to stare at the wedge of skin. But not really.

He was pretty damned obsessed with her. Touching her, kissing her, looking at her. Talking to her.

That day in Scallywag's kept biting at him. It had been the sweetest thing, the way she had stood up for him.

But he always felt as if . . . he had tainted her. By association. Even if she didn't feel that way. Even if he shouldn't feel that way.

He supposed the problem was that they had all lived in this town for too long.

Millie would have bad blood with Danielle anyway.

But his presence had drawn fire, and he felt bad about that.

Still, today, he was dressing as an outlaw, giving tours in the exact spot where Austin had been shot and killed. But he would be telling the real story, solving the historic mystery of what had actually occurred between Lee Talbot, Butch Hancock, and the Wilder gang.

So far, they had been unsuccessful in getting the town council to change the plaques.

A lot of people who had been on board with reviving Gold Rush Days were not necessarily on board with all this new information coming to light. They worried about how the new narrative would affect business. Or reduce the standing of their family. He had been right about what he'd said to Millie. People didn't always care about being good. They cared about being seen as good. And it was clear a lot of people worried that if they started turning over too many rocks, they were going to find inconvenient truths about their own ancestors.

Millie was incensed, which he thought was cute. But then, he had a much more cynical take on people, so he didn't bother with rage.

"You should write a newspaper article," she said.

"Right. Like the *Rustler Mountain Gazette* is going to print something written by Austin Wilder."

"They should."

He had been thinking about it ever since she'd said that. In truth, he had started fiddling with a piece. He was almost done with the book. It was just . . . writing the ending. Austin Wilder's untimely demise. He felt he was missing something. Maybe the emotional insight to write it. Maybe he was resisting for that reason. He really hated that idea.

But here he was, dressed all in black, and Millie had finally gathered together all of her notes, binders, handouts, sign-up sheets, and everything else, so they could drive down to the old town hall building, which was serving as their staging ground.

They had gone into her building the previous week, the one owned by her family, and had been surprised by the number of artifacts in it. It was like an antique shop, and he'd wanted to spend more time poking around, but they were just too busy planning for Gold Rush Days, while also holding down their jobs. Millie had left the keys with him and said he could go back and explore when he had time. They had taken out quite a few pieces of old mining equipment, which they were using for a display during the festival.

Every station was thoroughly manned, and he had to admit, the event was admirably presented. The festival would run during the week for schoolchildren on field trips, and then for the next four weekends it would be open to the general public.

The number of volunteers it had taken was staggering, but much as he might complain about the willingness of the town to change its version of history, he couldn't fault folks for the work they had put into the festival.

In the end, even Danielle and Michael had taken part. But he had a feeling it was because they knew it could benefit them.

He let Cassidy give him a ride down the main street in the covered wagon, and it felt surreal to jump out right there on Main where the original Austin had met his demise.

"Creepy, bro," Cassidy said, tipping her cowgirl hat as she guided the wagon down the blocked-off street. There were a couple of cars that came up to the yellow cone roadblocks and honked, expressing outrage as if news of the detour hadn't been printed in the paper, put on the local Facebook group, and generally bandied all about town.

But that was people, he supposed.

They wanted to complain.

He had a schedule that told him when each group of kids would filter through.

He knew a moment of fear, because schoolchildren were not in his wheelhouse.

Except then he thought of his sister. And how he had done his best to take care of her.

How he'd built a relationship with her, even though she had been a little girl, and he'd had absolutely no experience with girl children.

Maybe he could do this.

When the first group showed up, it took him a minute to work out the rough patches in his speech, to get used to the interruptions that occurred.

Children were not attentive listeners.

But later in the day there were some middle schoolers, and even if the boys were more preoccupied with trying to slam-dunk oranges from their lunch into nearby trash cans, he found he had a few captive members of the audience, including one girl with vivid green hair who frequently interrupted to talk about miscarriages of justice.

"Definitely agree with you," he said.

"That's good. You can always be a better ally."

"Agreed," he said, amused by all that fire.

But it was the people with fire who did things in the world.

The festival was nearly over for the day when Michael and Danielle approached the corner where he was standing. He fought the urge to curl his lip.

"Can I help you?"

"We need to have a discussion about the presentation you're giving the children," Danielle said.

"Why?"

"We haven't verified the facts you're relating."

He couldn't help himself—he laughed. "I'm sorry. You think you have a better handle on the facts than I do? Because I've been taking my information from primary sources, not handouts that I got back in fourth grade combined with my rudimentary knowledge of the *Oregon Trail* video game."

He had far more than a rudimentary knowledge of the *Oregon Trail* video game, but that wasn't the point.

"It's just that you've submitted a petition to change the town plaques. . . ." Danielle started.

"I didn't submit it. An entire historical review panel submitted it. Based on my research, and the research of several others. What we sent you is fact. You just don't like it."

"I don't see how it's relevant that the bank engaged in some unfair practices. Those policies were a product of the time," Michael said.

"Well, it was a shitty time, and I'm not really sure why we're pretending that it wasn't. You don't have to romanticize the past to make it interesting."

"I'm just saying," Danielle went on. "These changes all seem to line up in your favor, and we can't trust that Millie is being. . . . It seems she's been influenced by you. Poor girl."

That did it.

"If you knew Millie at all, you would know that she wasn't influenced by a damn thing. She knows her own mind. And she has no trouble speaking it, either. Just because you all have decided she's mousy, because you can't recognize the kind of strength she has, that doesn't make it true."

Millie started to walk up behind Michael and Danielle then, smoothing down the skirts of her prairie dress, her expression concerned. "What's going on?"

"I've got it," he said.

"Austin. . . ."

"I'm disappointed in you," Michael said, turning to Millie. "I don't understand. You were such a. . . . You are such a good girl when we were together. And now you're openly *sinning* with him?"

"How dare you talk to me about sinning?" Millie asked. "I wasn't a *good girl* for you. I was *bored* with you. You confused the two things."

Austin couldn't add anything to that, because it was one of the more scathing comebacks he'd ever heard in his life.

"Just a minute," said Michael. "Your father would be so ashamed of you. He wanted you to have a good life, a good reputation. He wanted you to be respectable."

"Did you ever want me to be happy, Michael? Because I wasn't with you. And I am now."

Austin had difficulty taking in her words, because he was starting to get angry. Very angry. Red haze descended over his vision such as he hadn't experienced since high school. A kind of startling, malignant, pure rage that he associated with the lack of brain cells in teenage boys.

It was the unfairness of it. The years of unfairness. The decades of it. The centuries of it. That a little weasel like Michael could stand there and pretend to hold his head up high, pretend he was the good guy, when in fact he represented everything that was wrong with the world.

"Don't you speak to her again," Austin said, squaring up to Michael right there in the middle of Main Street. There were no cars; the road was still blocked off. Danielle dipped to the side, and the two of them were there, staring each other down, like an old-fashioned showdown. Well, if he had to die in the fucking street, he was perfectly comfortable that it would be over this.

"You're not any good for her."

"Maybe not. I would venture to say that's true. But you are a weasel of a human being. Who doesn't understand what it means to take a shred of accountability for anything. You don't get to say what's good for her, you don't get to say what she wants, what her dad wanted, any of that. It's not up to you to stand there and tell her who she is when you don't even know who you are. You're a weak man. You would never have started a bank in the Old West. You'd have fucking died of dysentery on the way over."

Michael growled and took a step toward him, and without thinking, Austin cocked his fist back and punched him directly in the jaw.

Michael went down, and Danielle screamed.

And too late, he realized that there were police officers standing by, about to remove the roadblock.

"Did you see that?" Danielle shouted. "Officer Jamison! He just assaulted Michael."

There was no point saying that Michael hadn't been an innocent bystander. There was no point fighting it. Austin was about to be put back in handcuffs, and he damn well knew it.

"Don't," Millie said, rushing forward, putting her hand on his chest, standing between him and the police officer. "Michael was antagonizing him."

"I saw Austin punch Michael, Millie," Officer Jamison said. He looked genuinely apologetic, but also as if he felt obligated to do something. Danielle was shrieking hysterically and Michael was rolling around on the ground like a soccer player trying to get a penalty called.

Thank God all the kids were gone, so there were no small people around to watch as the handcuffs were snapped around his wrists.

"You have the right to remain silent," Jamison said.

"No," shouted Millie. "This is ridiculous. It was just a fight."

"It's assault," Michael said.

Austin looked at Millie, who was devastated, and he realized that the problem wasn't just him. It was the two of them together. Nobody was ever going to be okay with it. It was always going to be like this. This judgment, this bullshit. And then he was always going to do something like throwing a punch instead of just ignoring the provocation, not taking the bait. But he wasn't a big enough man to do that, apparently.

Because for all that he had tried to be better and do better, he'd wound up right back here.

He went easily, because he wasn't going to make a show on the street. Because he didn't aim to get shot where he stood.

Millie was crying and speaking words, so many words, but he decided not to listen.

He didn't know what he felt right now. Whether it was shame, or a bone-deep sense of relief. Confirmation. Because this was a reminder. Of who he was, of what he was.

He even knew how to put his head down so he didn't hit it when getting into the back of the cop car.

Millie was still shouting, and when the cruiser started to pull away, she ran after them.

He was dimly aware that Cassidy was out there too.

He leaned his head back against the seat. It was just a three-block ride to the station.

"I had to do that," Officer Jamison said, "but I have a feeling that once I get you back to the station, we're going to decide to let you go."

"Great," Austin said. "Always happy to be an example."

"I don't want to get sued. Or thrown out of a job. She's the mayor. But I have a feeling the DA's not going to charge you with anything."

"Well, you wouldn't think so."

He was pretty familiar with this dance. He'd never gone to trial.

No one had actually pressed charges against him. It was always catch and release, as though he was an inconvenient bass rather than a human being.

"Next time don't do it in front of a cop," Jamison said.

Austin barked a laugh. Because as pissed as he was, the guy did have a point.

"Wasn't really calculated."

"Well. He's . . . I'm sure he earned it, let's just put it that way."

It was gratifying to know that even the police officer thought Michael was a dick.

"As long as we agree."

But as he got out of the car, entered the station, and walked into the holding cell, as the door clanked behind him, Austin had a sense of finality.

It was a wake-up call.

He had tried to cross the line. It hadn't worked.

And he couldn't subject Millie to this degradation.

They had been playing house. It wasn't realistic. And it couldn't go on.

He was going to have to tell her so.

Probably after today, she would be all right with it. Yes, she had been upset—he could see that. But at the end of the day, his arrest reflected badly on her. After all, she was the one responsible for putting such a volatile, unstable man in contact with a group of kids.

Maybe she wouldn't think so today. But she would someday.

This, he realized, was the real test.

He had to do what the original Austin Wilder hadn't been willing to do.

He had to make sure he didn't drag the woman he cared for into his mess.

Chapter 23

The love she has for me is so deep and wide, but I've failed that love. I have a bad feeling we pushed it too far this time. That our crimes are about to catch up with us. In another time, maybe I could have given her a love to last a lifetime, not just a few happy years.

—Austin Wilder's journal, June 10, 1867

They wouldn't let Millie back to see him right away, and she was vibrating with rage by the time she was told she could go in.

Heather had been blowing up her phone ever since news of the incident had gotten out.

She was threatening to put together an angry mob, complete with torches to break him out.

Millie was just going to give the cops the scolding of a lifetime. Nobody wanted an angry librarian's finger in their face. And she was about to go completely off.

When Officer Jamison met her in the hall, he put his hands up in a defensive gesture. "He's going to be out in a few minutes. I had the mayor screaming that I had to arrest him. There wasn't a lot else I could do."

"Well. . . ."

She hated that he was sort of right about that.

He led her back toward the holding cell, and there was Austin, standing right in the center of it, the bars crossing his handsome features. She wanted to burst into tears at the sight of him, but she tried to hold them back. Still, she felt her lips quiver and her throat get tight.

"You didn't need to come here," he said.

And then she did lose her grip on a couple of tears, because what else could she do?

"How could I not come here? I had to come and get you."

He looked pained but didn't say anything as Jamison unlocked the cell and let him out.

"That's it?"

"I called the county, and they just think it's silly, so I'm going to let you go. Now if someone had an issue, it's with the DA. Not me."

She couldn't really fault Jamison for trying to cover his rear. Because Michael and Danielle were petty.

But they'd better not cause an issue, or. . . .

The feeling of not having power was a terrible one.

She was a Talbot, but that had never given her any clout before. Not the kind they wielded.

No. But she did have influence. She could influence people the way her mother had.

With firm and unwavering kindness. Because her mother had been kind, but she also hadn't let people get away with nonsense. She was no pushover. She pushed back when it was necessary. But not in the ways that Danielle and Michael did, making petty power grabs.

As soon as Austin stepped out of the cell, she rushed forward and wrapped her arms around him. He didn't hug her back.

He looked tired.

"Austin. . . ."

"Let's go," he said.

He didn't take her hand, he didn't say goodbye to Officer Jamison either, but she couldn't really blame him. And she wasn't going to go getting all weird about manners or anything.

"I drove your truck over," she said, pointing to the vehicle as they stepped outside.

He realized he must've left his keys somewhere.

"I actually found them on the ground," she said. "Your keys."

He looked spooked that she had read him so easily.

She handed him the keys, then went around to the passenger side.

"I'm going to take you home," he said.

"Okay. You can stay."

"I can't stay."

"Austin, will you please talk to me?"

"There's nothing to say. That wasn't a onetime thing. That's the state of things. Great. I'm out. But what's going to happen next to put me back in?"

"You're not going to get arrested. That was weird, and he was being—"

"Agreed. But I'm Austin Wilder, and no matter what we discover, nothing is ever going to change that. You're Millie Talbot. And everybody is always going to find the two of us to be some kind of object of fascination. Or something to poke at. And you don't deserve that treatment."

"You just ordered Michael not to tell me what I deserve. Now it's your turn. You don't get to tell me what I deserve."

He started the truck engine and began to drive toward her house. She felt panic clawing at her breast. He was trying to end it. She knew he was.

"Austin, I love you."

He didn't say anything. The only sound was the truck engine, the tires on the road. They passed the bar, the neon sign, and she wished they could go inside. And that it would be a different day. A different moment. Maybe a couple of weeks ago, and they would go dancing.

As long as it wasn't now. But they'd always been heading toward this moment. Toward the end. She wanted to go back to the middle. She wanted to go back to a time when she didn't know what was going to happen. She wanted to go back to when she could imagine that they might be able to love each other from now until forever.

"Austin, please," she said.

"Millie, those who don't learn from history are doomed to repeat it. And you know that. Bad boy, good girl—it's a great idea, it's a great love song, it's a great book. But it's not a great life, for people who are as different as you and me."

"No," she said. "No, no. Because we aren't different. We're the same. We lie in bed at night reading books, and we think about why people do things, and we both love it here, even though it can be a difficult place to live. We never run out of things to talk about. We are not that different from each other. We are more the same than I have ever been with any of those other people. With Michael, with Danielle. I love you."

"I'm sorry," he said. "But I'm never going to be able to give you the things you need. I want to. I do. I wanted to figure out how to be that guy. But when I looked at your face after I punched him and realized how badly everything was fucked up, I understood that I can't make all those set pieces fall into place. And that's what they were in my head. Set pieces. It wasn't real. I don't know the first thing about having a happy family. I did my best to piece one together, but my dad was useless, and my mother didn't love us. There are only two outcomes when it comes to loving a man like me. You leave like my mom because you can't stand it anymore, or you stay. And the staying just about kills you too. Because what did Katherine Wilder get for her loyalty?"

"But the thing is," she said, her heart beating hard, tears sliding down her cheeks, "you're not *him*. And you never were. It was always wrong for the town to make you feel that way. Always. And you knew it. In your heart you knew it. So why are you giving in now?"

"It's not the town. It's my own mother. She left us. Because she knew. She knew that it was a dead end. That we were."

"But you aren't. Look at you. You're alive, and that was supposed to mean something to you. I thought your thirty-fifth birthday mattered. I thought. . . ."

"I wanted it to. But this arrest reminded me of who I really am. I can't spend my life waiting for the other shoe to drop, Millie."

He pulled up to the front of her house. And she sat. Because she couldn't face getting out of the car, because when she got out of the car, then they were over, and this breakup was real.

"But didn't we mean something?"

He swallowed so hard, she could hear it. He was staring straight ahead. "Yes. The worst part is that we did."

That was what did it. That was what propelled her to unbuckle her seat belt. To get out of the car.

Because what could she say to that? He wasn't denying the reality of what they were to each other. He just didn't want to take the commitment on.

She could almost understand. Because there was a heaviness to this loss. It wasn't insubstantial. It also didn't feel like the grief she had experienced after losing her parents, or the pain she had felt when her relationship with Michael had broken up. It felt like a deep cavern of sorrow that existed alongside those other things. She was mourning the end of the growth she had experienced with him, the love she still felt for him.

"I guess I was right," she said.

"About what?"

"When I warned all those girls away from you back then. It was because I was afraid you would break their hearts. You broke mine. So I guess I knew more than I thought I did."

She got out of the car and stumbled to her front door. She unlocked it, and everything felt as though it was moving in slow motion. While he was just sitting there watching her.

She went inside and closed the door behind her, leaning up against it, dead-bolting it. Then she pressed her hands to her face and held in a scream that wanted so badly to escape.

She had lost so many people, so many things. Watched so many of her hopes and dreams shatter.

But this was the worst. Because it wasn't supposed to be like this. Because they were good for each other. Because she did love him.

Because at least losing your parents was the natural order of things, even if she had lost hers before she wanted to.

There was nothing natural about this. Nothing right.

They were supposed to be together. They were. And he wasn't going to let it happen.

She felt like she was being stabbed in the chest. She felt like she was dying.

Because she truly loved him. And it wasn't a matter of finding another man someday so she could get married.

She wanted Austin.

That wasn't going to change.

And nobody would ever be him. Not ever.

He was her one and only outlaw.

He was her hero. And she didn't have him anymore.

Chapter 24

Austin Wilder, 33, was shot dead on Main Street by Sheriff Lee Talbot, after refusing to be apprehended by authorities for the crimes of robbery and murder. His brothers were arrested for crimes of the same nature. They are believed to be responsible for a string of robberies of stagecoaches and banks all over Oregon. If these men are remembered, it will be for their crimes.

—the *Rustler Mountain Gazette*, June 12, 1867

When Austin got home, his siblings were all waiting in the house. They had been texting him, and he had been ignoring them.

"What the hell are you all doing here?"

"We've been trying to get hold of you. We didn't know if we needed to go down to the police station, but we thought that perhaps a bunch of Wilders showing up there would make things worse, not better," Cassidy said.

"Not wrong."

"What happened?" Flynn asked.

"I got put in handcuffs for punching that asshole. I don't regret it."

"And?"

"No *and*. It's not a case. It's not a thing. I'm not catching any charges."

"Oh," said Flynn. He sounded almost disappointed.

"Sorry if that damages your fantasy of me actually being dangerous."

"Are you okay?" Cassidy asked.

"Do I look like something's wrong?"

"You don't look *happy*," said Flynn.

"I'm not."

"What did you do, Austin?" Carson asked.

"Just leave me alone, Carson."

"You broke up with her, didn't you?"

He turned and looked at his brother. "How the fuck did you know?"

"Because actually, you look like a man with a broken heart. Not one that just got let out of prison."

"Prison and jail aren't the same thing."

"Whatever. Why did you do it?"

"Because look at me," he shouted. "I tried. I participated in her thing. I put on a costume, and I stood in the street and I did the thing. I participated and I supported her, and I got arrested. I punched her ex-fiancé because he was running his mouth. Because that's who I am."

"And did she at any point indicate she wanted you to be different?" Flynn asked.

"It doesn't matter what she wants. We know how this goes. It's a tired tale. Our dad could never get it together. He never could. Our mom left because she knew that we were never going to get it together. And you tried, Carson. God knows you did. But you're a bigger fucking disaster than you ever were before."

Carson sniffed and crossed his arms. "I'd be offended if it weren't true. But it doesn't have anything to do with you. And frankly, it doesn't have anything to do with Mom or Dad. I went through something awful. But that has nothing to do with you."

"It does," he said. "Because if I know who the Wilders are, and I understand that it doesn't matter how hard we try, life just doesn't come together for us, then why would I ever put Millie through that?"

There was a long pause, and finally Carson spoke. "I don't think you're worried about her. I think you're worried about you. Because you've been left before, and you know that sucks. Because you watched me lose my wife, and you know it was hell on me. I think you want to protect yourself. God knows I don't blame you. But don't pretend that you're protecting her. You're protecting yourself."

Austin was angry. He wanted to lash out. He wanted to deny it. But it felt too real. Carson's accusation sank down to the deepest parts of himself, and he found that he couldn't.

"It doesn't matter what the reason is. I can't do it."

"Then you're an idiot," said Carson.

There were so many unspoken words in his eyes. So much unsaid between them. And Austin was happy to leave it unsaid.

"Let yourselves out."

He walked away from them, but he didn't go to his bedroom. He went to his office, slammed the door, and shut it behind him. And then he sat there at his desk. With his manuscript open in front of him. Dry-eyed, his chest feeling as if somebody had taken broken glass and ground it up, then smashed it into his heart. He sat there until the sun rose. He didn't sleep. He barely moved.

Then he got up and walked to his truck. He still had the keys to the old building. The one where they'd found the mining equipment. It had been his intention to go back and go through all the artifacts there.

He felt driven to do it now. He felt hollow. He had so many unanswered questions. And maybe they couldn't be answered.

On the drive back to town, he cursed every jackrabbit that got in his way. But mostly, he cursed himself.

When he pulled up to the old Talbot building, he got out.

He shouldn't use the keys. He should give them back to Millie. And he damn sure shouldn't let himself in.

But he did anyway. And as he stood there in the darkness, surrounded by history, he didn't find the clarity he was seeking.

Instead, he was swept by a terrible longing for something that he knew he couldn't have. He had felt this way when he was a kid, on the outside looking in.

Except now he was a grumpy old man who had told himself he didn't belong. He was a grumpy old man who had told himself to get the fuck out. He was the one who hated himself. And he didn't know what the hell he was supposed to do with that.

He walked through the place slowly. There were ghosts hanging in the air. Or maybe they were just inside him.

Maybe his brother was right. Maybe he was a coward. Afraid for himself.

Maybe the real tragedy wasn't that everybody thought he was a villain, but that everybody thought he was a villain when he was, in fact, a coward.

There was nobody he could ask. Because his dad had never known him, and he was dead anyway.

His mom was gone.

And he thought back to his siblings, sitting in that house, looking at him, wanting better for him.

God dammit. They were his family. They *were* his better.

The ones who knew him, the ones who cared for him. And so was Millie.

He was strangled by the depth of that realization.

He took another step and tripped, his foot connecting with something hard.

He swore a blue streak, grabbed his phone, and switched on the flashlight. He shone it down on the bin he had just tripped over. Inside were books.

Of course there were books. Because there were always books. Because somehow it always came back to books. He bent down and started going through them. *Little Women. Pride and Prejudice.* A big family Bible. He grabbed hold of it and opened it up, looking for the family tree.

And there he saw it, in faint spidery writing. Austin Wilder. Katherine Wilder. The date of their marriage. This was . . . this Bible belonged to his family. These were *their* books.

This was their history.

The hair on the back of his neck stood up, and he actually sat there and asked himself what had made him hang on to these keys. What had made him drive here this morning. There had been a feeling. Something compelling him. Something he couldn't explain.

Goose bumps broke out all down his arms. He picked up another book. *Huckleberry Finn*. And then, he saw a little red journal, identical to the one that had been Austin's.

He picked it up. He opened it, and his heart hammered hard against his chest.

This journal belongs to: Katherine Wilder.

He opened it up to the first page, and read their wedding date.

This was the happiest day of my life. And he gave me this book to write all about it. To write about our lives.

This was it. This was what he needed.

How the hell had a woman like her loved a man like Austin Wilder? How did she bear it?

He sat down, there in that dusty building, and shone his flashlight onto the pages. And he began to read as quickly as he could.

The joy when she had found out she was expecting. Every time she was afraid that Austin was going to get caught.

She didn't like Butch Hancock. And she was against her husband's continuing his life of crime. But through all of it she loved him. Even if he was imperfect.

Sometimes I wonder if we agree on anything.

She had written that one day after a big fight. But she had never wavered in her love for him.

She didn't make entries every day. Especially not after she had the children.

A few days before Austin's death, there was one last entry, and then nothing. For two years.

He looked at that two-year gap. There was nothing written about those years, but he could feel the pain.

The emptiness.

And very slowly, he began to read the first entry she wrote after living in a world without her husband.

The boys are very tall now, Austin.

He gritted his teeth, taken aback by the shock of seeing that the entry had been written to Austin.

I think they'll be even taller than you. I wish that you could see them. I'm so damned thankful for the life that you gave me. Every day I find ways to be thankful for the happiness we had. So many people in this town have asked if I'll remarry. Marry a respectable man this time. I don't want a respectable man. I have always and only ever wanted you. And I had you. Gloriously. I miss you. Sometimes like a small crack in a windowpane, letting in a few raindrops. And sometimes like a whole flood. When you first died, I wondered if it would've been better if we had never met. But then I wouldn't be me. And our boys would never have been. And I have decided that I would rather live with your loss, than live in a world where I didn't love you.

It has taken all this time to write these thoughts out. I wanted to try to hold on to them, instead of just sending them out like prayers into heaven.

I do believe you're in heaven, Austin, even though you told me you never would be. And I got so angry at you and threw a water pot at you, because I told you there was no point to anything if we wouldn't be together in the hereafter. So you told me you'd do your best to get there. I believe you did.

It was never hard to love you. Only to lose you. But I would do it again. All a thousand times over. All those people, who asked me if I wanted a better man. There was no better man. Because no one could've loved me in the way you did. No one.

He stared at those words. They mirrored so closely what Millie had said to him. That they were perfect for each other. For Katherine there had been no better man, because Austin was the right fit for her.

Could he be Millie's?

Was she his? Maybe that was the most terrifying question of all.

Because if she was, and then he lost her. . . .

"You already have, dumbass."

Those words came right out of his mouth, seemingly from nowhere. Perhaps he had been possessed by his late ancestor—he wouldn't be surprised.

Katherine had loved Austin. And even though their years together had been short, they had been full.

He didn't want short years. Not with Millie. He wanted their years to be long.

He wasn't afraid that he couldn't have a happy marriage. He was a man who did what he set his mind to. It really was as simple as being afraid of losing the person he loved.

But if Katherine Wilder believed that loving and losing was well worth the cost, then maybe he could believe it too.

Maybe she had always been the missing piece. The missing lesson.

And he made a decision right then and there. If Millie would love him, still, after everything, then he would give her everything. He would stop trying to protect her. He would stop trying to protect himself.

He would put all the outlaw into that book. And not call himself an outlaw ever again.

Because she was right. He couldn't use his reputation as a convenient excuse when he didn't want to deal with something.

He was going to lay down his gun.

He was going to do what his namesake had never done.

He was going to change for the woman he loved.

In whatever way he needed to change.

Chapter 25

The women in town seem to think I should feel shame. In truth, I feel pity. For them. They do not know what it means to love with hope, as I did. Even if my hope was shattered, my love remains. I will never let go of it.

—Katherine Wilder's journal, July 7, 1869

Millie was exhausted, and unamused by the fact that she was going to have to take Austin's place on the tour that morning.

But she was there, in her prairie dress, because she would be damned if she would let anybody down just because she was feeling dead inside. Actually, dead inside would be an improvement.

She hadn't told Heather. She would have to eventually. But the pain just felt too raw to even speak of it. All the same, she was going to have to figure out how to say something, because she had to give this tour.

She realized that there had never been any resolution of Danielle and Michael's demand that they stop sharing the updated history. She didn't care. She would punch him herself. Maybe if she ended up in a jail cell, Austin would understand that they weren't so different.

Maybe he would stop. . . .

Running.

She sighed heavily, feeling tender. When she heard the sound of footsteps, she was afraid it might be the first group. She turned around and stopped dead. Because there was Austin. Backlit by the early morning sun, a black cowboy hat pulled low over his face. He was still wearing the all-black garb from yesterday.

And he looked . . . like every bad-boy fantasy a woman could ever have. But it was more than that. She loved him. So much that she ached with it, even though she was angry at him. Even though she felt hurt.

"What are you doing here?"

"I thought this was the best place to do it. And I know that you probably have a tour group soon. But . . . this was where Austin died. Right here," he said, pointing to the ground. "And if he bled out here, it's a good enough spot for me to do it too."

And then he did something completely unexpected. He got down on one knee.

"Millie, I love you," he said, his hands clasped firmly around hers. "I don't know when exactly I fell in love, but I did. I didn't recognize it, because I didn't understand it. I didn't want to understand it. I'm afraid of it. Because I'm terrified of losing people. Because I don't trust myself. Because I don't trust . . . anything.

"All my life, I've discounted the love I had. I have my siblings. And they've been there for me. I had your mother. And you. You were all there showing me that people could be good. That I could be good. But I wanted to protect myself so badly that I pushed it all away. I minimized it. I spent so much fucking time trying to figure out why other people did things, but I didn't spend nearly enough time trying to figure out why I acted as I did. Because I didn't want to know. Because too often, I acted out of fear. I'm much more comfortable writing words into a manuscript. I'm much more comfortable writing about people who aren't me. Thinking about people who aren't me. Because it hurts. I hurt you, and I hate that. I hurt me, and I hate that too."

"Oh, Austin," she said. She put her hand on his cheek. "I love you. Everything you are. Everything you've done for me, everything you are to me. You are the most wonderful man I have ever known. And I would consider myself lucky to be with you. To make our own legacy together."

"I found Katherine's journal."

"What?"

"I haven't slept. I read it. She . . . she never regretted loving him.

She thought it was worth it. All the pain. I never believed love could be like that. They had this perfect, singular love. They understood each other. The things she wrote about him—they're the most beautiful companion piece to what he wrote about her. They were soulmates. And you're mine. I want us to have the ending they couldn't have. They were happy. For a time. But I'm willing to change myself, to make an ending that'll last."

"You're on one knee," she said.

"Yeah. I am. I know you were just engaged a couple of months ago."

"Who cares? Honestly. Who cares about him? It didn't count. It wasn't real. This is real."

"Marry me."

"Yes," she said.

He lifted her up, his hands spanning her waist, and brought her in for a kiss.

He heard little gasps, and he and Millie separated and looked behind them. There was the first tour group.

"Oh," she said.

"Sorry," he said.

There was a smattering of applause. Two teachers looked at each other. "Was that not part of the show?"

"No," he said. "That right there was a genuine proposal."

"People are going to be weird about it," Millie said.

"You know, the only person whose opinion I care about at this point is yours. And everybody else can go—" He cast an eye over the kids. "I don't care what anyone else thinks."

"Well, I do. Because I want them to know that I'm going to marry the best man in town."

Epilogue

The very last thought he had was of Katherine. And even as the world around him grew dark, her love was his light.

—from the novel *Outlaw*, by Austin Wilder

"There's actually a line," Heather said, scurrying quickly into the library and over to the refreshment table. There was a stack of books sitting on a different table, manned by Eileen the bookseller, who had come all the way from Rebel Heart in Jacksonville for the event.

Austin was giving a talk about Rustler Mountain history, and there would be a guided tour later. And, of course, a book signing.

Outlaw had been picked up by a publisher a year earlier and had been an instant favorite of the publishing house. They were anticipating a potential spot on the *New York Times* bestseller list.

Austin was deeply uncomfortable with all of it. Millie was so proud she thought she might burst.

"I saw all the new plaques today," said Heather.

"And?" Millie asked.

"Perfect. My favorite is the one that goes on the bank, acknowledging that Gin Lin made the largest deposit in Oregon state history, and of course that he was charged unfair fees."

"I'm glad he got his acknowledgment."

Heather beamed. "Me too."

Millie looked around the room, her hand on her stomach. She felt nervous for Austin, even though she knew he could handle the attention.

"Once he got that article into the Rustler Mountain paper,

everybody's feelings on the plaques changed. The way he writes about history makes it real. And once people become real, it's so much harder to deny them," Heather said.

"That's true," she said.

She felt a little bit queasy, but she knew, thanks to the test she had taken an hour ago, there was a reason for that.

She didn't know if she should tell Austin tonight. Finding out she was pregnant during his release week seemed a little much. And letting him know about it on the night of his book launch seemed like stealing his thunder.

Austin came in through the back door then, all in black, as he always was.

"There's a crowd," Millie said.

"Good God," Austin said. "Why?"

"Because," Millie said. "Everyone cares now. About the original Austin Wilder. And you did that."

"I care a lot more about supporting the local economy. And the bookstore."

"You could also just be proud of yourself," she said. She kissed him on the cheek.

He held her there for a second. "You ever talk to your mom?"

She blinked. "I guess sometimes. I don't really mean to. It's kind of silly."

"Tell her thanks. I'm here signing a book in this library because she let me check out that first book. It means a lot to me."

Millie had a hard time holding her tears back for the rest of the evening. While Austin gave his talk and signed at least thirty-five copies of his book. Which to some people might not seem like a lot, but in this small town, was impressive.

They all talked long into the night, and by the time she had Austin headed back to the ranch, she was exhausted.

"You must be proud," she said. "I am."

"I guess so. I mean, I'm happy about the book, make no mistake. But the only thing I'm really proud of is us. Because from my perspective, given Rustler Mountain history, we are a damned miracle."

"Well," she said, letting out a breath. "Then maybe you want to hear about one more miracle we have coming up in about eight months."

He stopped the truck. "You're kidding me."

They were on the dirt road that led to the ranch, with no other cars in sight.

"I'm not kidding," she said.

He got out of the truck, and she could only watch as he rounded the front and opened her door. Then he dragged her outside and spun her in the beam of the headlights. She swore she saw a jackrabbit scurry off.

"I love you, Millie Wilder."

She couldn't help but remember the first time she had come marching up this mountain to ask for his help. She had found so much more than she'd bargained for.

She had found herself.

And then she had found the love of a lifetime.

"Thanks for being my hero," she said.

"Thanks for believing I could be one."

They swayed in the light for a few moments more, and then they got back into the truck. And Austin drove them home. To the happily ever after that had been more than a century in the making.

Please read on for a preview of Maisey Yates's next novel, *Outlaw Lake.*

Chapter 1

There is nothing left for me here. I'm going west.

—Mae Tanner's diary, June 15, 1899

Perry Bramble loved Carson Wilder with all her heart.

It was just that her heart had been irrevocably broken into pieces when she was a child, along with any trust she might have had in the world, and Carson was an emotionally unavailable hot mess who had fallen in love with another woman.

As caveats went, those were pretty big ones.

It was why Carson was her best friend in the whole world and nothing more. It was why she spent every evening with him, and many mornings, even though it wasn't convenient for either of them.

It was why they were attached—if not at the hip, then at the very least, the soul.

They had been like this since they were seven years old and her family had moved in next door to the Wilder Ranch.

"Stay away from them, they're not the right kind of people," her dad had warned in his neat clothes with a bland expression on his face. And later he would turn into a monster and roll up those same sleeves before hitting her mother, and if that didn't satisfy his rage—Perry herself.

Perry lived with a villain. She hadn't understood that right away. That was the problem. But what she had thought was that if her dad thought the Wilders were bad, she wanted to know about them.

She'd sneaked onto their property, and she could still remember, plain as day, meeting a nine-year-old boy in overalls—nothing else covering his skinny arms and bony chest—who looked her square in the eye.

Do you want to play?

I do.

They'd spent the afternoon playing pirates, and when the day was over they were best friends. As they had been ever since.

Not without trials, tribulations, and her dad trying to tear them apart, but one thing Perry had learned when she'd decided that Carson Wilder was her person: She was more than happy to be a rebel as long as she had a cause.

Her cause was Carson.

Though now she was thinking maybe—*maybe*—her cause needed to be herself.

She chewed the inside of her lip as she finished putting together her last arrangement of the day, which was due to be picked up just as she closed her shop. Then she was going to Carson's for dinner.

Instead of going on a date with Steven Lee. He'd asked her to dinner, and she would have said yes, but she had her standing plans with Carson—which were not firm or official and could easily be blown off, but she hadn't done it.

She wasn't *in love* with Carson.

She wasn't that foolish.

But it was hard to want a new relationship when the one she had was so all-consuming.

And also she was wary of men.

Thanks, Dad.

She had once loved her dad with all her heart too.

It would have been easier if he had consistently been a fire-breathing dragon, but he hadn't been. It was why she rolled her eyes when young girls on the internet talked about red flags in men. As if there were clear and obvious signs that were visible to anyone and everyone from the first—and sure, there were men like that.

Those men didn't scare Perry.

It was the ones who went to church every Sunday and Wednesday besides. Who had friends in the community, and a good job. Who smiled easily.

A smile that could quickly turn and change the temperature of the room. A smile that trained everyone in the house to walk on eggshells to avoid the explosion that could come if anyone stepped wrong.

Perry always walked carefully. Ironically, though Carson was an absolute mess, he never made her feel that she had to watch her step.

If Perry thought back, all the way back, to the last time she'd had something that counted as a boyfriend, she could easily say why those relationships worked so well.

She'd never cared about those guys any more than they'd cared about her. She'd always known walking away would be easy.

She'd never wanted her whole life to be wrapped around a man, not the way her mother's had been.

Joke was on her, she supposed. She had thought that sort of obsession only came with romance.

But she chose not to think of that. Instead she chose to think of the building in Medford—an hour away from Rustler Mountain—that had ivy climbing the sides and would be available in six months to house her new, larger florist shop.

The building that would require a heck of a down payment—one she wouldn't get with the sale of her house alone. And since she was renting this little building on Main Street, she wouldn't get anything from vacating it either.

She had some plans.

Most of which involved trying to grow a field of flowers for several weddings. And maybe working nights at the twenty-four-hour drive-through coffee stand off the freeway—also over an hour away, but beggars couldn't be choosers.

She had a plan. For the first time in a long time.

She finished up her arrangement and waited for the customer to arrive. And once the sale was complete, she turned the sign, locked the door, and zeroed out her register.

She took a deep breath, and her lungs expanded, her heart lifting slightly. She always felt this way when it was time to see Carson.

Which was why she was doing this.

It was the reason for the broken date.

And also for the dry spell of the last several years.

Her general *girl treading water in circles around a man* approach.

She loved Carson with all her messed-up, broken, crushed little heart, and that ended up looking a lot like codependency.

Or so a therapist she saw once eight months ago had said. She hadn't gone back because who wanted to hear that the most important relationship in your life was holding you back.

Not Perry.

But that assessment had wormed its way into her brain like a weevil, chewing and chewing and *chewing*.

She had sad news to tell Carson tonight, and yet she still felt so happy she was going to see him. As if she was racing toward the best part of her day even though tonight was going to be weird and difficult and maybe even terrible.

It wasn't as if she was moving to Canada. Or moving tomorrow.

They'd lived farther apart before.

But she was doing this . . . well, not because of him. It was because of her. Because she needed to get a life. A bigger life.

She told herself that as she drove down Rustler Mountain's quaint Main Street, and looked at all the beautiful hanging baskets of pink petunias, and smiled slightly at the new, updated plaques shining bright against the building facades.

Along with local wine and stunning mountain views, history was one of the big tourist draws in Rustler Mountain. A gold rush town eight miles from the California border, with the romanticized American West baked right into the red brick.

The biggest local legend was the death of notorious outlaw Austin Wilder right on the street Perry was driving down now. An ancestor of her very dearest friend in all the world.

Carson's brother Austin, named for the same man who was killed on this street, had written a definitive novel on that event. His research had changed a long-standing town narrative, and since then a lot of local history had been updated as people took a much deeper, broader look at Rustler Mountain's past.

She'd miss this place.

A hollow feeling filled her as she drove on, out of town and along the road that would carry her to Outlaw Lake, Carson's part of the vast Wilder Ranch.

When she pulled up to the modern ranch house, Carson was halfway out the door. Ready to greet her. She smiled and her heart squeezed.

She remembered him when he was a child. That skinny little boy in overalls. She could picture him so clearly, and she thought she probably always would.

But he was not that boy now.

Carson Wilder was well over six feet tall, with broad shoulders and the physique of a man who lifted tires and hay bales for fun. He had let his military haircut grow out over the last few years, his dark blond hair still short on the sides, but now longer on the top. It was rare to see him without his cowboy hat, but he'd clearly come in from working the ranch a while ago. His hat had been discarded, along with his boots. He was wearing a black T-shirt and jeans, his feet bare.

A common enough sight, and yet it also spoke to the level of intimacy in their relationship.

Intimacy was the wrong word. It was a nice word. But it made them sound like emotionally healthy human beings, and she had to remember that they were not.

She put her car in park, and Carson opened the door and held it, waiting for her. "Hey," he said, a smile on his handsome face.

His blue eyes were more intense than the sky.

She had to look away. "Hey, yourself."

She ducked under his arm and went inside. The house was always an indicator of just how Carson was doing. The level of neatness was a window into the state of his mental health.

Thankfully, right now it was clean. And it smelled great.

"Pizza?" she asked.

"Yeah, I had to go into Medford earlier, so I got a take and bake."

"Ooooh."

She smiled, and for a minute things felt normal.

The oven timer went off and she followed Carson into the kitchen. It was such a pretty kitchen. A lot more stylish than anything Carson would have chosen on his own, but then, that was true of the whole house.

The white countertops and emerald-green cabinets had been chosen by Alyssa, who'd died less than a year after the house had been finished.

And Carson still had to live in it.

She shrugged that thought off and looked at the white double oven with the gold door handles as he pulled the pizza out.

"Thank you," she said.

"You cook for me often enough."

"I do, it's true."

One of them did, every night. They were never alone. They went out together; they spent their downtime together.

It was a lot.

And never enough.

This was so perfect. And it was even more perfect when they sat at his dining table with their pizza. And they'd do it again tomorrow, and the day after that and the day after that and they would never, ever change.

"I wanted to talk to you about something," she said, setting her uneaten pizza crust down on his plate—she didn't like crust.

He picked her crust up and started to eat it like a breadstick. "Oh yeah?"

She looked at those blue eyes and emotion expanded in her chest, so big and bright it couldn't be contained. Carson Wilder was the love of her life.

And that was precisely why she had to leave him.

She let out a long, slow breath. "Carson . . . I'm moving."

Visit our website at
KensingtonBooks.com
to sign up for our newsletters, read
more from your favorite authors, see
books by series, view reading group
guides, and more!

BOOK **CLUB**
BETWEEN THE CHAPTERS

Become a Part of Our
Between the Chapters Book Club
Community and Join the Conversation

Betweenthechapters.net

Submit your book review for a chance to win exclusive
Between the Chapters swag you can't get anywhere else!
https://www.kensingtonbooks.com/pages/review/